1 2 3 4 5 6 7 8 9 10

ISBN: 978-1-9163520-6-3

First edition

Editing by Heather Osborne

Formatting by Dawn Nelson

Cover design by Terry Wells Brown

For Annmarie, Jane, Tracy and Anne-Janine who have always been there for me no matter what

Greed

D A NELSON

Chapter 1 - Dominika

The assassin followed her prey at a distance as he made his way down the busy Jerusalem Street. Although still young, she had many years under her belt of stalking and killing people for money. But this guy, this guy she was doing for free. And she was going to love every minute of it.

The man – ex-Mossad agent David Adelman – was taking his usual route to a small restaurant in Music Square where, she knew, he would order the same breakfast he did every time. She had spent the last few days learning his routines and today was the day all that work would come to fruition. Age and retirement have made you sloppy, Dominika thought, as she trailed him down a built-up city street. He seemed oblivious to her presence, something that a highly trained former spy should never be. She wondered if he now thought himself safe in his home city, safe from all the predators who might take him out.

Well, you're not safe from me, she thought as a smug smile played about her lips.

He turned left and quickly looked around him forcing her to duck into a shop doorway. It wouldn't do for him to see her following. She stifled a chuckle. This was her favourite part of being a killer for hire, stalking her prey before she pounced. She peered around the door sill to see Adelman disappear down the side street. He was out of her sight for a moment, but that didn't matter. She knew exactly where he was going.

David Abelman entered the small restaurant in the city's famous Music Square and sat down at his usual table close to the rear of the eatery. Sitting with his back to the wall, he waited patiently as the waiter took his order. He didn't have to look at their menu of delicious things to know what he wanted—poached eggs on sourdough with a cup of coffee and a sugar donut on the side. He was a small man with thick, white hair and piercing brown eyes that never missed a thing. Time had not been kind to him. Gone was the trim figure of his youth, replaced with a growing belly and wrinkled skin. His extra weight had added flesh to his once handsome face: where there had been a chiselled jawline, there was now corpulent jowls. What did he expect? He was nearly 73 after all. He had given his all to his country, and now it was his time to relax, hang loose a little. So, what if he had put on a little bit of weight? He'd earned the privilege.

Housed in a 200-year-old building, the café had been a favourite haunt of his in his youth. It had been where he had stolen his first kiss from Miriam Goldman, where he'd had his first taste of illicit beer and where he had first thought about joining Mossad. He had avoided it for years for fear of bringing bad luck to the place, only returning when he was well and truly retired. Now he could kick back and enjoy it again.

The waiter brought his dish to his table. Abelman thanked him, and before the young man had even returned to the kitchen, he was tucking into the dish with relish. There was something about poached eggs that perfectly set you up for the day.

Across the restaurant, the door opened and a young woman

slipped into the building. Tall, lithe and stunning to look at, her entrance did not bring even a flicker of attention from the old man, so rapt was he in eating. The same could not be said for the waiting staff and, after a tussle at the kitchen door, two rushed to her side eager to take her order. She ignored one and spoke quietly to the other before sliding into a seat at a window table, directly opposite Abelman. It had the advantage of allowing her to pretend to be looking at the busy street outside, whilst all the while watching her prey with the attention of a lioness stalking wildebeest. She observed and waited. She had all the time in the world.

Dominika Gagolin, codename Aggravate, was the top assassin in the world. Sure, there were others like her; other Sisters of Sin who worked for the same organisation, Conexus, but none were like her. She had a cat-like coldness that honed in on her victim and stayed there until the deal was done. And she enjoyed it. A little too much.

She sat back in her chair and waited. Normally, she would be paid thousands for killing someone of Abelman's status, but not today. No, today, this one was on her. This one was personal.

The waiter reappeared with a cup of mint tea and, hands sweating, carefully placed it in front of her. With a smile and a nod of her head, she dismissed him and watched as he bumped into the next table, reluctant to take his eyes off her lovely face.

Stupid boy, she thought as she lifted the cup, as if I'd be interested.

Taking delicate sips of the beverage, Dominika continued watching as the oblivious Abelman gorged on his breakfast. He was not a refined man; he used the fork to shovel food into his mouth in great lumps, letting egg yolk drip down his chin. Dominika flinched as a globule of yolk oozed out of the side of his mouth and landed on his immaculately pressed shirt. The man did not seem to notice and continued gobbling his breakfast in blissful oblivion. Minutes later, the eggs and sourdough were finished and he turned his attention to his coffee and donut.

"Do you want to join me, young lady?" he called as he took his first sip of steaming hot coffee. He had not even looked up. "Well? Are you going to sit there all day watching me or are you going to answer?" He lifted his eyes and caught her in a steely gaze.

Dominika turned on the charm. "Are you speaking to me, sir?" she replied matching his stare. She gave him her warmest smile. Fake, but she was good at faking it.

He returned the smile. "Well, I don't see anyone else in this place, do you?" He held his hands out to illustrate how empty the restaurant was.

"I don't know what you mean. I wasn't watching you, you know," she lied. "I'm just here for the excellent tea."

Abelman gave her an incredulous look that told her he was not fooled. "We both know that you were and we both know that you've been following me for the last few days," he said. "Now, are you going to join me or not?"

Dominika nodded and stood up. She collected her tea cup and saucer and sashayed over to the older man in the corner. A tall, striking woman, she was all in black: tight-fitting linen trousers and a shiny silk blouse that perfectly framed her cleavage. Her designer sunglasses acted as an expensive Alice band for her long, silky black hair which shimmered in the dull light. She pulled her chair so that they were uncomfortably close together and put an immaculately groomed hand on his thigh.

"Now, may I ask why you are taking such an interest in an

old man like me?" He ignored her hand and broke his donut in half. He offered her a bit. She shook her head.

"Who says I find you interesting?" she replied with a shake of her glossy hair and a coy smile. She was reeling him in slowly, slowly.

"You've been tailing me," he said. "You've been watching me."

She removed her hand. "You are the only other customer in this place," she said. "I had nowhere else to look." She shrugged.

"Is that so?" He studied her carefully, a smirk playing about his thin lips. "So, who do you work for and what do you want with me?"

"I don't know what you're trying say," she said as sweetly as she was able. "I'm a tourist just enjoying the sights of Jerusalem."

"Let's not play games here. I can spot a fellow agent from a mile away. The question is who are you and who sent you?" His dark eyes squinted as he tried to get a read on her. She was giving nothing away. He wiped his mouth with a napkin.

"No-one sent me." She took a sip of her tea, her icy blue eyes glittering at him over the rim of the cup. "I came all by myself."

"Who are you, and what do you want?" He threw his napkin on the table and turned to fully face her. She smiled; the cat who got the cream.

"Okay, so maybe there is something you can do for me and I'll get to that in a minute," she said. "But, let's first talk about you… You once knew my father, Gregory."

"Gregory? I don't know your father; I don't know a Gregory," he spluttered. "What are you talking about?" His face grew pink.

"Yes, Mr Abelman, you did know my father," she replied. "His name was Gregory Gagolin, and you left him to be captured by the KGB and taken to Siberia where he died soon after," she explained. There was something matter-of-fact about the tone of her voice. No emotion showed, and she delivered her words as she would have when asking a stranger for directions in the street. "My father used to spy for you, don't you remember? He trusted you and you let him die."

"I don't know what you're talking about," he said coolly, but the colour of his face belied his feelings. Gone was the calm of before replaced by a reddened complexion that told Dominika he did indeed remember her father. She put her hand to her back and pulled a small revolver with an attached sound moderator from the waistband of her trousers. She pointed it at his head. His face whitened, and he looked like he was about to be sick. He slowly put his hands up.

"Now just a minute," he said, voice wavering. "I don't know who you think I am, but I am just a retired civil servant. I don't know who this Gregory Gagolin was nor know anything about his death."

She made the sound of a game show buzzer. "Wrong answer," she said prodding him in the face with the silencer barrel. "Try again."

"It's true, you must have me mixed up with someone else," he pleaded. "I'm telling you the truth."

She poked him again. "We both know that's bullshit, Mr Abelman. You are an indeed retired civil servant… a retired Mossad agent whose job it was to liaise with my father when he worked as a scientist in the former USSR. You used to come to our apartment and have meetings with him. You are older and fatter…" She spat out that last word in disgust. "…now, but it's still you. I would know your face anywhere. I used to call you Uncle David, remember?"

He frowned, then realisation dawned on his face. "Nika? You're little Nika?" he asked.

"Yeah, that was me," she replied. "Although I'm not so little now."

"Okay, okay, so you're right, it is me, but how did you find me? Why have you found me?" he asked. His tone softened. "What can I do to help you?"

"Oh, it's too late to help now. My father died a horrible death in a labour camp in Siberia and my mother died soon after. You could have gotten us out of the USSR, we could have had a good life in the West, but you did nothing and there is nothing you can do to help bring them back," she snarled. "Is there?"

"What do you want from me, Nika?"

"And that brings me to why I'm here."

He gasped. "I couldn't do anything to save your family, Nika," he said. "There was nothing I could have done. My hands were tied."

"You could have smuggled us out, gotten us to safety," she said, her voice rising. "Instead, you left us to die. After everything my father did for you, for Israel."

"He served us well," Abelman admitted. "He was a good asset."

"He wasn't an asset; he was my father!" She felt herself losing her temper and reined it in. "And now you're going to pay for what you did."

"What? No, wait, you can't do that!" he said panicking. "I can give you money. I have lots of money, you can have it all."

Just then there was the sound of the kitchen door opening and closing, and the waiter came out to see if they wanted anything else. Dominika lowered the gun and hid it at her side, but she kept it trained on Abelman.

"Can I get you anything else, sir?" the waiter was talking to Abelman, but looking at Dominika.

"Nothing for us, thanks," she said smiling sweetly.

They waited until he had returned to the kitchen before resuming their conversation.

"Nika, look, I'm sorry what happened to your mother and father, I really am, but I was too far down the ladder to be able to help them," he said.

"You were in charge of the unit," she said. "You helped others escape. Why couldn't you help my father and mother?"

"No, that's not right," he began but was horrified when, with her free hand, Dominika removed a folded piece of paper from her bra and placed it on the table.

"This," she said, "details your career with Assad."

"How did you get that?" His face turned a sickly white and a bead of sweat trailed from his brow.

"It doesn't matter, but it shows that you were the lead agent at the time. From my research, I also know that you personally smuggled four different scientists and their families from the USSR to the West." She paused to let her words sink in. Abelman gulped. "So, why didn't you get my family out? Why did you leave us?" He swallowed hard. "Well?" she demanded and held the gun to his left temple. "Tell me!"

Eyes closed, shaking with fear, the older man cleared his throat before speaking again. "Your father wasn't important enough to be rescued," he said and opened his eyes to see her reaction. "I'm sorry, but there was nothing he could offer the West that would justify the expense of smuggling him and his family to safety."

There was a pause whilst Dominika let the words fully sink in. Her father wasn't important enough. She looked away, sighed and trained the gun on his head again.

"Wrong answer again," she said and squeezed the trigger.

The silencer muffled the sound as the bullet left the barrel and lodged itself in Abelman's brain. The former agent, blood running down his cheek, slumped to the right, his chin resting on his chest, his eyes open and glassy. Dominika lowered the gun and rose from her seat.

Another one down, she silently congratulated herself, but she had a whole list of others she still had to attend to. She tucked the gun into the back of her trousers, slipped her hand into a pocket and pulled out a five Shekel note. Throwing it on the table, Dominika stalked out of the café.

Chapter 2 - Greed

Alex Grier leant her left cheek on her L115A3 sniper rifle and peered through the scope. Lying on her stomach atop a five-storey building in Rome's Prati neighbourhood, she trained her rifle on an open window in the building opposite waiting for Luca Gallo. A prominent international businessman, the handsome Luca had been a bit of a naughty boy selling arms to warlords in central Africa. Now, someone wanted the charismatic Italian out of the way. He had recently upped his game with how much and what he was selling, and things were getting a bit too ornery for leaders in one of the African states.

Alex didn't know who had ordered the hit—she didn't care. All that mattered was she got the job done and got paid. She had her heart set on a new pair of diamond earrings she'd seen in Tiffany's last month. As she waited for the shadows at the window to stop flitting about and take form, she wondered briefly if she could also stretch to the matching diamond necklace or would that be going too far? No, she decided, nothing was too far for her.

"Come on," the 28-year-old murmured as she sought out her target. "I know you're in there. Just come to the window, just for a second, and let me shoot you, will you?"

She breathed deeply, keeping her heart rate steady and waited under the warm Roman sun. It was five o'clock in the afternoon and the sun was still strong. Its rays were starting to burn the back of her neck and she cursed herself for tying her long blonde hair up into a ponytail. She had a black baseball cap on, but it wasn't stopping the relentless heat beating down on her. She sighed.

Come on, Gallo, come to the window.

As if her prayers had been answered by divine providence, the slim, tanned figure of Luca Gallo appeared briefly at the window. Alex licked her lips. Gallo was a looker. She watched as he opened the second button of his tight-fitting shirt and ran his fingers through his dark hair. Then he leant against the windowsill, the shirt opening slightly to reveal a tanned torso and a smattering of dark chest hair. His handsome face was creased into a frown and he looked furious. Sexy, but furious, and Alex almost felt sorry that she had to take him out. Something must have grabbed his attention for he turned and began gesticulating with his perfectly manicured hands.

He is definitely a man who could warm my bed on a cold night, she mused. *Pity he's been such a naughty boy.*

Gallo disappeared back inside.

"Damnit!" she cursed softy, shifted her weight a little and continued waiting.

Suddenly, Gallo was at the window again. Leaning on the window sill and still arguing with the mystery person inside.

Got ya!

Alex took a breath, squeezed the trigger and bam, Luca was down, dead, shot between the eyes. His body slumped against the window and disappeared from sight. The only sign he had been there was a smear of crimson blood on the glass.

Screaming sounded seconds after the hit, and Alex ducked down out of sight.

Time to go, she thought as she quickly broke down the rifle, placed it carefully into her rucksack and fled the rooftop.

She took the back stairs down to the ground level at the rear of the building, jumping three steps at a time in her haste to escape. A minute later, she was at the rear door and, after checking the coast was clear, scurried out to a small city car she had left there for her escape. The hire car was quick and soon took her out of the Prati neighbourhood heading for the outskirts of the ancient city. She removed her baseball cap and shook her glorious hair out of the restrictive ponytail. It landed in magnificent blonde waves around her shoulders, her crowning glory.

Alex kept calm and cool as she continued her escape. Traffic was atrocious—it always was in Rome—but she soon found herself skirting the Vatican City and heading south-west down the Via Aurelia to finally join the A90. It was a laborious route, but better than trying to negotiate Italian drivers through the rest of the city. Somewhere in the distance, sirens screeched and she smiled. She was almost out. Just another couple of miles to go.

Alex headed north, stopping once to abandon her hire car at the Riserva Naturale Dell'Insugherata Nature Park and pick up her own vehicle: a brand new, hand-made silver Aston Martin. She stowed her rucksack on the floor of the car, removed the drab grey overalls she had worn for the job and slipped into a skin tight, red mini dress and high heels. Completing the look with a pair of vintage Dior sunglasses, Alex ran her fingers through her long hair and got into her car. Pressing a button to bring down the soft-top roof, she hummed to herself as she checked her makeup in the rear mirror.

Time to go, she mouthed to her reflection and she turned the ignition key. A thrill of delight ran through her as the car roared into life. She loved this car—a recent purchase. It was her baby.

"Take me home, honey," she murmured as she put the car into gear.

It was a long drive home and Alex was glad she had a quality music system in the car. As she drove the 15 hours to Berlin, she listened to her favourite bands. At first it was all the classic rock bands of the 80s and 90s, but as the hours dragged on, she found herself wanting a more peaceful vibe and opted for some gentle jazz. She stopped briefly in Innsbruck to get something to eat before carrying on north-east.

Alex arrived in Berlin just shy of eight am the following morning, exhausted, but satisfied she had done a good job. The city was already buzzing with rush hour traffic as she negotiated the busy streets.

She reached the Charlottenburg area of the city and sighed with relief. She was home.

Alex lived the expensive part of town in a beautiful building with carved stone window and door sills and secure entry. Occupied by business people and elderly rich people, it was exactly the type of place where Alex liked to be. She looked up at it as she drove closer and grinned.

Home sweet home.

Parking her in a nearby private underground garage, Alex got out of the car and stretched. Jesus those long journeys never got any easier. She yawned and fetched her bag from the passenger side. Slinging it across one shoulder, she made for her building. Felix the door man nodded to her as she made her way through the security door and into the lobby. She pressed a wall button for a lift and was relieved when one opened almost immediately. She dragged her tired body inside and a few minutes and three flights later, she was opening the door to her apartment. Discarding glasses, dress and shoes on an original Art Deco chair in the hallway, Alex made her way to her bedroom and threw herself on her bed.

Nick Walker entered the meeting room at MI6's Vauxhall HQ and sat down next to his colleague, Ben Littlejohn. Tall, dark, handsome and impeccably dressed, Nick looked more like a top footballer than the spy he was. He smiled at Ben. They had been friends since university and had joined the secret service at the same time. Both were field operatives and vied for the best jobs. Nick wondered if they would be teaming up for this next assignment.

"Lettis not here yet?" he said. A tray of glasses and a jug of water sat in nearby and he poured himself a glass. "Want one?"

"She's finishing a call," Ben replied, shaking his head to the offer.

"Any idea what this is about?"

"None."

The glass door opened and Lettis Green, small, slim and in her 40s, walked in carrying a laptop and a coffee mug. She took the chair at the head of the table and put her coffee down.

"Gentlemen," she said by way of greeting. Nick and Ben nodded. "Thanks for coming." She sat down and opened her laptop. "If either of you want to get yourself a coffee, now would be a good time," she said as she tapped some keys. Neither man moved.

"What's this all about, Lettis?" Although she was Nick's superior, there was no formality in the way they addressed each other.

"All in good time," she said, looking up at a large flat screen on the wall. "Ah, there we go."

Nick and Ben glanced up at the screen as it blinked into life, depicting an ornately embellished Victorian style office building with Italian stonework. It would have been a stunning structure, had it not been for the scorch marks and blown out windows.

"This, gentlemen," began Lettis, "is the headquarters of Conexus in Rome. As you can see someone planted a bomb there recently and killed a number of the Conexus board members."

"Yes, I read about it in the briefings," Nick said.

"What those briefings didn't tell you is that Conexus is not the international business that it seems – well, not in the sense you would think. Since the bombing, we've heard whispers that there is far more to them that at first appears," she said. "In fact, we believe that this is the cover organisation for an international gang of assassins called the Sisters of Sin."

Nick and Ben looked at each other, their faces belying the absurdity of it all. "The Sisters of what?" Nick asked.

"Sin," she replied. "Yes, an unusual name but one that's weirdly accurate. As far as we can make out, the Sisters of Sin is a group of female assassins who have been working around the world murdering various people. We don't yet know who, but we have our suspicions."

A new image appeared on the screen. It was of a tall, beautiful blonde with blue eyes. Nick whistled. What a stunner.

"This is Alex Grier, 28, currently living in Berlin. She's a former British army sniper. She grew up in Chelsea, London. At a young age, Alex joined the army, trained as a sniper and left three years ago, we believe, to join the Sisters of Sin," she said.

New images appeared of Alex on security footage at various airports and in city centres. The images were sometimes fuzzy but bore the dates of her journeys.

Lettis continued, "As you can see here, Miss Grier gets around. This is her in South Africa catching a plane back to Germany only a few hours after a local drug lord was murdered. Here she is again in Portugal and Luxembourg hours after another hit. We believe she is an assassin and linked to Conexus and the Sisters of Sin."

She turned to Nick. "Nick, I want you to seek Miss Grier out and try and infiltrate the Sisters. We need to find out how many of them there are, who are their bosses and how do they operate." To Ben she said, "And I want you to see what you can find out about the Conexus bombing. You'll find all the information you need in the system."

She shut down her laptop and stood up. "Nick, Stacey has organised a flight to Berlin for you this afternoon, so if I were you, I'd get home and get packed as soon as you can. She'll give you all the details."

"Thanks, Lettis."

"Ben, can you start off in the office and see what you can find out? I don't want to send you to Rome just yet. Don't want to tip them off that we're on to them."

"Sure."

"Thank you, gentlemen." Lettis rose and walked smartly out of the room.

Ben turned to Nick, grinning. "Trust you to get the job tailing a blonde. How come I never get those jobs?"

Nick shrugged and smiled. "It must be my amazing good looks and charm!"

"Yeah right!" Ben laughed.

Chapter 3 - Berlin

It was three pm before Alex emerged again, still sleepy but feeling refreshed. Her limbs ached from the long drive, but a half hour yoga session followed by a hot shower soon put her right. She dressed and went to her large kitchen to see if there was any food. Her stomach growled as she opened the fridge door of her huge American style fridge freezer to survey the empty chasm inside. Shit. She had forgotten to buy groceries this week. She had been so busy with various jobs her domestic arrangements had been badly neglected.

Not for the first time did she consider getting herself some sort of assistant, someone who could run errands for her, pick up dry cleaning, that sort of shit. She had mulled the idea over in her mind many times and once again dismissed it. Working for Conexus, being an active member of the Sisters of Sin, working under the code name Greed, she did not fancy having a civilian in her home, a civilian who could guess her secrets. Bugger! She would just have to go out and get herself something eat. There was a deli a few streets away that sold the best open sandwiches she had ever had. They were expensive compared to the street vendors that one could find in the city centre, but they were worth it. Axel Meyer's Delicatessen would be her first stop.

Slipping on a loose silk designer dress and flats, Alex grabbed her purse and slipped out of her flat. At the grand old age of 28, she was a connoisseur of the good life. She liked nice things and nothing was too expensive or rich for her. That was one of the reasons why she had left the British Army three years ago to join the Sisters. It had been a great career, and she had learned how to handle herself. She had excelled at being a sniper and was one of the Army's best, but they just didn't pay well enough to keep her in the designer clothes and fancy cars she so loved. So, when Mother had approached her in London and invited her to join, dangling the carrot of a very large pay day, she jumped at the chance.

The Sisters were a group of international women assassins who worked directly for the parent company, Conexus. Each had their own codename based on the seven deadly sins and carried out the assassinations in their own inimitable way. Managed by Mother, the hours were good, the travel was great and the pay was amazing.

She thought about Mother and wondered why she hadn't heard from her for a couple of days. She was her only link to the Sisters, her handler, the woman who kept pushing through the jobs earning Alex the big money she so loved. Must give her a call when I get back, she thought as she exited her apartment block and walked down the busy Berlin Street to the deli.

Axel Meyer's delicatessen was housed in a two-hundred-year-old building and was packed full of elderly Berliners picking up their daily loaves and bratwurst. A small shop with just one counter, it was so full of pensioners that Alex had to squeeze herself in in order to join the queue. When at last it was her turn to be served, she jostled her way to the counter and, leaning over the large glass display cabinet that divided the shop's workers from their customers, put in her order.

"Toast Hawaii, bitte," she said to the woman on the other side.

It was a strange combination for a sandwich, but one she loved. Toast Hawaii had everything in she enjoyed in a pizza, and it would just hit the spot today. She watched as her sandwich was assembled: first the white bread which was then topped with ham, a slice of pineapple, cheese and Maraschino cherry. It was topped with another slice of bread and toasted. It was very popular with the German people and Alex just loved it. When in Berlin, she often thought to herself when she tasted the local fare. Some of the city's dishes had been a hit or miss for her, but Toast Hawaii was delicious.

As she waited for her sandwich, her mind wandered to her recent activities. So far, she had taken out a local drug lord in Budapest, a human trafficker in Paris and the handsome Luca Gallo in Italy. Those had made her already healthy bank balance even fatter. She gazed out of the window wondering where the next job would take her. She hoped it would be Paris. For the shopping, naturally. Although she had a bulging wardrobe, she could always do with some more clothes. Or maybe she should treat herself to a spa break in Switzerland, at one of their exclusive luxury hotels

Or somewhere hot, she mused, I could do with some sun. I might even take a holiday afterwards.

Alex dismissed the thought of a holiday from her mind. Yes, she was tired and in need of a break, but she was unwilling to pass up any work until those Tiffany earrings and the matching necklace were hers.

The street outside was busy with people of all ages and backgrounds, and she amused herself by watching them as she waited. A group of women, smartly dressed in suits, walked by probably on the way to their office. She glanced at her watch; it was nearly 4pm. Well, maybe they were leaving their office. A grandmother and four grandchildren wandered by—the grandchildren enraptured by brightly coloured helium balloons they were carrying, the grandmother smiling benevolently behind them. A couple, dressed like tramps according to Alex's high standards, wandered by arm-in-arm gazing lovingly into each other's eyes.

Alex flinched. She hadn't been part of a couple for years now. It wasn't just the strict rules of the Sisters that there should be no romances which kept her from finding her other half. She had been in relationships before, and they had ended messily. There was no way she was going there again. But sometimes… well, sometimes, she thought it might be nice. Her thoughts were interrupted by the loud laughter and joking of a group of young men as they passed by. A family of four walked in the opposite direction followed by a woman cyclist. Alex smiled to herself. Here were all these people, going about their daily business, little realising that there was a deadly assassin in their midst.

"Fraulein!" The shopkeeper's voice cut through her thoughts and brought her back to reality. She turned back to the counter and handed over some money in exchange for the now completed sandwich from the server.

"Danke," she said and smiled.

Alex paused at the deli's door to unwrap her sandwich. She was hungry and could no longer wait to satisfy her growling stomach's demands. Just as she was taking the first bite, her attention was drawn to a familiar looking figure striding confidently past the shop's glass door. Was that -? What's she doing here? No, it couldn't be! Could it? All these thoughts crammed into Alex's head as she tried to make sense of what she had seen.

Or thought she had seen.

Forgetting her sandwich for a moment, she pulled open the shop door and ran outside. She looked frantically up the street to see if she really had seen Dominika stride down the road. Her colleague's tall silhouette was hard to mistake. Dominika was dark-haired and gorgeous. She had a distinct way of walking that was part confidence, part catwalk model.

Alex strained to see up the street but could not see Dominika. Dismissing herself as having been "seeing things", she slowly walked back to her apartment in the opposite direction stopping briefly on a street bench to demolish the sandwich. As she sat there, in the cool shadow of a tree, Alex thought about what she had witnessed. She was not one for doubting herself, but there was no way she could have seen Dominika, was there? As far as she was aware, Dominika was in the States. Why would she be in Berlin? Berlin was her town, and if Dominika really was there – and she was almost sure it was her she had seen earlier - why hadn't she contacted her? She decided to call Mother for an explanation.

Back at her apartment, Alex picked up her cell and dialled the familiar number. She waited for the ringing sound, but got a long melancholy tone instead. The phoneline to SOS headquarters in Rome was dead. Alex frowned and dialled again but only got the same low-pitched monotonous tone of a deceased line. Strange. She would normally get through quickly. Had something happened? She tried Mother on her cell and after a couple of rings, Mother picked up.

"Greed, I'm so glad you rang. I've been trying to get you all," Mother said using Alex's work name.

"I couldn't get through on the landline. Has something happened?" Mother sounded flustered and that worried Alex.

Mother, handler of the all the assassins, upper class British and strong, was normally unflappable. Alex waited for her to answer.

"Something terrible has happened," she said. "Someone's blown up the headquarters!"

"Oh my God! Was anyone killed?" Fear made her stomach tighten, and it felt like someone had poured a bucket of frozen water down her back. What the fuck?

"It happened in the boardroom when the Board was meeting." Mother's voice faltered. "No-one survived."

"And the staff? Did they get out?"

"Yes, we managed to get all the staff out… eventually. The explosion took out the first floor of the building and caused extensive cave-in in the underground lab and in our offices. A couple of lab staff were trapped, but we got them out. They're recovering in hospital."

"Were the police involved?"

That was the last thing SOS needed, police poking around the building. Conexus was what Alex liked to call a shadow organisation, one that pretended to be an international legitimate business whilst making lots of money doing a number of shady activities behind the scenes. "They didn't find the arms' cache, did they?"

"No, Finn managed to secure it before he got himself out." Finn Rogers was in charge of SOS's lab and forge. His ideas for adapting and developing weaponry for the Sisters gained him the nickname of Father, and he had a bit of a thing for Mother. "They'll not find it."

"Do you know what happened?"

"The Fire Service investigator and the police say it was a bomb," Mother said, her voice tight and controlled.

"Shit! Any idea who or why someone did this?"

"Well, we are an international assassination organisation," Mother said. "We're bound to have enemies. Although who would want to take the entire board out at once, I don't know?"

"Maybe they were trying to put a stop to our business," Alex said. "Take out the board and you take out the whole organisation."

"I think there's more to it. One thing is for sure, Sisters of Sin will continue. I have a number of jobs still to be carried out and that will keep us afloat until a new board can be established and we re-open the headquarters."

"Are you alright?" Alex asked, relieved the organisation was still running. Her dream of owning those diamond earrings and matching necklace had suddenly gone up in a puff of smoke when she heard about the bomb. "You haven't been hurt, have you?"

The girls were all very fond of Mother. She was more than just their handler and giver of jobs. She had helped and supported every single one of them in some form or another. Alex was forever grateful to her for giving her the role of Greed in the first place.

"I'm fine, just a little shaken, that's all," Mother replied.

"I'm so glad," said Alex. Then she remembered why she had called in the first place. "Look I'm sorry I'm disturbing you right now, but I just need to know something. Is Dominika in Berlin? I thought I saw her earlier."

"No, she should be in South America right now, taking out a corrupt war lord," replied Mother. "You must have seen someone who looked like her."

"I could have sworn it was her," Alex said frowning. "Anyway, you mentioned jobs that need doing. Is there anything for me?"

"There's another assignment for you on the website," Mother said. "It needs done pretty quickly. The client paid extra to have the target taken out by the weekend."

"That's not leaving me much time," Alex said. "Where is the hit taking place? Have I got far to travel?"

"No, it's right on your doorstep," said Mother. "In Berlin. Details on the site."

"Cool."

"I must go, Greed. I have to find us some temporary offices until I can get builders in to sort out the mess in the HQ. We're not sure if the bomb affected the foundations. It's an old building, and it could have damage that we've not been able to see with the naked eye."

"Do you need me to be there? I can help."

"No, retrieve the assignment papers and get on with the job. I'll be in touch." With that, Mother ended the call, leaving Alex feeling like she had had the rug pulled from her.

Who would attack the Sisters and why? It was unfathomable. The Sisters of Sin had been running for centuries. A secret organisation, it was based in a two-hundred-year-old building in Rome. On the outside, the headquarters looked like any other business based in beautiful old premises. The front door, at street level, led into a tastefully decorated reception area. From there, huge wooden doors led into the boardroom and several other offices, which were empty. Apart from one gorgeous dark-haired receptionist, all the staff worked in the basement beneath. Down there, safe in the bowels of the earth, were the real offices and other rooms required by the organisation.

The underground offices stretched right under the building and those next to it. Accessed by a wood-panelled elevator, the doors opened out into a large modern workspace. There was the forge and armoury at the south end of the underground lair and a large lab next to it. The north end housed a series of offices and training suites where the Sisters of Sin regularly trained in a range of martial arts and firearms. In the middle, were a range of offices, the staff kitchen and a relaxation space filled with large leather sofas and the latest newspapers and magazines. It was unfathomable that someone had tried to destroy it.

Alex sat down on the sofa and opened her phone's browser. She was feeling pretty shitty about the attack, but wasn't going to let it stop her. Mother was right: if they were going to rebuild, they had to keep going. She did a quick search and got on to the dark web where she knew she would find her instructions. Sure enough, on the SOS pages, her next job was there in her section of the site. She downloaded the information and sat back to peruse them.

Her next target was a well-known Berlin business owner and local gangster. On the surface, Felix Weber was a good guy—he was a highly successful entrepreneur and philanthropist. The file SOS had given her on him showed images of him donating large sums of money to Berlin charities, and he was a leading light amongst the city's rich for his philanthropic work. But what you saw was definitely not what you got with this particular thug, for Felix was suspected of racketeering, prostitution and people trafficking. The German police had tried many times to get him for the murder of three people, but the slippery Weber had always outwitted them.

She looked at his picture. Hmmm, not bad. If he hadn't been such a nasty character, Alex might have fallen for him herself. She had a thing for handsome men with dark hair and dark eyes. And he was intelligent, a definite plus in her books. He had been a straight A student and had a degree in physics. So why was he such a nasty man?

"Money and power," Alex murmured. "It's always about money and power."

She put her phone down and wondered what to do next. Weber owned the trendiest nightclub in all Berlin, but she wouldn't be able to go there until midnight to scope him out. She had several hours to waste. She looked around her apartment, and suddenly, she knew what she wanted to do. She had been feeling a little stiff after the marathon drive from Italy and needed loosening up.

Gruber's gym was three streets away from her home. Aimed at men, the gym specialised in boxing, and Alex had had a hard time convincing the owner, Arni Gruber, that she was keen to join. It took her several visits and a box of Havana cigars to persuade the giant Gruber to let her join. It wasn't the most salubrious of places. Gruber kept the place basic. There was no steam room or pool. The interior design looked like it had been done by an amateur painter and decorator, and the changing rooms were non-existent (she changed in Gruber's private toilet as there were no ladies' toilets). There was a shower room, but as it was usually occupied by tall, muscular bare-arsed men, Alex always showered at home after a work-out. However, it was one place where she felt welcomed, where she felt safe and where she could get a great workout courtesy of the guys.

Alex arrived at the gym in a pair of yoga pants and exercise top, and carrying a gym bag that held her water bottle, a clean towel and a hooded cardigan. As she stepped through the double entrance doors she was met with the familiar smell of sweat and metal. The gym was housed in old police stables and accessed through a small wooden door. A tidy hallway, its concrete floors echoing with her footsteps, took her to a converted, large open plan workout area. A large boxing ring dominated the centre and was surrounded by weights and other exercise equipment around its sides.

"Ah, Alex, my lovely, how are you today?" Gruber called to her in German from across the room. He was a man in his 50s, an ex-boxer, grey-haired but still in very good shape. He had short hair cut in a Boho style and a trendy goatee beard. His face was barely lined and he had a boyish smile.

"I'm very well, Arni," she replied in German. "How's business?"

"Good, good," he replied, giving her a hug. "So, do you want in the ring today?"

"Yes, give me half an hour to warm up and I'm there," she said. "Who's in? Who will fight me?"

"Jorg and Yusuf," he replied, motioning to where two large and powerful men were training with weights. Both acknowledged her with a nod.

"I'll take them both on," she said decidedly. "I'm feeling a little stiff. A good bout will help iron the knots out."

"Are you sure?"

Alex grinned. Her blue eyes sparkled. Oh yes, she was sure.

Jorg was first to get in the ring with her. A tall blond man originally from northern Bavaria, Jorg smiled at her as he allowed Gruber to place a guard in his mouth. He touched gloves with her and the round began. Alex had told the men many times not to hold back on her just because she was a woman, and Jorg and Yusuf were the only two who kept to that agreement. Jorg swung several punches at her which she easily dodged. She jabbed, caught him on the jaw and left him stunned and shaking his head. He laughed and got back into the fight. He came at Alex, huge and menacing, and she easily dodged all his punches. She gave him a right hook in the abdomen and winded him slightly. He responded with a throw to her head which caught her on the left temple. Despite wearing head protection, Alex felt the punch connect. Dazed and staggering slightly, she moved away from him and regrouped. Then the grit and steel that saw her through years in the British army kicked in and she turned on him again. One-two-three punches and she put Jorg on the back foot. A final upper cut connected with his chin and sent the big German staggering back against the ropes. He laughed and called time out. Breathing heavily, he removed his mouthguard and grinned.

"You're getting better, little one," he said in English.

"I have a great teacher," she replied. "You want to go again?"

"Sure!"

An hour later, following several bouts with both Jorg and Yusuf, Alex had worked any kinks she'd had out of her body. Exhausted, sweaty and happy, she took off her gloves and shook their hands.

"Thanks for the workout, boys," she said in German. Sweat was pouring down her face, and she fetched her towel from her bag. Then took a long drink from her water bottle relishing as the cool liquid washed down her dry throat. As she was drinking, she glanced over to where Arni was talking to a tall dark-haired man dressed in a suit. They were in a deep conversation, then Arnie nodded and gave the man's right arm a pat. It was then that then man looked over to Alex and stared at her for a few seconds longer than was comfortable. She frowned. Arni escorted him out of the gym before approaching her.

"Who was that?" Alex asked.

"Some tourist who'd gotten lost. He was asking for directions to the city centre," Arni replied.

Alex wasn't convinced. She looked over to the exit. Her gut was telling her something was wrong and to be careful leaving. There was something not quite right about the stranger. She couldn't put her finger on it.

"Never mind him," Arni interrupted. "How is life for you, my dear? You have a boyfriend yet? Yes?"

"No," she replied with a small smile. The truth was Alex had not had a boyfriend for years. It was not something she was sad about and she did not dwell on it, but when someone like Arni made her think about it, there was as small slither of regret in her stomach. "You know me, Arni. I'm too busy for boyfriends."

"What? A beautiful woman like you? You should be chasing them off!" He grinned.

Alex smiled and picked up the gym bag. "Nah," she said. "Not interested." She slung the bag over her shoulder and smiled. "Tschuss (bye)!" She moved to the door.

"Next time I see you, I will have a boyfriend for you," Gruber called after her. "I promise! I know many good men who would make a good husband for you."

Alex laughed, as she pulled open the door. "Thanks, but no thanks, Arni," she called as she walked out.

The street was quiet as she exited the gym. She looked up and down checking for any sign of the strange man, and, seeing he was not there, cautiously headed for home. The walk back to her apartment was uneventful, and when she reached it, she dumped her gym bag in her kitchen before stripping off and jumping in the shower. It was now 10pm, and she had two hours to get ready for her job. She always studied her targets before taking them out. It made the jobs easier and lessened the possibility that she would fail. Not that she ever had failed, but there was a first time for everything. Her years as a soldier and latterly sniper had drummed into her the importance of preparation, and that's what tonight would be all about. She wanted to get there early to scope out the joint.

Alex had been in the nightclub before, but as a paying customer not for a job. She knew the basic layout, but it was the outside that interested her most. If she could lure Felix Weber outside, away from the public and his bodyguards, it would be so much easier to kill him. The sniper rifle might not be the thing for this job. She would pack a wire ligature and a small handgun in her evening clutch bag. Hmmm, should she take a syringe of poison too? She mused over the decision as she dried herself off. Maybe poison would be too much. The ligature and the gun plus a silencer should do the job just fine.

She stared at her naked frame in her floor length bedroom mirror. She was tall and willowy, but had the powerful shoulders of a swimmer. A bruise had formed on her rib cage where Yusuf had caught her in the ring earlier, and there was a mark under her left eye. She would disguise that with makeup. Now, what would she wear? It would have to be something slinky, sexy, hot. Something that would make Felix Weber stand up and take notice of her. She had the perfect dress in her wardrobe.

The dark-haired stranger arrived at his Berlin hotel trailing a small suitcase on wheels, and entered his room. After carefully hanging his clothes up in a small, but functional wardrobe, Nick stashed his suitcase under the bed before eagerly investigating the briefcase left on a tallboy by a local MI6 colleague. It had a digital lock and, already armed with the password, he tapped it in and the case opened with a satisfying click. Inside, nestled in cut out dark grey foam, was a gleaming Glock 17 handgun and a brown A4 envelope that had been sellotaped shut. He took out the gun, examined it carefully, aiming at himself in the long wall mounted mirror and making gunshot noises before replacing it in the case.

Although he worked for MI6, Nick didn't often handle a gun, so any excuse to hold one was a chance for his playful side to come out. He patted the gun in place. Then his attention focussed on the envelope. Ripping the top off, he stuck his hand inside and pulled out a wad of Euros. He'd use this to seduce Alex Grier into revealing the secrets of the Sisters of Sin. He would wine and dine her until she was putty in his hands. He smiled when he thought of her in the boxing ring at Arni Gruber's gym earlier. He had gone there en-route from the airport to see who he was up against and been caught by the owner. Passing himself off as a lost businessman, he thought he might have gotten away with it. Anyway, Alex Grier was everything he had hoped for. A tall, blonde woman knocking the stuffing out of an enormous man was certainly a turn on. He looked forward to getting better acquainted

Re-locking the case, he stashed it under the bed beside his suitcase. Then he did a quick check of himself in the mirror again and smoothed down a stray hair. He stared at himself for a few moments and smiled.

Still got it, he thought giving himself a wink. Right, time to go and find this Alex Grier again.

Chapter 4 - Nick

Dressed to thrill in a skin tight red mini dress and killer high heels, Alex glided into the nightclub and took up a spot at the bar. Club Eis was a trendy place in the Mitte area of the city and attracted both locals and tourists. From the outside, it looked like an abandoned office block, but inside were five floors offering a variety of spaces and music from chill-out to high energy techno. Open for only a year, Alex had already been in it a handful of times with friends and had always enjoyed herself. Attracted by the sparkling ice-themed dancefloors and bars, her favourite spot was on the third floor where they played a hypnotic mix of old school drum and base blended with newer European dance artists. It also happened to be where Weber had his office and where there was a bar selling delicious cocktails with names like Eisbrecher (icebreaker) and Icicle Atem (icicle breath). But she wasn't there for the ambience or the alcohol—she had a job to do. She ordered a whisky and cola from a buff barman and perched herself on a stool to watch, legs crossed and eyes keen.

The club was already filling up with regulars and newbies alike, all dressed up in their best for a night of revelry. There were girls in impossibly high heels and the skimpiest of designer dresses gathered in clumps of colour in the seated area or wriggling suggestively on the dancefloor. The men, many of who were enjoying the free sexy dances, were also in top brands, dressed in expensive suits and Italian footwear. This was not a club for the poor. Only the most successful, richest clients were allowed to frequent here.

The air was a heady mix of strong exclusive perfumes and the deep boom, boom of the music. Lights flashed, people danced and writhed, their bodies pulsating to the intoxicating beat.

From her vantage point, Alex was suddenly aware of a tall, handsome man standing near the exit. Like a hunter seeking prey, he revolved his head slowly, fully taking in the crowd before moving off. Walking with the ease of a big cat, he slunk around groups of people as he carefully made his way towards the bar. She noted him observing the faces of each person he passed—but why?

Then, as if he could feel her gaze on him, turned and looked straight at her. Alex did not flinch, but she found herself unable – no, unwilling – to look away. It was as if she was mesmerised by him. It was the man from the gym earlier. Alarm bells began to go off in her head. Who is he? she wondered, taking in the muscular form under his smart jacket and slacks, his dark hair and eyes. What is he doing here? And why alone? Who is he meeting? People did not normally go to a nightclub by themselves, not men anyway so he must be something to do with Weber.

The man finally broke eye contact and turned his cool gaze to the dancefloor. Some people walked by and she lost sight of him. It was as if he had just melted into nothing. Well, that was odd, she thought, biting her lip. She took a sip of her drink and dismissed the incident. She didn't have the time to think about some hunky mystery man. Not now. She had a job to do. A job that had a big pay-out, and she wasn't going to miss her chance this time.

Resuming her surveillance, Alex's attention was drawn to Weber's office door. Two goons appeared and stood either side of the entrance like the guardians to the underworld. Huge men, all height and muscle, they wore white shirts under dark suits and surveyed the crowd around them. Alex sat up, now solely focussed on the office.

One of the men cracked the door and had an animated conversation with someone inside. The door was pushed fully open, and Weber himself emerged like a bear from hibernation. He was tall, slim, but had not been blessed with good looks. Too small eyes, a bulbous nose and large fleshy lips made sure he would not win any male modelling competitions any time soon. But that did not put off a gaggle of scantily attired young women who, on seeing him surface, gathered around him clucking and fussing like hens on heat. He put his arms around two of the girls closest to him, and together they walked off in the direction of a private area of the dancefloor that was roped off just for him. The other girls, disappointed to have not been chosen, began to follow, but were blocked by the heavies. Weber had made his choice; they would not get near him again tonight.

Alex downed her drink and slid off the bar stool. Skirting the bar, pushing her way through the crowd, she made her way towards the VIP area. The music pulsated, the lights flashed and an army of young men and women danced with joyous abandon. Ignoring it all, only interested in her quarry, Alex moved towards the VIP area like a lioness hunting deer. Completely absorbed with what she was doing, she did not see the handsome man from before slide up to her. It was only when he blocked her way that she finally noticed him again.

"Hey!" she shouted over the music. "Get out my way!"

"I can't do that," the man shouted back in a well-to-do English accent. He was leaning over her, and she could feel his warm breath on her ear as he talked. He was tall and dark-haired with dark brown eyes that looked almost black in that light. Under his expensive suit, he was fit and muscular. Alex could see by the way his shirt clung to his torso that this guy worked out, and she had to fight the urge to lift a hand and touch his abs. He was even better close up. She frowned.

"Why not?" she demanded. She had a job to fulfil, and she was going to do it. She had a gun and a wire ligature stashed in her clutch bag. If she was able to take him out tonight, she was going to do it. She just needed to get close enough to Weber to use it.

"How can I possibly let a gorgeous woman like you go by without offering to buy you a drink?"

Alex looked at him like he had sprouted two horns from his head and hissed, "Is that supposed to be a chat up line? Am I supposed to be impressed by that? Well, it's fucking awful. Get the fuck out of my way before I knee you where it hurts."

"Oooh, I like my women feisty," he replied with a smirk.

She threw him a dirty look before putting a hand on his shoulder and pushing him out of the way. He grinned and stepped back.

"If you're going to see Felix Weber, he's already gone," the man pointed out.

Alex looked at the VIP area and it was empty. Shit! She searched the club frantically and could see no sign of the owner or of his two companions. The bodyguards were also missing. How did that happen? He was just there! Shit, shit, shit.

"I know where he is," he shouted.

She turned on him. "Look, I don't know who you are or care what you know, just stay out my fucking way," she snapped and began to push through the crowd in the direction of the exit. Before she even saw him, she sensed he was coming after her. As she went through the exit, he caught her by the right arm and stopped her in her tracks. She spun around, furious, left hand raised in a fist. He let go of her and held up two placating hands.

"Wow! Calm down, Tyson! I just want to talk to you, that's all," he said. The door had closed behind him, and the music was now a muffled dull throb in the background. "Look, I think we got off to the wrong start," he said. His face seemed honest and he was smiling. "Can we start again?" He held out a hand.

Alex sneered at the outstretched palm. "What's that for?"

"Well, traditionally you shake hands when you first meet. Did no-one teach you that?" he said. She glowered. "My name is Nick Baker. And you are?" Nick always used an alias in the field.

She glanced around the corridor looking for Weber, but saw no sign of him. Distracted by her quest, she mistakenly told Nick her real name. "Alex Grier."

"Well, Alex Grier," said Nick, taking her right hand in his and shaking it, "I'm very pleased to meet you."

She yanked her hand away and glared at him. "Well, I'm not pleased to see you," she snapped. "You've made me miss him!"

Before he could answer, Alex made her way to the stairwell and began to descend. This time Nick did not follow her right away. She looked back and saw him leaning against the wall looking amused. She scowled and continued her on her way.

Alex cursed as she searched the stairwell for the club owner, but he was nowhere to be seen. Buggery bollocks, she thought as she made her way outside to see if he might have gone out.

Three bouncers were standing chatting at the club's main entrance and they didn't notice her approach until she tugged the sleeve of one.

"Excuse me," she said in perfect German, "but has Mr Weber left?"

"What's it to you?" the smallest of the bouncers asked. He was about her height, but built like a house. His broad, overly muscular frame was squeezed into a dinner suit and was topped by a shining bald head. He had dark blue eyes and an expression on his face that said: don't mess with me.

"I was supposed to meet him inside," she said. Then in a coy voice, she added, "He said he might have some work for me."

"I bet he's got plenty of work for a lady like you," the bouncer smirked. He leered at her, staring down the low cleavage of her dress.

"I can't find him," she said. "Has he gone?"

"Mr Weber has gone out for the night and is not expected back," the man told her. "Perhaps you can try tomorrow."

"Perhaps I shall," she replied. With a flirty smile and a light touch on his enormous arm, Alex leaned in and whispered, "Any special time I should show up?"

He grinned, happy to be singled out by this stunning woman. "If I were you, I'd come around 8pm. That's when he usually gets in. He likes to be early to make sure the club runs smoothly."

"Okay," she said, licking her lips. "I'll see you tomorrow at 8 then."

A few metres away, hiding behind the doors, Nick watched and listened.

Alex was furious when she returned home. How could she

have let that man distract her? She had gone in there to do reconnaissance on Weber, she could have maybe even gotten close enough to kill him and then that buffoon got in her way. Shit! Still in her nightclub attire, she grabbed a bottle of white wine out the fridge and poured herself a glass. She kicked off her shoes and padded into the living room where she slumped on to the sofa.

Taking gulps of her drink, Alex thought about what she was going to do next. She would have to go back tomorrow. The job needed a swift conclusion. If she went at 8pm as the bouncer suggested, there would be fewer people around, but maybe more opportunities. Glancing at the clock, Alex realised it was 2am and exhaustion began to overtake her body. She downed the rest of the wine. Tomorrow, she would take out Weber.

Nick stood outside Alex's apartment block, watching. From his position in the shadows of a nearby building, he saw her lights go off and assumed the plucky assassin would not be leaving again tonight. A quick glance at his watch and he made the decision to leave her 'til later. Time to get some shut eye himself. He walked round to where his hire car was parked and got in.

Fifteen minutes later, Nick drove into the car park of his hotel. Housed in a less salubrious area of the city, the hotel was still a welcome sight to the tired spy. MI6 might pay decent wages, but they didn't splash out when it came to housing their agents in nice places. His hotel was small, but clean and comfortable, so at least they got that right. He went into his room and stripped for bed. Naked, he slipped under the cotton covers and turned off the bedside lamp. He lay back and closed his eyes, but sleep would not come. He thought about Alex and that red dress. She was even better looking in real life and that feistiness! He loved a strong woman. Was she really one of the most dangerous women in the world? She seemed so normal. He would enjoy getting to know her better.

The following morning, Alex rose late and went for a workout at the gym. None of the guys were there to fight her, so she took her anger about missing Weber out on the punch bag. That bloody man who had intercepted her! Who was he? I could kill him, she thought as she savagely punched the bag.

Arni Gruber watched her with amusement. "If you're not careful, you'll punch a hole in my bag," he joked as she walloped it once more. He folded his arms. "What's got you all uptight? A man?"

"Yes," she puffed, jabbing at the bag again, "but not in the way you think." She stopped punching and took a breather. Sweat ran down her face.

"Well, maybe you should not let this man upset you so much," Arni replied.

"He hasn't upset me," she lied.

"You could have fooled me, Liebling," he laughed. "My punchbag has never taken such a beating."

She grinned and wiped her face with a clean towel. "Maybe, but I feel so much better for it," she said.

Outside, drinking coffee from a takeaway mug, Nick sat in a dark coloured BMW. Alex had been in the gym for well over an hour, and he wondered what she was doing there. For someone so well turned out, that particular gym was not the type of place he expected her to go to. She was the type who would frequent an exclusive gym and spa in one of Berlin's top hotels, not some fleabag boxing club in the worst part of town. It didn't fit with her profile.

The door burst open, and Alex, carrying a gym bag over her shoulder, walked out. She looked around her and Nick quickly slid down in his seat so she would not see him. It wouldn't do for her to know he was following her. Not yet. He had made the mistake of letting her see him at the gym yesterday, he would not do the same thing today. He gave it a minute before gingerly peering up over the steering wheel. Alex was walking down the street in the direction of her apartment. Nick gave her a few minutes before starting the engine and slowly moving off.

To Nick, Alex appeared to have no set plans for the rest of her day. She went food shopping to the local grocery store and butcher's shop. She ate lunch at a local deli. Laden with bags, her last stop was an independent book store and Nick tailed her inside. As she browsed the shelves closest to the door, he stole past her and joined the queue for the coffee bar. As Alex perused the displays, Nick kept a close eye on her.

"What can I get you?" the girl barista asked in German.

"Ein Kaffee und Schinken-Sandwich zum Mitnehmen," he replied, still distracted by Alex.

The girl fetched his coffee and a ham sandwich and passed them over the counter. Nick handed her a ten Euro note and she returned with change.

"Danke," he said and strolled away.

It was his intention to "accidentally" bump into Alex before he left the shop, but that was proving to be more difficult than he thought. His target had left the aisle displays and was examining history books in the back of the shop. Shit. He casually tailed her and ducked down another book aisle to emerge at the other side of her. She did not look up as he approached.

"Well, fancy meeting you here," he said, taking a small bite from his sandwich.

She scowled up at him. "What do you want?" she said, returning to the tomes on the shelves.

"I saw you there and I thought I'd come over," he replied. "It's nice to meet a fellow Brit abroad. Aren't you even going to say hello?"

She gave him a dirty look, her lips curled in disgust and her eyes narrowed. "Hello," she replied. "There, I've said it. Now go away I am busy."

"Sorry I disturbed you," he said with fake sincerity. She blatantly ignored him. "I'll just go then, shall I?"

Alex sighed and peered up at him. "You just do that."

"There's no need to be rude," he said.

"Look, I came in here with the strictest intention of buying myself a new book. I did not come here to get picked up by a stranger."

"I'm not a stranger. We met last night, remember? My name is Nick, and you are Alex."

She gave him a cold hard look which told him exactly how she was feeling.

"Okay," he said turning away, "I get the picture. You do not want to talk to me right now."

"I don't want to talk to you ever," she said. Then she rounded on him. "Why were you at the club anyway?" she asked. Then she said: "And why were you at my gym? Are you stalking me?"

"No, it was just...coincidence."

"Well, I don't believe in coincidence," she said. She poked him in the chest. "Leave me alone. If you don't, you'll be sorry."

"Okay, I get it," he said backing off. Shit, he'd overplayed his hand. "I'll leave now." He paused to see if she would reply. She did not. "Well, have a nice life."

He turned heel and walked away. He did not look back, but could feel her eyes boring into his back. Good, he had nettled her.

Chapter 5 - Weber

At 7.30pm on a roof of an office building across from Club Eis and dressed in black trousers and zip up leather jacket, Alex lay on the smooth flat surface with her eye to the scope of her rifle and watched the front door. It was closed, locked, she assumed, and no soul went near it. Ten minutes went by, fifteen, and then a gold limousine drew up and stopped at the entrance. One of the thugs from the night before, emerged from the front passenger seat, observed the area and then opened a door in the rear. A man wearing a dark suit got out and nodded to his man.

Felix Weber then adjusted his suit jacket before looking around him. He had all the confidence of someone who knew himself to be untouchable by law and by morals. He smiled to his guard as the man put out a hand to usher him inside the club. With a last look around, Weber walked up to the door and waited whilst a third man, who had also disembarked from the car, hurried in front of him with a set of keys. The nightclub was unlocked and the door opened.

From her perch above, Alex, breathing slowly, waited for the perfect moment to pull the trigger, but the bodyguard was forever in the way. Felix was in shot one minute and out of it another. Shit. Weber stepped toward the opening, his man right behind him. Get out of the way! Alex desperately searched again for a shot, but the nightclub owner was inside before she could pop him. Shit! She drew back and bit her lip. She needed a new plan. She would have to regroup.

Alex knew the nightclub boss was unlikely to reappear at the door any time soon, so she packed her gun away in a rucksack and exited via the internal stairwell that led from the roof to the ground. She paused at the door, taking a baseball cap out of her rucksack to cover her glorious blonde mane. Satisfied her hair was all tucked up inside the hat, she peeped outside. Happy there were no witnesses to her departure, she carefully left the building and, sticking to the shadows, scuttled down an alleyway heading for the U-bahn or subway at Freiderich Strasse.

Taking care to not draw attention to herself, she walked smartly to the station and purchased a ticket from the machine using cash. Following a group of young men down into the underground, she stood on the platform to wait for the next train to take her home. As she waited, her brain mulled over how and when she was going to take out Weber. He was always surrounded by bodyguards, or so it seemed, and she wondered if she might be better going after him in his home. She was so caught up in planning, she did not see she was being tailed until it was too late.

Alex couldn't pinpoint what made her glance over to the tall man at the other end of the station, but all of a sudden, her Spidey senses were tingling. There was danger about. He was also wearing a baseball cap, but she recognised the fit frame. Damnit, she thought as she realised who it was. A group of teenagers bounced noisily down the stairs and walked past first him and then her. She took the opportunity to use them as camouflage while she slipped behind the nearest supporting pillar. She waited. A few moments went by and then a tall figure walked by her hiding place. She sprang out behind him and pinned a knife to his back.

"Why are you following me?" Alex hissed in his ear.

"I'm not following you," Nick replied, turning around.

She stepped closer to better disguise the weapon. The underground train rumbled into the station. Passengers got off and passengers got on.

"I'm just here to get a train."

"Really? So, you're not following me?" she said. She stood with her arms crossed, trying to be fierce and threatening. His face softened.

"Honestly, I'm here to get a train," he said, taking a step forward. The knife touched his belly.

"Bull… shit!" she growled. "I'm not stupid, you are following me and I want to know why."

"A pure coincidence," he said. "I'm heading back to my hotel now. I have a dinner appointment."

"I don't believe you." Her grip held firm to the blade. "What do you want from me? The truth, mind."

He bit his lip, silently staring at her for a brief moment. Alex could see in his face he was trying to work out what to tell her. At last, he spoke. "Look! You're right," he said. "I am following you."

The confession made her angrier. "Why?"

He leant forward. "I want to join your organisation," he whispered.

"What organisation?" She, too, lowered her voice.

"The Sisters of Sin." He stepped back and watched her reaction. Alex felt a flush creep up her cheeks and couldn't stop it. Damnit!

"I don't know what you're talking about," she replied. How did he know about the Sisters of Sin? Fuck. They were a secret organisation. Who are you and what do you want with the Sisters?

"Cut the crap, Alex," Nick replied. "I know who you are. I know what you are. And I know all about the Sisters of Sin and I want to join."

Alex searched his dark brown eyes for any signs of duplicity and could find none. He seemed sincere, but how a person seems and what a person is can be two different things in Alex's book. She didn't trust many people and she certainly did not trust him. She did not respond.

"Look, I've been wanting to approach you for some time. I'm ex-Navy and I'm looking for a job. I've tried Civvy Street, but it just doesn't feel right for me. Too vanilla. I'm great at hand-to-hand combat, I'm a trained sniper and I have no qualms about taking anyone out for the right amount of money," he said. "I've seen the evil people who populate this world and I want to do my bit to take them out. That's what you do, isn't it? Kill bad people?"

She eyed him suspiciously.

"If you don't believe me, here's my dossier." He stuck his hand into his pocket and pulled something out. She flinched and pushed the knife towards him again. He put his hands up and she relaxed a little. "I'm just getting something." He put his hands down and handed her a memory stick.

"How do I know you are who you say you are?" she wanted to know. "How do I know you're not police? And how do I know that won't corrupt my computer?" she asked. She didn't take it.

"You don't, but that won't. It's against my interests to do

something stupid like that." He offered her it again. "I'm sure your organisation could do with another person who's handy with a gun. All I ask is that you look at my resume or give it to the person in charge."

She snatched the stick with her free hand and shoved it in the pocket of her trousers.

"Thank you. Now if you'll lower that knife, I'll leave you to go about your evening," he said.

Alex stepped back and stashed the knife in her jacket pocket. Never taking her eyes off him, she watched as he backed away.

"Goodbye, Alex," he said, moving towards the exit of the subway station. "I hope someday we will see each other again."

He gave her a nod of farewell and turned and climbed the stairs. Alex waited until she was sure he was gone before she moved. Something was off here. She would call Mother and find out what to do. She glanced at her watch. Another train was due in five minutes. She decided to wait for it and call her handler when she got back to the safe private space of her home.

Chapter 6 - Bratwurst

Mother was preoccupied with the bombing when Alex called, but she didn't seem overly worried about him.

"I don't know who this Nick Baker is," she said, "but tell him nothing about the Sisters. We don't exist, got it?"

"What about the memory stick?"

"Take a look at it, copy it and then hand it back," Mother said. "Send the copy to the lab and get Finn to go through it. He may be able to detect code that could tell us more about this Mr Baker." She paused. "Greed, I'm sorry, I'm going to have to go. There's so much to do to try and get the headquarters back up and running. Just do as you see fit. I trust you."

"Thank you, Mother."

"And for God's sake, get that job done!" she added. "Our client is waiting!" The phone clicked off.

"Damnit," Alex muttered. When Mother said the client was waiting that meant they wanted a quick result, which would mean returning to do the job tonight. *What about Nick Baker?* she thought. *What will I do about him?* She plucked the memory stick from her pocket and considered what it might hold. *He can wait until I get home.*

It was past eleven when Alex found herself outside Club

Eis again. The streets were empty apart from habitual night-club goers who were only beginning to emerge. Gaudily dressed spectres, they made their way towards Club Eis, laughing and singing, flirting and dancing. Still in her dark work gear, Alex stuck out like a sore thumb, so moved into the quieter streets off the main thoroughfare, cap pulled tightly over her eyes, rucksack slung over one shoulder. She reached the office building a few minutes later, picked the security lock on the fire door and began the climb to the top. Her legs were aching by the time she reached the summit on the eighth floor—two journeys up here in one evening was giving her an unexpected and unwelcome workout. She emerged on to the roof just as a full moon appeared from the clouds and lit up the nocturnal world before her. As she skulked across the rooftop, she kept as low to the ground as possible fearful that its brightness would highlight her tall, slim frame and give the people below warning that she was coming. She again took up position at a point overlooking the main door of the club and waited.

Club goers came and went all night. The front door opened and closed. Music blasted and waned. There were four bouncers on the front door again tonight, and they spent the evening filtering out unwanted guests and surveying the streets like they expected an invasion any moment. An hour went by and still no Weber. Alex, lying on her front, eye to eyepiece, shifted slightly to ease the stiffness in her back. It was a small movement, but gave her momentary comfort. This was part of the job she hated: the waiting. Once she had waited for four hours in the one position to take out a target and that had nearly sent her body into spasms. She hoped she wouldn't have that kind of wait tonight.

By midnight, the club was packed with revellers and the

street outside became still and quiet. The bouncers, convinced that most of the crowd were now inside, took turns having a break. Two went off at a time: one went around the corner for a smoke, another disappeared inside. Half an hour later, they returned and took up their positions again whilst their colleagues took their breaks.

At 1am, a gold limousine drew up to the entrance and Alex perked up. At last, this was her chance. She concentrated her gun on the door and waited. A bouncer made a call. There was some animation amongst them as they smartened up and stood up straight. Then one of Weber's bodyguards emerged from the doorway and looked around. He motioned to someone inside, and Weber stepped out into the arena. He moved towards the open door of his car oblivious that far above him, the angel of death had squeezed the trigger.

The bullet hurtled towards its target and caught him smack between the eyes. He crumpled to the ground, dead. It took all of three seconds for his bodyguards to realise what had happened. As two frantically trying to drag their boss inside, others drew handguns and began to scan the area, searching for the gunman. There were shouts for help and screams could be heard from inside. More men hurried out with weapons, and all eyes sought the murderer.

Up above, Alex quickly broke down her rifle and put it in the rucksack. She peeked over the parapet and saw the bodyguards searching in her direction. One pointed to her building and she knew she only had a few minutes before they would discover her position. She ran to the roof exit and rushed down the stairs, taking them two at a time. Emerging into the back street below, she looked left and saw no one there. She looked right, and a man emerged from the shadows and blocked her way. She immediately got ready to fight.

"Stop! It's me!" Nick said putting his hands up in surrender. "I can help you."

"I don't need your help," she said. The sounds of men running and their shouts filtered down to them.

"I think you do," he replied.

"Get out of my way," she said, pushing past him.

"I've got a car," he said, "I can get you out of here."

Just then a bodyguard came running around the corner. "Hoi!" he shouted. "Hier!" More shouts came from behind him and Alex needed to leave. Fast. He was running towards her.

"Alright," she said. "Let's go."

Nick's BMW was parked down the alleyway, and he and Alex just barely made it inside when the bodyguard stopped, raised his handgun and fired. The bullet hit the wall above the car, she heard it smack into the brickwork.

"Hurry!" she screamed as Nick fumbled with the keys. He switched the engine on and the car roared into life. Putting his foot down, he drove the car down the alley and then skidded left on to the brightly lit main thoroughfare. Alex spun to look behind them, fearful Weber's men were in pursuit, but there was no sign of them. She relaxed back in her chair and put on her seatbelt. Breathless, she placed her rucksack at her feet and wiped the sweat from her brow. Nick, keeping his eyes on the road, slowed down a little to make them seem less conspicuous.

"That was close," he said.

"Yeah."

"So, did you get him?" he asked.

"Who?"

"Felix Weber? I'm assuming that's who you were there to assassinate," he said.

"I don't know what you're…" she began.

"Look, Alex, you and I both know what you are, so why hide it?"

She took a breath. She couldn't trust him, but there was no point in lying any more. "Okay, and yes, he's dealt with," she admitted.

"Good," Nick said with a smile. "By all accounts he was a nasty piece of work."

"What were you doing in that alleyway? How did you know I was there?"

"I knew you would go back. You had a job to do and it needed to be done quickly," he replied.

"How do you know that?"

"We're the same, you and I. It's what I would have done," he said.

She didn't know how to reply to that so stayed quiet, and they sat in silence for a while whilst Alex wondered who this man actually was. She had so many questions to ask him about how he knew about her and the SOS, but she did not want to say anything, not until she had done her own digging into Nick Baker's background. She remained tight-lipped as they continued on their journey west.

"You're going the wrong way," she said at last.

"What do you mean?"

"You're going out of the city."

"I know," he replied. Suddenly she grew fearful and tried the door handle. It was locked. Shit, he was kidnapping her.

"Let me out! Let me out now!" she screamed trying the door again. Then she fumbled for her knife.

"Relax," he said. "You don't need to worry, and you don't need to use that. I'm not going to do anything to you. I'm just taking you to a little late-night place I know where we can get bratwurst and a beer. You must be hungry, right?" She nodded. "I was always ravenous after a hit. I think it's the adrenaline rush," he added.

Alex stared at him and tried to work out if he was telling the truth or not. She decided to let this play out and relaxed a little again, but the knife remained in her hand.

"Another five minutes and we'll be there," he said, giving her a smile. "I promise that once we've eaten, I'll take you straight home. Okay?"

She nodded and said nothing more. As they drove, Alex took furtive peeks at the handsome man beside her. He had a square jaw and short dark hair. His nose was straight and long, his eyes blessed with long dark eyelashes that gave them their boyish look. She wondered if she could trust him at all. She didn't know why, but she found this man, this stranger, somewhat beguiling. She hadn't felt this way about anyone in years. He fascinated her and she felt it would be fun finding out more about him. She could not trust him, no, but she would allow him to get to know her better.

Who knew where that might lead? Bed?

There was a quickening in her groin as she thought about having sex with this man. It had been a while since she'd last bedded anyone and maybe he could be her next conquest. What Alex Grier wanted, Alex Grier made sure she got, and she suddenly realised she wanted Nick Baker. There was something tantalisingly masculine about him. Just her type. He caught her staring at him.

"What? Why are you looking at me that way?" he asked.

"No reason," she said. Was that heat rising up her face? Was she blushing? She never blushed. He smiled and carried on driving.

A few minutes later he drew up to an all-night burger van in a seedier part of town.

"You bring me to all the best places," Alex drawled as she got out of the car.

"You're hungry, aren't you?" he asked.

"Yes."

"Well, let's eat."

They ordered a bratwurst in a bun and a beer each, and sat down on a nearby bench under a street lamp to munch happily on their food. Despite finding herself attracted to Nick, Alex was still wary of getting too close. What did she know about him? Nothing. He could be anyone, police or secret services or another assassination team, she had to remain alert. If any of that were the case, she thought, why hasn't he arrested me or taken me out by now? She peered over the top of her bun at the man who had helped her escape. He was busy taking a swig of beer and grinned when he saw her looking at him.

"It's good?" he asked.

"Oh yes," she said, taking in his handsome face and firm body. Then she blushed. Shit, he meant the food.

"Are you alright?" he asked, sliding closer to her on the bench. He put his arm around the top of the seat and swivelled around so he was facing her. Her peered at her under the pale white glow of the streetlight. "Are you blushing?"

"No. I'm fine," she squeaked, inhaling the deep manly aroma of his aftershave. His aura was mesmerising. "You were right, this food is great."

"Glad to hear it," he said, wiping his mouth with a paper napkin in his other hand. "Are you nearly finished?"

"Yes, why?"

"Well, I thought I'd see you home," he said, leaning in to her so closely that she could feel his breath on her face.

She gulped. Get a grip, Alex, get a grip. She did not need any kind of complications in her life right now, especially a new lover.

"No, that's alright," she said. "I can make my own way home from here."

"If you're worried about me knowing where you live, don't," he said. "I already looked you up."

Fear gripped Alex. "What?"

"I followed you home last night."

"Why?" Fuck! Did she have her very own stalker?

"I told you. I'm interested in joining your organisation. I thought if I got to know you, one of their employees, you might be able to help me get in." He shrugged nonchalantly.

Alex frowned. She studied his face and he seemed genuine. Not that she felt she could trust him, not yet.

He moved in a little closer, his arm now around her shoulders and his mouth dangerously close to hers. "Of course, I had no idea how deadly attractive you'd be," he whispered and went in for a kiss.

"Just a minute!" Alex said, extricating herself from his arms. "I don't know what your game is, matey, but you can't just seduce me to get into the Sisters."

"So, you are a member," he said, sitting back and laughing. "I knew it!"

Furious she had slipped up; Alex threw the remnant of her burger at him.

"Hey!" he shouted, moving back.

"That's for being such a dickweed!" she snapped and folded her arms. She sat there for a few minutes, angry at him, angry at herself. He wasn't interested in her, he was just using her to get access to the Sisters. Nick bit his lip, his dark brown eyes displaying genuine sorrow for his actions.

"I apologise," he said. "I shouldn't have tried to kiss you."

"It wasn't that."

"Or trick you into admitting you are a member of the Sisters," he added. Alex made a noise that sounded something like Hmph. "Look, can we start again? I'm sorry if I upset you."

"I'm not upset!" she growled.

"Well, you seem to be." He tried to touch her hand, but she yanked it away. She got to her feet, unable to hold in her anger any longer.

"Well, how would you feel if someone stalked you and then tried to seduce you just so he could get a job?" She glared at him.

"God, you look magnificent," he said, drinking in her beauty.

"Oh, fuck off!" she replied and stalked away. He scrambled to his feet, grabbed her arm and stopped her in her tracks. She rounded on him ready to fight, her right fist raised.

"Look, it's true that I was watching you for a bit, but it was only to find out more about the Sisters, that's all. You'd do the same in my position."

"Doubt it."

"I'm out of a job. I heard about your organisation, I decided to approach one of their members, you and – well – I am sorry if I upset you," he said. He let go of her arm and then, when she did not react, took a step towards her. "I didn't mean to, Alex. And if I offended you by trying to kiss you, I'm sorry, but you've got to look at it from my point of view. You're bloody gorgeous."

Alex relaxed a little. She could not look at him yet, but her anger quickly dissipated and allowed him to come closer to her.

She lowered her fist. He took her other hand, gently pulled her towards him and caressed her cheek. She gazed up into his deep brown eyes and knew then she was lost. What was he doing to her? Nick put his hand on her back and pulled her to him. Then he bent towards her and kissed her gently on the lips.

Weakness trickled into her knees and made her stomach do cartwheels. Alex hated feeling weak—especially for a man. However, she allowed herself to go deeper into the sensation, breathing heavier and getting lost in the touch of his soft, soft lips. His hands rose up her back as he kissed her with the passion of a lover. Then, all of a sudden, it was over and she was released. The loss of the delicious sensations had her frowning.

"Am I forgiven?" he asked.

"Maybe," she said. Stepping back, Alex touched her tingling lips and took stock of what had just happened. Jesus! This man was hot. He was handsome. He was fit. And he wanted her.

"What are you thinking about?" he asked.

"I'm thinking it's time I went home," she said, deciding she needed time to muse over where this could go. "Will you take me?"

"Do you trust me to?"

"Well, you already know where I live, so I suppose I'll have to," she replied. "There's no point pretending otherwise, so I might as well take advantage of the fact."

Nick dropped Alex outside her apartment building. Neither had spoken a word about that kiss, but before she got out of the car, he leant over and gave her another one on the cheek. It was disappointingly chaste.

"Good night, Alex," he said softly.

For a brief moment, Alex wondered if he would kiss her

again, but he didn't. Unexpected disappointed coursed through her as she got out of the car. "Night," she said.

Without another word, Nick drove off, leaving her alone and upset on the pavement. What had just happened? First, he could hardly keep his hands off her and now he was kissing her like he'd kiss a relative. And why was she now sad about it? It was ridiculous. She had only just met him. They had kissed and that was it. Why was she feeling her world had just fallen apart?

"Get a grip, Alex," she muttered to herself as she let herself into her apartment block. "He's just a guy."

She went to bed as soon as she got in. The assassination of the night club host, their flight from his bodyguards and that kiss had taken it out on her physically and emotionally. She gratefully slipped naked under her covers, her body still singing with desire for Nick. Alex willed sleep to come, but every time she closed her eyes, all she could think about was him. Bugger, get out of my head Nick Baker, she inwardly screamed as she tossed and turned.

She must have finally fallen asleep some hours later for it was 1pm when she awoke to urgent knocking.

Chapter 7 - Dominika

Throwing on her ivory silk Chanel dressing gown, Alex ran barefoot to answer her door. Her heart was beating wildly as she ran down her hallway, her imagination going wild with the possibility that it could be him. She didn't even bother to look through the security peephole before unlocking the heavy wooden door and yanking it open.

"Nick?" she said, hope rising.

"Hello." A tall dark-haired woman stood before her. "How are you, Greed, and who the hell is Nick?"

Dominika was standing at her door in all her gorgeous glory. Dressed in tight black leather trousers, a silk shirt and a long, black leather coat, she looked for all the world like she had just stepped out of vampire fantasy. Dominika was no warm and friendly heroine. No, if she were one of the undead, she would be the nastiest vampire of them all. Her long, black hair was straight as a die, her face was pale and her lips were a perfect sneer of blood red. Yes, she would make the perfect vampire queen, Alex thought as she opened the door to let her sister in.

"Dominika, welcome," she said, managing a smile and choosing to ignore the question. "What brings you to Berlin?"

"Alex, darling," the willowy Russian said with a nod of the head. That was about the warmest greeting Alex had ever had from her. Dominika slunk into the spacious apartment with the confidence of a panther and settled in the living room. She stood, cold and aloof, slowly taking in her surroundings, abject disapproval in her face. Alex's cosy home obviously didn't meet with Dominika's high standards.

"Please, have a seat," Alex said, motioning towards her designer leather sofa. "Can I get you something? A coffee? Tea?"

Dominika wrinkled her nose at Alex's sofa and her face said it all. Her lips curled back like she had stepped in something nasty. Instead, she chose to sit in the adjacent armchair.

"No thank you," she said with all the warmth of a corpse. She turned her ice blue eyes on Greed. "I'm not here to socialise. I'm here to find out what you know about the HQ bombing. I hear the entire board were killed."

Alex found Dominika intimidating at the best of times, but was not about to let her know that. Sitting down opposite, Alex relaxed into the sofa's back and held Dominika's gaze. "I only know what Mother told me…" She began picking invisible lint from her dressing gown. "That someone had blown up the HQ and that all the board members were dead."

"Do they know who did it?" the Russian asked as she rifled in a pocket of her coat. She pulled out a black and gold cigarette packet, Sobranie, and a solid gold lighter. She held them up. "Do you mind?"

"Yes, I do actually," replied Alex. She did not like to be rude to any guest, but was staunchly anti-smoking. She hated the smell of it and would not entertain it in her home. Dominika grimaced and stuffed the cigarettes and lighter back in her bag. Her cold eyes returned to Alex.

"Well? You didn't answer me. Do they know who did it?"

"No, they've not a clue," Alex said. There was a tense pause.

"I wonder if it was a rival company? Someone trying to get us out of the way so they can dominate the market?"

"Hmm, maybe."

Dominika's dark eyes flitted around again like she was searching for something. She finished her assessment of Alex's home and stood up, giving Alex a nod. For a brief moment Alex thought she was also going to click her heels together as well like German and Russian characters did in old movies.

"I'm going now," she said after a beat, turning toward the door. "If you hear of anything, please let me know."

"Just a minute," said Alex, scrambling to her feet. "Before you go, I'd like to ask you something. What are you doing in Berlin? Mother said you were in South America." She walked towards her to see her out.

"I was in South America and now I'm here," Dominika snapped. She strode into the hallway to the front entrance.

"What for?" Alex knew her question was futile. Dominika liked to hold her cards close to her chest, but she had to try.

"Well, that's my business, isn't it?" the Russian growled. She placed her hand on the handle of the front door.

"Of course," Alex replied, catching her up. They were face-to-face now. Dominika was a few inches taller than her, but she wasn't about to let her bully her. She looked straight into her eyes. The other woman snorted and a nasty smile played about her lips.

"Good," Dominika said. She yanked open the door and then paused. She turned to look at Greed again. "When I came to the door, you said someone's name. Who was it?"

"What? Did I?" Alex replied.

"Yes, it was Nick," Dominika said her eyes narrowing, boring into Alex's.

"Oh, him! He's no one." she replied. Her stomach clenched and she fought to keep the fear out of her eyes. It would not do to let this particular Sister know she had a new man in her life. Dominika was known to be brutal and was rumoured to have killed the partners of fellow Sisters in the past. Alex didn't know how true this was, but she wasn't about to find out. Her feelings for Nick would have to remain secret if she wanted to keep him alive.

"Hmmph," the Russian said. "Well, I hope for his sake that he is really a no one. You know the rules, Alex. It's forbidden to have relationships."

"I don't have a relationship with him. He's a contact, that's all," Alex reassured her.

Dominika nodded but didn't look convinced. "Make sure he stays that way," she snapped as she strode out into the outside corridor. "Goodbye, Greed."

Alex closed the door, gave it the bird and went to the window of her apartment that overlooked the front of the building. She waited until Dominika exited the main door and watched her walk up the pathway to a waiting black car. A large, heavy man in a black suit was standing at the rear passenger door and opened it as Dominika walked up. He then closed the door and went to the driver's side. He slid in, started the engine and the car drove off. As it drove away from the kerb, the window at Dominika's side slid open and Alex observed her fellow sister lighting a cigarette. Now wearing dark sunglasses, Dominika looked every bit a queen.

Queen of the Damned, Alex thought as she came away from the window.

As she made herself some coffee in her kitchen, Alex mused

over the visit. Why had Dominika come? Surely, she could have gotten the news of the bombing from Mother herself? Why bother her? Why was she really in Berlin? And who was the man driving her?

The Sisters did not hire staff, especially bodyguards as that man so obviously was. As he had bent over to open the door for Dominika, Alex had caught a glimpse of a gun holder strapped to his inside left breast. The Sisters worked solo and in secret, so why was Dominika flouting the rules? Her instincts were tingling, setting off warning flags.

Maybe it's all to do with a job, she thought, taking her first sip of coffee. She let the strong bitter taste slide over her tongue and enjoyed the delicious first hit of caffeine. Alex contemplated speaking to Mother, but didn't want to really bother her, seeing as she was busy trying to rebuild the organisation.

What if Dominika's visit had been totally innocent? The Russian was a cold fish at the best of times, and they had never got on, so why would she expect her to be warm and cuddly now? But something was nagging at the back of Alex's mind and she decided she had best speak to Mother.

"Hello? Greed? This isn't a good time right now," Mother said when she called her. "I'm up to my eyes in it."

"I know, but…"

"Is this really important or can it wait 'til later?" Mother said.

"Well, I…"

"Great. Look, I'll call you, all right? Good. Goodbye, Greed." And with that she hung up.

Alex stared at her phone for a few minutes. Had that really just happened? Had Mother hung up on her? Shit! Now what? I'm just being silly, Alex thought. There's nothing sinister behind Dominika's visit or the fact she's here. She told that to herself, but she didn't really believe it. She would keep an eye out for her sister, just to make sure.

Dominika had her man drive to an industrial area on the outskirts of Berlin and pull into an abandoned engineering works. The factory building was a cavernous rusting hulk of corrugated metal, its concrete floor cracked and stained. The place was empty save for a small, weak looking man in his 50s standing beside a small pale blue car. Worry marred his face until the car pulled inside. Dominika waited for the driver to open her door before emerging from the limo. She paused for her moment at the car, removed a compact from her pocket and checked her lipstick. The trembling little man could wait.

Dominika knew the effect she had on men and enjoyed every moment of their awe, their lust. She could feel his eyes on her as her tongue flickered over her lips, and he was almost drooling when she finally shut the compact and slipped it into her pocket. She approached him, her full heavenly gaze never wavering. He gaped at her like she was some sort of goddess come down from heaven to bestow on him the secret of eternity. He gulped as she came close, placed her hands on her hips and smiled at him.

"I hope you have good news for me, Wolter," she said in perfect German.

"M-m-miss Gagolin," the man stuttered. He offered to shake her divine hand, but she put it up in the universal motion of 'stop' and he quickly retracted it. "I did everything you asked, now may I be released from our contract? There's really nothing else I can do for you. I've done everything I can. You did promise." His eyes were full of hope.

Dominika smirked. "Wolter, you have served me very well. That bomb maker you sourced for me in Rome was spot on," she said. Then she remembered how the HQ had gone up in flames, and her grin widened. "But I'm still in need of your services. I have another small job for you and then you're free."

Wolter shook his head. "I can't keep doing this, Miss Gagolin," he said. "I just can't. I'll be found out. They're already suspicious."

"Wolter, I'm shocked at you," she said, giving him a fake worried look and placing her hand on his shoulder. She could feel him trembling as he averted his eyes. "You've been so faithful to me so far, and you've done so well. Surely, another few weeks working for me won't be too hard. You're such a clever man, Wolter, you can do it. I have faith in you."

Breathing hard, Wolter took a handkerchief from his breast pocket and wiped his sweating face. "My colleagues are growing suspicious."

"Well, no wonder…especially if you look like a frightened rabbit every time I ask you for some help!" Dominika snapped. She removed her hand and held it up as if she was going to slap him. Wolter flinched. Then she calmed down and changed tack, slowly lowering her outstretched hand. "I know it's difficult for you right now, but it won't be forever. I just need you to track down this man for me and then that's it." She handed him an envelope. He took it and slid the contents out. It was sheet containing the name of a top FBI agent and a photograph.

"Why do you need to track him down?" he asked.

"I think you'll find that's my business," she said coldly.

"Of course."

"I will pay you handsomely as usual," she said. "That should give your Interpol pension a good boost. You'll be able to buy a nice house in Bavaria and live your life out in peace."

"If I do this for you, will this be the last request you make?" he asked. "I'm only an analyst. I shouldn't be tracking people for you."

"Yes."

"Promise me."

"I promise," she said with a pout. "Hand on heart and hope to die." She placed a carefully manicured hand on her chest and crossed herself.

"Alright," he said, gazing into her beautiful eyes, "but this is the last job I do for you. I just can't keep doing it. It's too stressful. I'm developing an ulcer, you know."

"Poor baby," she crooned as she gently stroked his cheek. "I do appreciate everything you're doing for me, Wolter, you know that, don't you?" Her voice was low, sultry.

"Y-yes."

"Good." She stood back and folded her arms. "Now off you go. I need that information as soon as possible. I have plans to make." She gave him one last smile before shooing him away with her hands. She watched as the little man got into his car and drove off. Then she returned to her own vehicle. "That one may become a problem in the future," she said to Wolfe, her bodyguard and chauffeur, as he opened the door for her. "I may need you to sort him out."

"No problem," he said.

Lying back against the plush seat, Dominika smiled to herself. Well, this has been a good day, she thought. Not only do they have no idea who hit them, but I'm pushing on nicely with my plan.

"Where to now, madam?" Wolfe asked.

"I have a business meeting with some investors," she said.

"Take me to the city centre, and I'll give you directions from there."

Chapter 8 - Flowers

Alex spent the rest of the day alone. She went to her gym to try and burn off some of the pent-up energy she was experiencing after being with Nick last night. Although she tried hard not to, thoughts of him steadily worked themselves into her brain and would not go out again. Every time she closed her eyes, all she could see was his handsome face smiling down at her. When she tried to concentrate on the weights or skipping rope, she found her brain drifting off to his buff body and killer smile, with the result that she tripped over the rope twice. She pounded on the punch bag as hard as she could, but he was still there.

Fuck, I've got it bad, she thought as she got ready to take on Yusuf in the ring.

The dark-haired Turk grinned as he and Alex touched gloves. The assassin had beaten him the last time they had fought, and she was angling for another win. He was tall and powerful, but she was quick and sneaky. She had feigned a move and then quickly gotten the upper hand, punching him on the chin and sending him flying against the ropes. She wouldn't do that to him again, that was for sure. Yusuf threw the first punch, which Alex easily blocked. Then the fight really began.

At first, Alex was determined beat him again. She was lighter, faster than he with a quick mind that worked out her next move in half the time his brain took to work it out. As they fought, her mind drifted to thoughts of Nick. She was distracted by the Englishman's good locks and her opponent took advantage of it. As she moved left, he brought his right fist up and caught her square across the jaw. Her mouthguard flew out as she fell to the ground out cold. Her body must have fallen heavily on the ring floor for when she came round seconds later she was aching all over. She looked up to see Yusuf pulling off his gloves and removing his mouthguard. Discarding them to the side, he went to Alex's side just as Arni and Jorg leapt over the ropes. Yusuf knelt down at her side.

"Alex? Are you okay?" he said looking at her with concern in his eyes. She managed a weak nod. Her head was ringing and her jaw was numb.

"Yusuf! What have you done?" Arni wanted to know. "I told you to go easy on her. She's just a woman."

"You told me no such thing," the Turk growled. "You said that if she beat me again you were going to ban me from the gym for being a disgrace to men."

"That was a joke. Can't you take a joke?"

Alex groaned.

"Help her up," Jorg said.

As Yusuf assisted as she got into a sitting position, Arni removed her gloves. She sat there for a minute before trying to talk: "What happened?" She winced as pain shot through her jaw. She touched it. Ouch.

"Yusuf gave you a hard, right hook," Arni said, throwing the Turk an angry look. "He shouldn't have done that." Wagging a finger, he demanded, "Apologise to the girl."

"I'm sorry, Alex, I didn't mean to hit you so hard," Yusuf

said.

She clutched her jaw and began to slowly move it side to side, checking for any damage. "Well, I don't think it's broken," she said, "but I'm going to have a corker of a bruise tomorrow."

"I'm sorry, Alex," Yusuf said again. The big man was close to tears. Alex smiled and winced. Then she put out her hand for Yusuf to help her up. Once on her feet, a little unsteady, she gave him a hug.

"Don't worry," she said. "I'm fine."

"I shouldn't have hit you so hard what with you being a…"

"A woman?" she finished the sentence for him. "How many times have I told you I do not wish to be treated any differently from anyone else who uses this gym?"

"Yes, but…" Yusuf looked to Arni for help. The gym owner shrugged.

"So, you got me with a right hook," she said, rubbing her jaw. "Good on you! It won't happen next time," she added with a grin. Yusuf returned the smile and looked relieved.

"Want me to run you to the hospital? Get it checked out?" Arni asked.

"No, I'll be all right," she assured him. "It's just a bruise."

At home, in a hot shower, Alex reflected on what had happened at the gym. Yusuf would have never been able to get me like that if I had not been so distracted, she thought as she soaped up her long, blonde hair. I need to get Nick Baker out of my head and out of my life. I cannot go on like this. It's too dangerous. Besides my career is everything to me. I will tell him to leave me alone the next time I see him. She mused over when that would be and was horrified when her stomach flipped with excitement just thinking about it.

"Stop it, Alex Grier!" she chided herself. "You are being ridiculous!"

Clean, a little sore, but determined, Alex got out the shower and slipped on some comfortable clothes. She walked barefoot into her living room and took up her cell phone. She flicked open the internet and went into the dark net to check for any new jobs. There were none, and she cursed. She was getting closer to buying her diamonds, but she was still short of a few thousand. A new job would have gotten her there.

Alex sat back in her sofa and thought about what she was going to do next. With no job to go to, she had a few days of free time on her hands. How would she spend it?

With Nick, a voice in her head said.

No, not with him, she thought crossly. I need to get away from him, he's not good for my health or my career. She touched her bruised jaw and flinched.

Or your looks, the voice pointed out.

A few days away might do me some good, she thought. Maybe I should go the seaside? Or should I jump on a plane and go visit my folks?

Her parents—with their high expectations and perfect lives. She had to lie to them about her career and found it stressful keeping the pretence up that she was a high-flying executive working for an international bank. She had told them she worked in the most boring industry she could think of so they wouldn't ask too many questions, but her mother insisted on knowing everything her children did so would ask question after question after question.

No, going home would be too stressful. A few days away at the seaside or in the mountains would do the trick. Somewhere relatively near. Alex was sick of international travel, so it would have to be in Germany. She flicked through the web and landed on Sylt Island in the North Sea. One of the North Frisian Islands, Sylt had a distinctive t-shape and a long sandy beach that was 40 kilometres long. A favourite holidaying spot for Germans and tourists, the island would be the perfect place to recharge and forget about Nick.

"Yes, Sylt it is!" Alex said aloud. She suddenly felt back in control of herself again, like taking herself away from the temptation of Nick would somehow bring her back to herself. Then something occurred to her. It was the middle of the tourist season. She checked for bookings and found nothing was available.

Shit! Now what? "Well, I suppose I'll just have to stay at home. Fuck!"

But home meant being in the same city as Nick, breathing the same air, seeing the same stars. What if she ran into him? Could she resist the urge to kiss him again? That would be fatal for her calm state of mind. The memory of that kiss filled her head, and she felt a great longing to be in his arms.

"Fuck's sake!" she growled. "Get a grip!"

She had never fallen this hard, this fast, for anyone before, and it was doing her head in.

There was a knock at the door, pulling her back to reality. Does everyone bypass the security door downstairs? Alex thought irritably as she stomped down her hallway. She pulled open her apartment door. It was her neighbour, Frau Fischer, and she was carrying an enormous bouquet of flowers.

"These were delivered to you when you were out, fraulein," the elderly woman said, shoving the bouquet into Alex's arms. "So, I took them in for you. You never know who is wandering about these corridors. These could have been stolen."

"Thank you, Frau Fischer," Alex said wondering who had

sent them to her. "I appreciate it."

"Ah, a new admirer, I'll bet," her neighbour said with a smile. "I remember when my Hans used to send me flowers. When we met, we were so in love. He used to bring me flowers all the time," she added wistfully.

"And does he still bring you flowers?" Alex said hopefully.

"No, the lazy sod just sits in front of the television all day watching his programmes while he leaves me to clean the house," Frau Fischer said. "He won't even lift a finger to make coffee when our children come round to visit. I don't know why I married him. To think, Ernst Wagner wanted to marry me, and I said no. If I had married him, I would be sitting in a big house right now with someone coming in to clean and a big car." She shook her head. "Still, I fell for my Hans. It just shows you can't decide who you fall in love with. The heart wants what the heart wants."

"It certainly does, Frau Fischer," Alex replied.

"So, aren't you going to find out who the flowers are from?"

"I will," said Alex. "Thank you for taking them in for me. Good bye."

"But-!" Frau Fischer said as Alex closed the door.

Frau Fischer was a nosey old bat and Alex wasn't about to let her know any of her business. She was a nice enough old lady, but was someone who once you allowed her into your life even an inch, she would take a mile. Alex knew the type—they tended to be lonely and latched on to whomever they could. She felt sorry for Frau Fischer, but what could she do? She had work to do, and the last thing she needed was a curious neighbour feeding that curiosity by looking into to her life. Besides, the old woman had five children. Let them take on the brunt of their mother's snooping.

Alex carried the bouquet into her kitchen. It was an enormous bunch of pink peonies, her favourite. She placed the flowers on the counter top and searched for an envelope. Finding it, she tore it open and pulled out the card. It read: Saw these and thought of you, Nick xx

"How did he know?" she said aloud.

Dismissing it as a coincidence, she went to her kitchen and got out her best crystal vase. Filling it with water, she leisurely arranged the flowers and smiled. Nick had bought her flowers. She barely knew the man, but he had spent a lot of money on buying her flowers. She hadn't been bought flowers in years, and these were beautiful. She stooped over to inhale their fragrance. Lovely.

Hold on a minute, the little voice in her head said. Why is this man buying you flowers? You barely know him. You only met him a couple of days ago. What's in it for him? Is this his way of buying himself into your affections so you'll lead him to the Sisters of Sin?

Oh my God! That's it! That's what he's doing! He's trying to buy your good will so you will get him into the organisation. She stood back from the flowers and frowned. She read the card again.

"What do you want from me, Nick Baker?" Then she tore the card up and threw it in the bin. She turned her attention to the flowers, which had suddenly lost their beauty in her eyes. These were bribe flowers. "If you think you can get to me through flowers, you're very much mistaken, Nick!" she said, grabbing the vase.

Alex lifted it to the bin, yanked up the stems and then stopped.

Why waste these lovely flowers just because a using arsehole sent them to you? her inner voice reasoned. It's not like he put the bouquet together by himself. He just ordered them from a florist's shop. He never touched them, so it wouldn't be wrong to keep them and enjoy them.

She bit her lip. Yeah, why should these lovely things go to waste just because of him? Fuck! She took the vase and walked into her living room where she placed them on her small dining table. They created a lovely centrepiece, sitting there all pink and wonderful.

Damn you, Nick Baker!

Her head was telling her to ditch them, but her heart wanted them kept. She huffed, grabbed the vase again and took it into her kitchen where she placed it on the window sill.

"I'll leave you there until I decide what to do with you," she said, sorting a stem that was leaning the wrong way.

Chapter 9 - Sex

Alex was awoken early the next morning by her door buzzer going again. Fuck! What now? She got up and took a moment to come round before climbing out of bed in a state of sleepiness. Hair mussed, makeup undone, only the silk dressing gown to cover her nakedness, she stumbled to her door and peered out of the peephole. A smiling Nick stared back at her. Shit! What was he doing here? And how did he get through that damned front door? The security door that was supposed to keep people out! She quickly patted down her hair, tightened the belt on the dressing gown, licked her lips and opened the door.

"Nick," she said somewhat breathlessly, "what are you doing here?"

"I was in the neighbourhood and thought I'd pop by and see you," he said. He was wearing a smart shirt and designer jeans. "Nice hair, by the way." He pointed up to the mussed-up mess of her normally glamorous hairstyle. Her hand flew to it as if to fix it, but Alex knew there was no point. Her hair had a mind of its own. "Can I come in?" he added.

"How did you get up here?" she asked, stepping aside to let him into the apartment. "Who let you in the security door?"

"I snuck in after one of your neighbours," he admitted, looking a little ashamed. "Hope you don't mind. Nice apartment."

"Thank you," she replied. "Now, what is it that you want?"

He frowned. "I came round to apologise again for the other night," he said, following her into the living room. "May I sit? Thanks. Look, I'm honestly not trying to seduce you to get into the Sisters. I really like you, Alex, and I'd genuinely like to get to know you better. I think we have a connection, and I'd like to see where it goes." She sat down on a chair opposite him. He was perched on the edge of her sofa. "Well? Am I forgiven?"

The hope in his gorgeous brown eyes melted her heart. She couldn't resist them. "All right," she answered, unsure of where she was going with this. "I forgive you."

He smiled, and Alex's whole world lit up.

"Great, so, here's my second reason for coming round."

"You had more than one?"

"Yes. Alex, would you come out for lunch with me?"

"What now? Today?"

"Yes." He grinned, his white teeth sparkling. "Of course, you'll have to get changed into more appropriate lunching material, but yes, today, if you're free."

She thought for a minute. He was asking her out for a date. What should she do? Should she go and risk falling for him even more? Or should she just brush him off and get on with her life? He was so stunningly handsome, sitting there on her sofa. She sighed. Fuck it!

"I'd love to," she said. She stood up, and her dressing gown flapped open showing off a toned thigh. Embarrassed, she quickly pulled it back to cover her legs. "I'll…errr…just go and get showered and changed."

"Don't wear anything too fancy," Nick called to her retreating back. "I'm not taking you to that type of place."

A quick shower, fresh clothes, full makeup and a spray of Chanel No5, and Alex was ready. She re-joined Nick in her living room where he was examining her bookcase full of leather-bound classics. He whistled when he saw her.

"Will this do?" she asked, giving a twirl. She was wearing tight black trousers, a black and white polka dot halter top and a leather jacket. On her feet, she had on black wedge heels. She looked great, but not over-dressed.

"You look…" he paused whilst he searched for the word, "…perfect." He offered her his arm. "Would milady like to accompany me to my waiting chariot?" he joked.

Alex smiled. "Milady would," she said and felt a frisson of excitement shoot through her body. Shit, what was she letting herself in for?

Nick drove them in his hire car out of the city. It was a lovely fresh day, and Alex was looking forward to her lunch. He headed north-west and, about an hour later, he pulled into a layby alongside the banks of the River Havel near the small town of Hennigsdorf.

"I thought we were going somewhere to eat," she said, looking around her. The spot he had chosen was beautiful. The layby was perfectly located alongside a private stretch of grass next to a copse of trees and the slow meandering of the river.

"We are," he replied. "Wait here."

He got out of the car and walked around to the rear. Withdrawing a wicker picnic basket and blanket from the boot, Nick headed a few metres onto the river bank before flicking out the blanket. Nick grinned back at Alex as he set the basket down and seated himself alongside it.

Alex, unsure whether this was a good idea or not, got out of the car and joined him. As she sat down, Nick, looking really pleased with himself, opened the basket and offered her a plate and some cutlery. Then he proceeded to unpack plastic boxes. Alex was astonished to find they contained sausage rolls, quiche, sandwiches and boiled eggs.

"I thought you might like a little reminder of home, so I did not pack German food, but instead made you some British picnic fare," he explained.

"But what if I had refused to come out?" she asked. "How did you know I would?"

"It was just a hunch," he said, taking a sandwich and smiling. "Everyone eats lunch." Sheer wonder crossed Alex's face. Who was this man and what did he want with her? She inspected the food and hesitated. He clocked her worry right away. "Don't worry, I haven't poisoned or drugged any of them. They are just ordinary, run-of-the-mill picnic foods. Here, have some."

She took a cheese sandwich and bit into it. He had put Branston pickle in it, and it tasted delicious. All at once she was transported back to her childhood in England when her mother used to make her cheese and pickle sandwiches.

"Good?" he asked. She nodded. "Here, have an egg. I don't know about you, but I love a cold boiled egg. There's nothing like it!"

They sat in silence happily, munching for a few moments before Nick suddenly gasped. "Shit! I forgot!" he said rummaging about in the basket. "We need drinks." He pulled out a bottle of dandelion and burdock soda.

"Where did you get that?" she asked, her mouth agape. She hadn't had a bottle of dandelion and burdock in years.

"I have my contacts," he replied. He fetched a wine glass

from the basket and filled it. "Well, it was actually from a British shop in Berlin, but you know they are 'contacts' now!"

"I can't believe this!" she said as she accepted a glass. "Do you always create such thoughtful picnics?"

"Only when I'm trying to impress a beautiful woman," he replied. It was cheesy, but Alex couldn't help smiling.

"Well, thank you for supplying it," she said, losing herself in his wonderful eyes.

"Well, thank you for eating it," he said with a grin.

They sat in companionable silence for a while, the only sound the gentle flow of the river and the odd rustling and tweeting of birds.

"Look, I know I said I was interested in joining your group, but actually that desire has fallen somewhat by the wayside."

"It has?"

Nick captured her intense gaze with his own. "Yes," he said, eyes full of meaning.

Alex's heart skipped a beat. "Why would that be?"

"I've become bewitched," he said.

"You have?"

"Yes, you've put a spell on me, Miss Grier."

"I have?" Shit! He likes me! Her heart pounded faster.

"You're one of the most beautiful women I have ever seen and, with your permission, I'd like to get to know you better." His voice was sincere, his face serious. Before she had time to answer, Nick leant towards her and removed her glass and plate. He looped his arm around her waist and gently pulled her towards him. Barely able to breathe, Alex found herself on a trajectory she could neither pull away from or wanted to. Her lips met his, and worlds collided.

The kiss was gentle at first, softly pressing against her mouth.

She closed her eyes and let herself dive in. He smelled great, of a light citrusy aftershave, and his lips were oh so soft. He was tender, then his caresses became more urgent, hungry. Before she knew what was happening or could object, he had her enveloped in his arms, her soft curves met his hard, muscular form, and he was kissing her face and neck. She moaned with pleasure as he followed the lines of her neck down to her décolletage. His hands slid up the back of her jacket and undid the halter strap. Alex felt her breasts release from their binding, and his hand skimmed up her side to cup her right breast. He stopped kissing her for a moment to slide her jacket off her shoulders and discard it to the side, then latched on to her breast. He licked and sucked on her flesh, causing the nipple to harden. He flicked it with his tongue, and she arched her back, moaning gently. She had not been touched this way in such a long, long time. Too long. It was amazing.

"Oh Nick," she moaned as he moved to her other breast. "Oh my God!"

He was back at her face now, kissing her passionately on the lips. Then stopped.

"Why have you stopped?" she asked, pouting. He grinned.

"I haven't stopped," he assured her. "I'm just moving position. Come on!"

He sat up, threw all the food and drink back into the basket and put it to one side.

"Coming?" he said, putting a hand out for her.

She scrambled to her feet, covering her nakedness with her halter top, and took his hand. He grabbed the blanket and led them into the thicket. There were only six or seven oaks and elm trees to hide them, but it was enough. Nick spread the blanket before drawing her down beside him, resuming his intense kisses. His hand moved to her breasts, and she let her top fall again. She felt a cool fresh breeze come off the river as he laid her down and whispered in her ear.

"I want you so much, Alex," he whispered. "You are so beautiful."

He stopped kissing her and removed his own shirt. Alex marvelled at his chiselled physique and wondered at the bulge in his jeans. He saw her watching and slowly unbuttoned his trousers. He had gone commando, and his cock, long, thick and hard, was out in the open for all to see.

This was really happening. She was going to have him and relish every moment of it. They were going to have sex out in the open and she didn't care. Fuck it, why not? she thought as she wriggled out of her own trousers and panties, and opened her legs for him.

The birds were twittering in the trees, the river gurgle nearby, somewhere in the distance were the noises of vehicles, but Alex was oblivious. All she could think about was him. She shivered in excitement as he climbed on top of her and manoeuvred himself so that he was lying between her legs, his penis just touching her pussy. She gulped and her breathing became somewhat shallow.

"Are you okay?" he asked. "Is this okay?"

She nodded. "It's just that…it's been a while."

"We don't have to if you don't want to."

"Oh, I want to," she said wrapping her arms around his neck and pulling him to her. She kissed him hard and felt him shiver with excitement. Yes, I definitely want this, she thought as she completely surrendered herself to him. He kissed her passionately on the lips, running his tongue around her mouth, teasing her with small bites, making her greedy for more. She responded; her hand dove south, gently caressing the shaft of his penis, driving him to distraction until he eventually pulled away. He removed her hand and placed it back around his neck.

"Uh-uh," he said. "No touching!"

"But- "

He covered her mouth with a long, wet kiss before making his way down her neck. Every touch, every kiss sent shivers down her body. She moaned, taking in every hot caress, every flick of his tongue and she felt herself getting oh-so-wet. Oh fuck, this was good. Don't stop. I want more! She thought as he moved down to her breasts, running his strong hands over each mound before choosing one on which to focus. He cupped her left breast in one hand and then bent down and ran his pink tongue over her straining nipple. His lips engulfed the hard nub and he sucked, making her arch her back and groan in pleasure.

"You like that?" he murmured as he sucked some more. Alex felt her eyes roll in her head as wave after wave of sheer pleasure washed over her. She liked it very much. Then he began to slowly move south, kissing her stomach and making his way down to her groin where he slotted two fingers into her moist vagina. She shuddered as a red-hot burst of desire ran through her. She heard him chuckle softly as he slowly rubbed inside her, bringing her to the verge of orgasm. She waited for him to come inside her, but he did not. Instead, those magical fingers kept rubbing and moving in and out of her. She pushed her hips up, encouraging him to dive deeper. Her body ached for him to take her now. She began to move rhythmically, pushing her hips into his erection, willing him to enter her. Oh God Nick, please just come inside me, she thought desperately. She could feel his hardness touching the entrance to her vagina at was agony that he hadn't taken her yet. Nick continued to tease her, running his fingertip back and forth over her most sensitive area. Low moans escaped Alex's throat. She wanted more, her nails bit into his shoulders. Finally, after what felt like hours of excruciating torture, Nick widened her thighs and slowly slid inside her waiting body. He was gentle at first making sure she was ready for him, moving rhythmically until they were in time with each other. Then his thrusts became faster, stronger, harder, until the pair of them were in a steady, steamy tempo. Oh my God! The familiar ripple of pure pleasure began to build as her body began to rise to orgasm. She closed her eyes.

Oh. My. God!

She arched her back, pushing herself against him as a veil of sheer joy swept over her. She held that position, unable to move as they came together, man and woman, reaching true pleasure as one. Nick gave one final thrust, and she felt her orgasm wash over her in waves of sheer ecstasy.

Fuck. A. Duck.

Nick collapsed on top of her, breathing hard. He kissed her cheek. He kissed her nose. She opened her eyes and saw that he was looking at her, his eyes soft.

"That was amazing," he said breathlessly, gently stroking her mussed up hair. "You are amazing."

"Yes," was all she could reply. She felt adrenaline rush through her body in a rush of hedonistic gratification. "Fuck!" she said between heavy breaths. "That was just what I needed. I feel…so alive."

He laughed, his eyes shining brightly. "Well, I was very happy to oblige."

He carefully slid out of her and came to lie by her side. He cradled her in his arms, and they lay there for some time, basking in the quiet warmth of each other's bodies. As she lazed there,

Alex could not remember ever feeling this happy. She barely knew this man, and yet here she was, lying in a German wood, fully naked and having just had sex with him. What was she thinking? That totally went against her usual behaviour. Yet, she did not feel that what had just happened was wrong. Quite the opposite. This felt right. She wondered if he fancied having another go.

"What are you thinking about?" he asked.

"Nothing much," she lied. "I'm just enjoying the moment."

"Me too," he said and kissed the top of her head. "But, you know, we'll have to get dressed soon and I'll have to take you home."

Disappointment ran through her. "Oh nooo!" she whined. "I don't want to go home just yet. It's so nice here."

"I know, but we can't lie here forever. Someone will find us…eventually."

"Just a couple of minutes more," she said, snuggling into his neck.

He smelled of expensive aftershave, and she was so relaxed she could have fallen asleep in his arms. But the breeze was picking up, and it was getting colder. She shivered causing Nick to react. He pulled her in closer and kissed her gently on the lips again.

"I think," he said between kisses, "you and I need to get dressed now."

"Yes, okay," she replied, disappointed her bliss was over.

Giving him one last kiss, she sat up and began to dress. As she did so, she took furtive peeks at her new lover and liked what she saw all over again. Nick was fit. Nick was hot as hell, and she loved that she had just had him.

When they were both ready, Nick shook off the blanket and

rolled it up. He held out a hand for Alex and she took it. They walked hand in hand to the car, grabbing the picnic basket as they went. Nick ditched the blanket and the basket in the back of the car then he pinned her up against the side of the vehicle and kissed her passionately again.

"Oh, Alex, what are you doing to me?" He pushed himself against her. She could feel his manhood tighten and stiffen again, and giggled. He kissed her once more. "Right, into the car with you before I lose my resolve to get you home without having you again." He gave her a playful slap on the backside before walking around to the driver's door. She got in the passenger side and sat down. As he took his place behind the wheel, Alex couldn't help but look at him and grin.

"What?" he said.

"I just can't stop smiling," she replied.

Nick laughed and switched on the engine. "Good."

Alex spent the journey back to Berlin in a state of unadulterated bliss. That had to have been the best picnic she had ever been on. She couldn't stop smiling and peeking at Nick. He grinned and put the radio on. All the way home they listened to rock music and sang, content in each other's company. The happy haze began to fade when they reached the city, then her street, then her building.

Nick dropped Alex off at her apartment, and she got out of the car reluctantly. She did not want this dream to end. It was the happiest she had been in forever. He rolled down the window as she walked around the car and beckoned her over to have one last kiss. Holding her hand, he drew her in and kissed her softly. She closed her eyes and drank it all in; the sensation of his lips on her, his scent and the warm strong hand that held hers.

"Are you busy later?" he asked as she finally opened her eyes and pulled away.

"I don't think so," she said. I know I'm not busy, she thought, but he doesn't need to know that.

"Can I take you out for a proper dinner tonight?"

"Yes."

"Alright, I'll pick you up around 7pm. That okay with you?"

"Yes," she said giving him a final peck on the lips, "see you then."

"That's a date! Until tonight!"

He rolled up the window, started the engine and gave her a wave before driving off. Alex watched the car disappear down her street before turning in towards her apartment. Nearly floating, Alex slid the key into the lock. That would certainly be a lunch she wouldn't soon forget.

To say Alex went about the day with a smile on her face was an understatement. She felt like she was walking on air. She tried to have a lie down, to get a couple of hours' sleep so she would be fresh for her date later. But every time she closed her eyes all she could think about was him and their love making in the German countryside. After tossing and turning some more, she rose at 4pm and spent the rest of her time getting ready for her date that night. Mother had not given her another assignment, so she had plenty of time to get herself ready to see Nick again. He was all she could think about.

First up: a luxurious bath. Bubbles, scented candles and a face mask were in order. An hour later, she got out, dried herself and wandered naked to her wardrobe to pick out her clothes for that night. She went to her wardrobe and fingered some of her sexiest dresses. There were three options: one red and strappy, another black and glamorous and a third, a white Grecian style cocktail dress. She stood back and pondered as to which one to pick. She tried to imagine herself wearing each one as she sat with a glass of wine in her hand.

Shit! Wine! She had forgotten to pick some up in case he came back to her apartment. What was she saying? Of course, he'll come back.

She hurriedly got dressed in distinctly non-date clothes, leggings and a sweater, with the intention of running down to the local grocery store to pick up some wine. Alex smiled to herself as she grabbed her door keys and skipped out of her apartment. Her life usually revolved around her job which was all about death. It didn't bother her, the killing, but it didn't make her happy either. She couldn't believe how light she felt in that moment.

The store was only a couple of blocks away and, as she pushed open the glass door, an old-fashioned bell tinkled somewhere above her. Grabbing a basket, she slung it over one arm whilst she headed for the wine section to select something for that night. So engrossed was she in her task, she did not see a tall, dark woman enter the shop nor was aware that the same woman was watching her closely.

Humming softly to herself, Alex stood at the rows of wine on shelves and wondered what to pick. She wished she knew his preference, but she didn't, so she slipped two bottles of each colour into her basket. Now for some nibbles. They were going out for dinner, but Alex liked to have food in the house in case they got hungry later.

Would he stay the night? she wondered. Best to pick breakfast stuff too. She slipped some crusty bread, cheese and butter into the basket followed by some Danish bacon, eggs and blutwurst (black pudding). Not sure she had enough, she also picked up a large packet of paprika flavoured Crunchips, or as she preferred to call them in her very English way, crisps. Alex stared down at her overflowing basket, contemplating if she had enough. Oh, that will have to do.

Alex paid by card at the cash desk, stuffed her goods into a plastic bag at the checkout, and made her way home. Unbeknownst to her, a dark-haired woman also left the shop and followed her at a distance.

It was a lovely day that July early evening, and Alex could just make out the birds singing in the trees over the traffic sounds. Although she loved living in Berlin, she was really a country girl at heart. She had been brought up in a mansion in the English county of Surrey, one of the most expensive areas in the UK. Her father was an investment banker in the city, her mother a wealthy heiress, so her upbringing had been privileged. She had gone to the best schools money could buy, and was to follow her father's footsteps and go to Eton when she decided to join the British army instead. Her parents, aghast at her decision, threatened to cut her off, but she joined none-the-less.

Six years as a soldier had taught her all the life skills her upbringing had not. Her parents came round eventually, especially when she left the army to take up a new job. Of course, she had lied about what that new role would be. Well, would they really understand her desire to be an assassin? As far as she was concerned, she was doing the world a favour by killing bad people. She doubted her parents would get it, so as far as they were concerned, she worked for a large German bank.

On days like this, Alex missed the countryside of her childhood. If she were back at home, she would be out horse riding or walking on the North Downs with her family. I must make plans to go and see them soon, she thought as she opened the outer door of her apartment building and walked in. Alex had just placed her shopping back on a kitchen cabinet when there was the loud scratching sound of her security buzzer. She went to answer it.

"Hello?"

"Alex, it's Dominika. Let me in, will you?"

"Okay."

Alex buzzed her fellow sister in, but was perplexed as to why Dominika was at her door again. They weren't particularly close – Dominika wasn't particularly close to anyone – so what was she doing here? There was an angry rap at her door and Alex pulled it open. Dominika stood, face like stone, waiting to be invited in.

"Dominika, so good to see you again…so soon," Alex gushed. "Come in."

The tall Russian glided in and came to rest in her living room. She did not sit down; despite being invited to by Alex. Instead, she stood and an imperious expression on her sharp features. Alex glanced at her wall clock. It was six o'clock. Nick would be here soon. She pushed thoughts of him out of her head and turned to her visitor.

"So, what can I do for you?" Alex asked, perching herself on the arm of her sofa.

"I have come to visit you," Dominika said matter-of-factly.

"Yes, I can see that," Greed replied. That wasn't like Dominika at all. Alex could count on one hand how many times this tall, willowy sister had been in her apartment and that was twice. And this was the second time.

"Yes, I have come to find out if you have any more news about HQ? I tried to call Mother yesterday, but she was so busy, I did not want to annoy her with my questions." Dominika, shifting her eyes around the room, grimaced at Alex's taste in paintings.

"No, no more news. They are still investigating. It will probably take some time. I assume Finn and his team will be pulling together all the evidence as we speak. I'm sure they'll find out who it is and then we can get our revenge," Alex replied.

"Good, good," Dominika replied.

Alex's brow furrowed as she swore a smile played over Dominika's lips. Surely she couldn't be happy that HQ had been bombed. The question lingered on the end of her tongue, but she thought better of asking.

"Well, it was nice seeing you, Alex. I must go now."

"Already? But I haven't offered you any refreshments." Alex didn't want the Russian to stay; she had other plans with Nick, but British politeness forced her to at least offer.

"Thank you, but no, I must go." Dominika walked to door and pulled it open. "Oh, and by the way, I'd look into that man who's been following you around. He's not what he seems."

"What do you mean? Have you been spying on me?" Alex's neck warmed at the intrusion into her personal life. How dare she?

A cat-like smile emerged slowly on Dominika's lips. "Well, someone's got to look out for a sister. Goodbye, Alex."

Before Alex could say anything else, Dominika strode out of her apartment, shutting the door behind her with a bang. Alex stared at the door and wondered what all that had been about. And what did she mean about Nick? She should have looked into his background. Why hadn't she? That was so not like her. She quickly fetched his memory stick from her desk and stuck it in her laptop.

"Alright, Nick Baker. Time to find out who you really are."

Chapter 10 - Dinner

There were only two files on the stick: one was Nick's resume, the other a list of the weapons he could use. He was 32, four years older than she, and had ten years in the British Army behind him. During his stint as an officer, he had managed to complete two degrees—one in Arabic, the other in engineering.

So, he is a bit of a nerd, Alex thought.

After the army, he had worked as a mercenary in Africa and also did a year as a bodyguard. He was unmarried and currently living in Berlin seeking work. He was proficient in many different types of weaponry—both handguns and rifles—and was adept with a knife. There was also a bit of bomb experience.

That could be handy, she thought. That's if Mother decided to hire him.

She pulled back from the desk and gave herself a mental shake. Why on earth would she hire Nick? The Sisters of Sin were all women. They didn't hire male assassins. Maybe she should introduce him to Mother anyway and maybe Mother could find something for him to do.

Nick's handsome face flitted through her head and Alex smiled. Then the smile faded. It was too soon to be falling for him, and Dominika's warning rang through her head. What did she mean that Nick wasn't what he seemed? She would ask him tonight.

Nick arrived clean shaven and smelling of expensive after-shave at 7pm on the dot, carrying a bunch of pink roses. Dressed in a smart Armani suit, he presented the flowers to Alex along with a long and lingering kiss. Alex, still in her dressing gown and black lacy underwear, returned the kiss with less enthusiasm than before, causing Nick to pull away from her, frowning.

"What's wrong?" he asked. "And why aren't you dressed?"

She took the flowers and skipped away, feigning a search for a vase. Dominika's words still bugged her, and she was beginning to feel this new relationship was going a bit too fast.

"Nothing," she said, walking into the kitchen and searching for a beautiful antique cut glass vase she had bought at auction only three months before. He followed her in.

"There is something wrong. What is it?"

Upon finding the vase, Alex placed it on the counter alongside the flowers. "Don't you think we're going a bit fast?"

"What do you mean?" There was hurt in his eyes and he was frowning.

"Well, I hardly know you, and we've already been intimate…"

"Been 'intimate'? You mean we had sex."

"Well, yes, well," she stuttered. She didn't know where she was going with this, but Dominika's comments had really stung. "I mean – I never have sex with someone I've only known for a couple of days. I don't really know you, and it was so out of character for me to do it."

"What are you saying? That you didn't enjoy it?"

"No."

"Well, what then?"

"I'm just saying that I hardly know anything about you, that's all," she said, taking the vase to the sink and filling it with water.

"What do you want to know?" he asked, his dark brown eyes looked worried. "Ask me anything!"

She arranged the flowers in the vase and kept her eyes averted from his. He had put her on the spot. Her mind was whirring. "I can't think of anything to ask right now," she finally said.

"Well, I don't know what else I can say to make it better," he replied. "What's brought this on anyway? We were fine earlier. No, not fine, we were great earlier. Have you gone off me already?"

She looked up and shook her head. "No, of course not."

"Well, then, come here and give me another kiss," he said, holding his arms out so that she might go into them. She smiled and allowed herself to be engulfed in his rock-hard body. She inhaled the scent from his aftershave and buried her face in his shoulder. Oh God, he smelled amazing. She angled her head, meeting his bemused eyes.

"Are you going to sniff me all day, or am I getting a kiss?" he murmured, bending down towards her and planting his lips on hers.

Gentle at first, then building in intensity, the kisses sent tremors through Alex's body. She closed her eyes, a low moan emanating from her throat as Nick backed her against the kitchen counter. Strong hands deftly slipped under her robe and encircled her hips, hoisting her up. The feeling of his hard cock through the dress trousers drove Alex wild as she tangled her fingers through his hair. Fingers drifting upward, Nick cupped her breasts, teasing her nipples with his thumbs. His lips travelled over her jawline to her neck, then to her ear, where he nibbled suggestively. One hand slipped down to her thigh, teasing the edge of her black lace panties, barely grazing the sensitive flesh beneath. Her legs turned liquid as strained against him, wanting more. Wanting release. Internally begging him not to stop.

Then, Nick did just that. He removed his hand from her robe and eased her feet back to the floor. Then she felt him shudder as if…as if he were laughing. She opened her eyes. He was laughing.

"Enjoying that, were we?" His eyes were liquid with desire. He'd obviously been enjoying it too.

Alex drew her robe back around her body. "Maybe." She bit her lip. "Why did you stop?"

"We've got a reservation, remember? I don't want to be late."

She placed both hands on his chest and looked him straight in the eyes. "Couldn't we just be late for a few minutes?" This man had gotten her all hot and bothered, and now he was refusing to close the deal.

"I promise, there will be more of that later," he said, voice hoarse, eyes twinkling. He coughed to clear his throat.

"There had better be."

They stood there, still close, looking at each other for a few seconds before Nick burst the passion bubble. "Go, before I change my mind."

"Well, I'm not against us just staying in," she murmured, touching his shirt, but really having a sneaky feel of his hard, taut chest. "We can always eat later."

He laughed. "Oh no you don't! You don't say you don't really know me and then expect me to bed you!" He tenderly took her hands and stepped back, holding her away from him. He grinned. "No, missy, we are going on a date like a proper couple so we can learn more about each other." Nick leaned in and murmured close to her ear, "Then I'll strip you naked and bed you when we come home." The rumble of his voice in her ear sent a shiver through Alex's body.

"Deal?" he said with a cheeky grin.

"All right, deal," she replied with a soft laugh.

Smiling, she hurried into her bedroom. Discarding the dressing gown on her bed, she shimmied into a slinky black dress and then gathered up her shawl and evening bag. She gave her hair and makeup a quick check in the mirror. Her reflection glowed back at her - she was happy.

There was no way Dominika actually knew Nick. She'd probably told her that Nick wasn't what he seemed to wind her up. Dominika was like that. She hated any of the Sisters to be happy. Alex liked Nick. She liked him a lot. And she wasn't going to let someone as bitter and twisted as Dominika ruin it for her. One last check in the mirror and she turned about and sashayed out into the hall.

Nick whistled when she appeared at the living room door. Alex knew she was gorgeous in a skin-tight black dress, killer high heels and red glossy lips. She wore her long blond hair loose and in waves, and there was a light scent of French perfume in her wake. At her ears were two-carat diamond studs. She held her hand out for him, and he went to her. Kissing her lightly on the nose, he opened her door, and together they went out.

In the street, right outside her doorstep, a black limousine awaited them.

"Milady," Nick said with a small bow as their chauffeur for the night opened the rear door for her.

Alex giggled as she slid inside swiftly followed by her beau for the evening. The cream leather interior smelled divine. The chauffeur made sure the door was properly closed before getting into the driver's seat and starting the engine.

"Where are you taking me?" she asked Nick as the car drove off. "Another picnic? I hope not. I don't want to ruin this dress. I only bought it last month. It's Gucci."

"You'll see," Nick smiled as he took her hand in his. He held it while the car wove in and out of traffic into the city centre.

"Okay, so this place is in the city centre," she said, trying to guess where he was taking her. "Can you give me a clue?"

"No," he replied.

"Is it an Italian restaurant? Asian? International?"

"I'm not saying," he said with a smirk.

"Just tell me!" Alex could be impatient and hated surprises. Her stomach growled, and she hoped that wherever they were going would have a quick service.

"Just wait and see!"

"I just like to know where I'm going!"

The car skirted around the Tiergarten, Berlin's equivalent of Central Park, past a number of excellent restaurants. They drove on a for a few more streets until the car drew up outside the Mandala Hotel in Potsdamer Strasse. The chauffeur got out of the car to open the door for them.

Alex emerged, delighted. "You're taking me to Facil?"

Facil was one of Berlin's top restaurants. Found in the Mandala Hotel's fifth floor, the restaurant had two Michelin stars and won awards for its fare. Known of its excellent food, gorgeous surroundings and fine wine list, it was one of THE places to see and be seen in the city. Alex had been there only once before and was excited to be back.

"But this is so expensive," she said, wondering how an out-of-work mercenary could afford such a place.

"Yes, but you only get what you pay for and Facil is brilliant," he said.

"You've been before?" she asked as he ushered her inside. Maybe he took all his women here to impress them. Alex's stomach sank. She didn't like the thought that Nick had had other women.

"No," he said, "but I read restaurant reviews."

Alex smiled as he put his arm around her waist and escorted her to the lifts. A few moments later and the lift doors opened revealing the restaurant in its full glory. Modern, exquisitely furnished, with large picture windows letting in natural light during the daytime and the stars at night, the restaurant had everything the modern diner could want. It was already half full when they arrived and they were greeted by the Maître D'.

Tall, thin and greying at the temples, the Maître D' had the stuffy air of a waiter who thought too much of himself. Nose in the air, he sailed forth and escorted them to a table close to one of the large windows. As they walked into the restaurant, Alex and Nick turned heads. They made a handsome couple.

The Maître D' helped Alex to her seat before assisting Nick and then offered them the wine list. Nick took it and studied it. "What would do you fancy to drink?"

"A nice pinot grigio will be fine for me," she said. "Something light like that."

"Not champagne?" he asked.

"Not right away," she answered. The truth was that despite all her love of expensive things, champagne was a costly beverage that did not appeal to her. She liked her wine expensive, sure, but also without bubbles. However, she was not about to admit that to Nick right now, she did not want him thinking her unrefined.

The meal was lovely. They had a starter of seafood followed

by a main of roast duck. The food was exquisite; fresh, delicious and beautifully cooked. Alex enjoyed every mouthful. By the time the dessert menu came around, she was so full, her taut stomach threatened to burst and she could eat no more. She sipped on her wine and surveyed her handsome beau. He had been a wonderful dinner companion, regaling her with tales of his army days and being interested in hers. He had made sure her wine glass was always full and that she felt she was the only woman there.

As she watched him happily looking at the dessert menu with the enjoyment of a gleeful five-year-old, Alex felt a surge of…something…feelings…wash over her. Shit. She REALLY liked this guy. Oblivious, Nick closed the menu and handed it back to the waiter.

"Actually, I'll not have dessert either," he said. "Could you just bring us some coffees? Thank you."

The waiter left, and Nick turned his attention back to his date. He reached over and took her hand in his. "I'm so happy you're here, Alex Grier," he said. "I know we've only known each other a short time, but – and I can't believe I'm saying this – I already can't imagine life without you."

Oh shit! What should she say back? What was he expecting? "I like you a lot too," she said.

It was the best she could think of. She couldn't say she loved him because it was too soon to say the 'L' word. She didn't want him thinking she didn't like him, but there was no word for that in-between place in a relationship where 'like' goes to a middle area before it becomes 'love'. She could have said 'lust' and that would certainly have been true, but there was no romance in lust and she wanted to have romance in her life so much. She hadn't realised it, but she had missed having someone special.

The waiter returned with coffee, and the pair sat amiably drinking and finding out more about each other. Nick had two brothers, had never been married and was a dog lover. He had grown up in Dorset, a lovely part of southern England, and had been schooled at a local high school. His favourite food was Italian and he loved opera.

"Opera?" Alex said impressed. "Me too."

"Well, maybe I'll take you to one, some day."

There really was no doubt about it—Alex was falling hard and fast, and she desperately hoped it wouldn't be a crash landing.

The limousine was waiting for them when they came out of the hotel after Nick paid the bill, and they snuggled in the back seat all the way back to Alex's apartment. A plethora of emotions rolled through Alex. Fear unexpectedly dominated the list. She had been in love once before and that had ended in disaster. Was she ready to give her heart again? She tentatively peered up at Nick's face silhouetted against the car window, and he smiled at her. Part of her screamed that she was, but another part pushed doubt into her euphoric brain.

The car drew up and stopped outside her apartment block. The driver quickly exited and opened the door for them. Alex got out first, followed by Nick. He stood close beside her and kissed her passionately on the lips, his hands warm and strong on her hips.

"Do you want to come up?" she whispered.

"I thought you'd never ask."

He instructed the driver to leave and, taking Alex by the hand, led the way up to her apartment.

As soon as they were through the door, the pair couldn't keep their hands off one another. Kissing Nick passionately on the lips, Alex removed his jacket, tossing it across the living room before tackling his tie. As she struggled to undo all the buttons of his shirt, Nick unzipped her dress. She drew his shirt over his shoulders as he slid her dress over her hips. She paused for a moment to let the dress glide to the floor before attacking his belt buckle and fly. He was already firm and ready for her as he kicked off his trousers and slid his thumbs into the top of his briefs.

With a wicked grin, Nick slid the briefs down his muscular thighs and stepped out of them. Naked, he went to Alex, flicked open her bra and removed it. He slowly descended down her stomach, leaving a trail of kisses, until he reached the waist of her lace panties. Lowering them to her ankles, he parted her thighs and left several teasing licks on her exposed flesh. Spasms of sheer pleasure rocked Alex's body and she moaned softly. That was all the encouragement Nick needed. He drew himself up and kissed Alex on the lips again.

"Come on," he said taking her hand. "Let's go to the bedroom."

Alex led the way to her large, opulent bedroom. Lit only by the hall light, they tumbled on to the king-sized bed, Alex on top. She could barely contain her excitement as Nick's hot lips sought hers, and his hands ran up and down her body, exploring every nook and cranny. She felt herself get wet and a thrill of excitement rushed through her. He kissed her some more, trailing his lips from the nape of her neck all the way down her back. Every touch was electricity, every lick made her gasp. Then he flipped her onto her back and kissed her from her neck all the way to her breasts—hot, yearning kisses that promised a night of sheer pleasure. He found her left nipple and gently gave it a suck as one hand slipped between her legs. Her body arched as the hand went in deeper, probing her most sensitive area gently before sliding two fingers into her.

"Oh my God!" Alex murmured as she felt a flush of heat. She heard Nick chuckle softly as his fingers delved a little deeper, curling upward. "Oh shit!" She arched her back as he found her g-spot and began to rub. Alex couldn't help herself; she found her body moving rhythmically with every touch of his hand. Breathing heavily, she sought his lips and kissed him with the urgency of a woman on the edge.

"I want you right now, Nick Baker," she said. "I need you right now. Come inside me, now."

She could hardly wait for a moment longer so ready she was for him. He needed no other invitation. He gently spread her legs and moved on top of her. She felt the warm weight of him as he positioned himself properly. Breathing quickly, she almost burst from longing as he gently made his first thrust. She gasped as his penis slid inside her. She pushed her hips up, enjoying every thrust as he pushed in harder. As he began to move his hips faster, she moved with him until the two were in synch, rocking together in perfect harmony, spiralling upwards to heaven. The thrusting grew more intense, more urgent, as he took them both to orgasm. Oh. My. God! It was all she could do not to scream the words out as a wave after wave of orgasm crashed over her. Fuck. Me. She arched her back, her head hit off the headboard as she climaxed. Nick gave one last mighty push as he came with her.

"Oh!" he gasped.

Panting hard, Nick held himself inside her for a few moments whilst they both reeled from the spike of oxytocin rushing through their bodies. Then he collapsed on top of her and, breathing hard, kissed her ear. She turned her head and kissed his lips. She was soaking with sweat, but very very satisfied.

"That was amazing," he whispered, kissing her again.

"Can we go again?" she whispered.

He pushed himself up on to his elbows and looked at her.

"Well, we are a greedy girl, aren't we?" he joked.

"Well, can we?" she asked running her hand up his damp back. He grinned.

Two further sex sessions later and they were both spent. Sleeping soundly, wrapped in her lover's arms, for the first time in ages, Alex felt safe. In her line of work there was always the worry of being caught or of an enemy tracking her down to kill her. But thoughts of her own mortality faded into nothing as she lay there next to Nick. Feeling protected, invincible, she drifted into a deep and dreamless sleep, cocooned in true happiness.

The following morning, Alex left Nick sleeping to surprise him with a cooked breakfast. Dressed in her beautiful ivory silk dressing gown, she went into the kitchen and began to cook. She put on a couple of sausages to fry and placed the kettle on to boil for coffee. Two eggs sat by the cooker ready to go in the pan at the last minute. As she waited for the food to cook, Alex went into her living room to tidy up the detritus of clothing they had discarded the night before.

She slung her own dress over the back of a chair along with her underwear before moving on to Nick's clothes. She placed his trousers and shirts over the chair that held her own clothes and went to pick up his jacket. When she lifted it, his wallet fell to the floor. She lifted the jacket to her face and sniffed. It smelled deliciously like Nick. Then she picked the leather wallet. She was just about to put it back in his pocket when curiosity overcame her. With Dominika's warning ringing in her ears, Alex opened wallet and began to explore. She liked Nick a lot and she told herself she was just looking to see that he was who he said he was, that was all.

He'll never know. It'll take me just a minute.

Alex glanced towards her bedroom where through the gap in the open door she could see Nick was still sleeping. Biting her lip, she began to search through the wallet. There were credit cards, all with Nick's name of them, some receipts and then she found it: a security badge with his picture and name of it, except this said his surname was Walker. She frowned. The logo on the badge had SIS on it. The only organisation with that logo was the UK's Secret Intelligence Service, also known as MI6.

Fuck! Nick was MI6! Fuck! The using…fucking…bastard!

Ignoring the smell of burning sausages, she charged into her bedroom and threw Nick's wallet at him. It bounced off his head.

"You lying bastard!" she screamed as she dragged the covers off him. "You lying, sneaky bastard!"

"What? What's up?" Nick sat up, his dark hair dishevelled and face a mask of confusion.

"You! You bastard! You've been lying to me this whole time!" she shouted. "I thought you were genuine. I thought you were telling me the truth, and then I find out you're fucking MI6!"

She flicked the security card at him and stomped out of the bedroom. Before Nick could fully comprehend what had happened, she returned with his clothes in her arms. She threw them at him.

"Get dressed and get out! I never want to see you again!"

"Alex, I can explain!" he protested, but she had already gone.

Nick quickly got dressed and went looking for her. He found her in the kitchen throwing a wasted cooked breakfast in the bin. She spun around, hot frying pan in one hand, a spatula in the other.

"Alex," he began.

"Just leave." Alex fought back hot tears as she placed the frying pan back on the cooker.

"It's not what you think!" he said.

"It's exactly what I think!" she snarled as she rounded on him, using the spatula to emphasise every single word. "You came here with the specific purpose of seducing your way into the Sisters. Didn't you?"

He hung his head.

"What was I to you? Part of the job? A bonus? Just a good fuck?" Her own shame and embarrassment at being taken in so easily had Alex's skin burning. What's more, it annoyed her to no end that Dominika had been right.

"No," he said, taking a step towards her. She raised the spatula ready to wallop him with it, so, hands raised in a conciliatory manner, he backed off.

"I've genuinely fallen for you Alex. I really have. Yes, okay, at first, I was told to get close to you to find out more about the Sisters, but as I got to know you, I realised what an amazing person you are. I was going to tell you I just didn't know how." And then he dropped the bombshell: "I love you, Alex."

"Just leave." Alex clenched her jaw until it hurt. When he didn't move, she screamed, "Leave!"

Defeated, Nick put up his hands once more. "Okay, okay, I'm going," he said, slipping on his jacket, "but I'm not giving up on you, Alex. I know you feel the same way about me. Last night was…fucking amazing. We can have more of that, I know we can. I'm not giving up on us."

Unable to look at him, Alex turned her back, staring through the mist of unshed tears out the window. He had used her, in the most unforgivable way. She heard him sigh, then the sound of his footsteps walking towards the front door. The door opened and closed. Then silence.

Back at MI6 HQ, Ben Littlejohn was trying to get in contact with Nick for the last time. He was supposed to have checked in the previous evening, but had not. He frowned.

He'll be okay, he thought. Nick's a big boy and can take care of himself. I'll try him again later.

Lettis strode up and saw his concerned face. "Everything alright, Ben?" she asked.

"Yep. Hunky dory," he replied, but his instincts were telling him differently. I'll give him another hour, and if he doesn't respond, I'll get one of our other operatives to go and see what's become of him.

Chapter 11 - Florence

The first thing Alex did after Nick left was to remove all memory of him. She stripped her bed and replaced the sex-stained ones with a fresh duvet cover and sheets. She threw the used set in for washing. She tidied the living room, pausing only to touch the back of the chair where his jacket had once lain.

How could I have been so stupid? she asked herself for the hundredth time. Mother was always warning us not to get involved with anyone, that a lover would distract us from the job, and now here I am out of my head with grief over a man I barely know.

Alex wondered if she should tell Mother about Nick. Did Mother really need any more worry at this precise moment when she was dealing with so much back at HQ? Plus, the Sisters were not allowed relationships. A quick fuck was fine, especially if it was for a job, but a full loving relationship? It was not on. Alex bit her lip worrying about what to do for the best and then decided she would tell Mother about Nick, but not right now. She had to sort out her own head before she told anyone about him. Fighting back the fresh sting of tears, there was only one more thing she had to do to totally rid herself of Nick.

The scent of his sex was all over her body, and she scrubbed herself mercilessly with soap in the shower, wanting to banish all memory of him. Tears cascaded down her face as she remembered his touch of the night before, of the amazing love making.

Well, he's certainly good at his job, she thought bitterly as she washed her hair. He had her fooled. He had made her feel special, like he genuinely cared or maybe even loved her. He had got her into bed and had his way with her, and she had just let him. They probably taught him all his seduction techniques at MI6 school, she mused. Well, that fucker won't be using any more of his techniques on me ever again! Alex angrily rinsed the shampoo from her long hair.

Alex finished her shower and, wrapped in her dressing gown, retired to her bedroom to put her face on. She had been sobbing hard in the shower and now she had let most of her grief out, it was time to hold her head high again and get on with life. She would get dressed, take a look on the dark web for any jobs and prepare for that. Yes, a good death would keep her mind off Nick Walker. Maybe she would strike lucky, and it would be him she would be tasked with taking out. Death, now there was a thing. What if she hunted down and killed that bastard for what he had done to her? Alex's stomach lurched as she thought of driving a knife into Nick's toned body. She knew then there was no way she could ever murder Nick.

Fuck, he's really got to me, she thought. For the first time in her life, Alex had truly and irrevocably fallen in love, and the man she loved had turned out to be a lying bastard MI6 agent. She put her head in her hands and sobbed some more.

"I hate you, Nick Walker," she wailed.

A few hours later, exhausted from crying, a now dressed and made-up Alex listlessly grabbed her laptop and put it on. Getting to the SOS's site on the dark web, she checked for any messages. There were two job offers for her, plus a round robin email to all the girls. She opened that first. It was from Mother.

Dear Girls,

As you all are now aware, someone has got to the very core of the Sisters of Sin and bombed our headquarters. Our entire board has been killed, along with three members of lab staff. Our thoughts and prayers are with their family and friends at this time. Investigations as to how our high-tech security was infiltrated are currently being carried out. However, it is clear that whomever carried out this heinous attack must have had access to our codes. Please be extra vigilant at this time when it comes to security, for the Sisters and for your own selves. I will be in touch in due course with any further findings.

Mother

A cold chill encompassed Alex, thinking the attack had come from the inside. She couldn't think of anyone at HQ who would turn traitor on them. All the staff had been with Conexus for years. They were like a family. Who would have done such a thing? It was incomprehensible.

She shook her head and bit her lip. No point worrying about that right now. There was nothing she could do to help at HQ, but she could keep the business going by taking a new job.

The first job offer she looked at was in Florence. A hit on a mob boss. Alex liked Florence; she had been there many times before, usually on holiday, staying at the best hotels and putting a dent in her credit card at the local designer shops. This time, she was to take out Dino de Luca, a nasty piece of work who was trafficking underage girls from the Philippines to his brothels across Italy. He was suspected of the brutal murders of three young women and a local police chief who had tried to bring him to justice.

Alex briefly wondered who had called the hit out on the sick bastard, but decided she didn't care. She was taking out an evil man, and this job would take her mind off the fucker who had broken her heart. The thought of Nick made her stomach lurch, and she suppressed the need to cry.

Fuck! I am better than this, she scolded herself.

Alex printed off the details of the job and stuck them in an envelope. She was old fashioned in this way. Most of the girls just transferred the details to their cell phones, but Alex didn't totally trust technology and always made a back-up on paper. That way she always had her job spec, and if she was caught, she could always set the envelope on fire. The client wanted de Luca killed by the end of the week. She would make that happen.

She began to prepare.

An hour later, Alex had an overnight bag packed and was working on cleaning and maintaining her small arsenal of munitions. Sitting at her dining table, she had spread out before her: her rifle, two handguns, several knives and three ligatures. She liked to have doubles of all her weapons, not only did it please her to have so many in her cache, but she was cautious. Two of nearly everything meant that if one failed, she had another ready. She did not yet have two rifles, but was in the process of purchasing another from a contact in Hamburg. She broke the rifle into pieces and began to clean and oil the parts. It was a slow process she liked to take her time on this particular piece - and as she cleaned, she fantasised about using it to blow a hole in Nick's lying head. Bastard! She would never, ever trust another man as long as she lived. She promised herself that.

Alex was just slotting the rifle back together when there was a buzz at her door. Someone was pressing the external buzzer on the outside door. Her stomach lurched.

Pressing a button on the control panel, she gasped as the external viewer switched on to reveal Nick standing there. She stepped away from her door and held back from letting him enter. She did not want to see him ever again. He was MI6, for fuck's sake! He was the enemy. What did he think he was doing standing there outside her apartment block? She should kill the fucker now. But as she thought of Nick dead, tears sprang to her eyes, and she knew she could never do it.

The buzzer went again, this time more urgently, and she jumped. Her hand rose to press the entry button almost all by itself, but she made herself stop. She lowered it again. There was no way she was letting him in. He had lied to her about who he was and why he was romancing her. He had wanted access to the Sisters of Sin and its parent company, Conexus, and like a fool, she had let him in. He was just using her, she knew that. She looked through the viewer again and saw Nick shrug and give up. Then he walked away and she relaxed.

"Good, he's gone," she murmured, but she wasn't happy at his departure. A small part of her was devastated that he hadn't tried to get her attention for longer. He obviously didn't like me at all, she thought miserably. "Oh, for fuck's sake, Grier, get a grip of yourself!" she said aloud. Alex drew herself up and let out a long, reviving breath. "Right," she said aloud. "Time to forget that arsehole and get on with my life. I have a job to do and money to earn. Those gorgeous diamond earrings won't buy themselves and neither will the matching necklace." Fantasising about jewellery put a smile on her face and she returned to the table.

Packing her weapons into a large rucksack, Alex placed it and the overnight bag at her apartment door. She was planning leave first thing in the morning. It was a long drive to Florence from Berlin and she wanted an early start. Shuffling to her bedroom, Alex threw herself into the soft, clean bed and fell into a dreamless sleep.

As Nick drove back to his hotel room, a feeling of utter desolation lay deep in his stomach. He admonished himself for not being more careful, and worst of all, getting too close to his assigned target. His head swam as he analysed the situation. He liked her. Yes. That was true. He fancied her…also true. He… loved her? Nick flicked the car's indicators and turned into the street where his hotel was. Do I love Alex? Was love even possible so soon after meeting someone? The turn in his stomach told him something he was barely able to acknowledge himself. He drove into his hotel car park and found a parking space. Do I love Alex? he repeated and, again, the lurch in the stomach. He turned off the car engine.

"Fuck, I'm in love with her!" he said aloud. "Fuck!"

Just then, his cell phone buzzed in his jacket pocket. He removed it and answered.

"Ben," Nick said.

"Alright stranger! Where have you been? I've been trying to get you for ages," Ben said. "Just checking in. Everything going okay? Anything to report yet?"

"Yes and no," Nick replied.

"Explain."

"Everything's going as plan, contact has been made with the target and relations begun. However, I have nothing to report back yet on Alex," he said.

"Alex?" Ben replied.

"Sorry, the target," said Nick, then silently cursed himself for over-familiarisation.

"And how is the target? Is she as tasty as she looks?" Ben asked, causing Nick to bristle.

"The target is as expected," he replied through gritted teeth. "Intelligent and professional."

"And your cover's intact?" his colleague and friend asked.

Nick paused. "Yes."

"Good to hear," Ben said. "Calling off now. I'll be in touch."

The line went dead, and Nick switched the phone off. He got out the car and made his way to the car park doors. Tomorrow he would go back and see her. He would make her understand that he had never meant to hurt her. He had to tell her…he had to say…had to make her see that he loved her and couldn't live without her.

At seven the next morning, Alex was up, showered, dressed and ready to go. Taking a look around her neat apartment, she checked she had switched off all the electrics before grabbing her bags and taking the lift down to the parking area in the basement.

Her car, her pride and joy, sat pristinely in its private parking space. She threw her bags into the backseat and slid into the driver's seat. Key in ignition, a quick turn and the car roared into life. She loved the sound of its engine; it was as mesmerising as a cat's purr. She put the car into gear and within a minute, she was driving out of the parking area and onto the busy Berlin Street.

Alex took a route heading roughly south-west of the city. It took her an hour to get completely out of Berlin's suburbs, and she began to enjoy herself as she drove into the German countryside. The weather was lovely; it was one of those summer days where there was hardly a cloud in the sky and everything seemed perfect.

Well, almost everything, she thought, and felt the pain of her loss again as she drove past a small lake surrounded by trees. It reminded her of their picnic. I am not going to let that arsehole ruin my day. I am going to Florence and I'm going to enjoy myself, she promised herself as the car zoomed along.

Alex drove through Germany, passing Nuremberg, where the Nazi trials had taken place after World War II, and the former Olympic city of Munich. Stopping twice for quick refreshment breaks, she reached the German-Austrian border a little over six hours later. She stopped off at a bed and breakfast in the town of Kufstein in the Austrian Tyrol, resuming her journey the following day. It would take her another six hours to do the drive down to Florence, but she really had no other option. If she had flown, she couldn't have taken her weapons. A bus would take too long, and the train was too public. Besides, the long, lonely drive south helped clear her head.

By the time Alex reached the busy and beautiful city of Florence, it was just after lunch, and thoughts of Nick had all but left her. Now she would concentrate on the task ahead and that was killing Dino de Luca. She would enjoy taking this one out. He was a nasty bastard by all accounts. Not only was he into trafficking, but was suspected of the torture and murder of several people, drug running and extortion. The police couldn't pin anything on him, so he thrived, and his empire continued to grow and strengthen. Cut off the head of the snake and his organisation would crumble—that was what she would do. The fact a turf war would break out between the factions of de Luca's own organisation had occurred to Alex, but she didn't care. All she cared about was doing her job and getting a big pay-out for it.

Alex negotiated the busy streets of Florence with care. The Italians drove like crazy people in her eyes, and it took all her concentration to stop the car from being hit or hitting someone else. Italian pedestrians were just as bad, running across the street without warning. So, it was with utter relief when she finally got to her hotel in one piece with her beautiful Aston Martin unscathed.

The Grand Hotel was situated off the main tourist thoroughfare and, unlike its name suggested, was small and intimate. Alex had stayed here before and enjoyed its quiet, family-run ambiance. She checked in and walked up the two flights to her room.

Room 12 was basic but neat and tidy. A large king-sized bed took up most of the room, but the owners had managed to cram in a vanity unit and a small chair as well. The walls were decorated with watercolour prints of old Florence and to one side was an en-suite with shower and toilet. The room had a view of a small piazza and had its own stone balcony. She dumped her bags on the double bed and went to the balcony doors. Opening them wide, she let in the warm breeze and the city noises.

Alex walked out on to the balcony and breathed in deeply. Yes, there it was: the smell of Florence. That heady mix of warm soil, pollution, Italian cooking and the faint hint of flowers. She smiled to herself and took in the scene: red-roofed ancient buildings, hot summer sun and a city so beautiful she could almost cry from the joy of it. She would need a couple of days to survey de Luca and his goons before deciding the best plan of action. But before that, she could afford to spend the rest of the afternoon relaxing. Florence had some of the best and most exclusive shopping in this part of Italy. Perhaps she should go out and spend some of her hard-earned money on new clothes and, oooh, hand-made Italian shoes.

It's to cheer me up, she told herself as she grabbed her purse and got ready to go out. Besides, I need to look the part if I am going to lure de Luca somewhere on his own, so it's for work. Alex always justified her purchases to herself, knowing full well her love of the good life, her desire for nice and expensive things, were the real reasons she spent so much on herself. She worked hard, and she deserved it.

Snapping her bedroom door shut behind her, Alex slid on her designer sunglasses and made her way out of the hotel.

As usual, Florence was hot and busy. The dusty streets were packed with late season tourists, skinny white legs in shorts and loud shirts and tops. While she loved the city, she did not love the thousands of foreigners who flocked there to stop every two minutes to take photos of yet another amazing building or statue. Frustrated and overheated, Alex made her way to the Palazzo Pitti where she knew she would find some of the best clothing stores in the city. She would go to her favourite shops and spend too much money on the very best of gear.

Now, normally, when presented with a whole row of designer stores packed full of goodies, Alex's heart would lift. However, not even Chanel could raise her spirits high enough to make more than a half-hearted attempt at perusing the rails. Instead of being delighted with expensive things, Alex found herself thinking of Nick. Damn him! She went to Prada, determined to lose herself in the gorgeous dresses. As she pulled an evening gown from a rail, listlessly inspected it and put it back, she realised resistance was futile. Nick's handsome face with his come-to-bed brown eyes refused to get out of her head. He was all she could think about. Shit, he had really got to her. She left the store and stormed back in the direction of her hotel, more furious with herself for being such as sap than with him for his betrayal.

"Bastard man," she muttered to herself as she walked up the street.

Alex was so caught up in her woes that she nearly missed the grumbling of her stomach. She had not eaten since that morning. She stopped at a street stall and paid for a coffee and a pastry. Devouring them as she walked back, she finally felt the magic of Florence wash over her. It was getting into early evening, and the sun was beginning to fall behind the stunning skyline of the ancient city. Birds twittered in the trees; Italians went about their business dressed to the nines and at every corner was a breathtakingly beautiful building or statue.

What am I doing? she wondered as she walked down her street. I'm in one of the greatest cities in the world and I'm wretched.

The skies grew darker, storm clouds gathered overhead and a large raindrop plopped on to her face. It was the regular early evening downpour that added so much to Florence's charm. Every day it arrived to wash the heat from the pavements, the dust from the air, making the city over again. Alex had forgotten all about it and, running the last few blocks to her hotel, she arrived soaked to the skin. She ran up the stairs to her room, stripped off and jumped in a hot shower.

Luxuriating in the warmth of the water for a full half an

hour, she finally emerged clean, pink and feeling oh-so-much-better. She slipped on her work uniform of black trousers and long sleeve t-shirt before pulling her long blonde hair into a ponytail, tucking it under a black baseball cap. Tonight was all about reconnaissance, about learning her prey's habits. Tomorrow she would make the first attempt. She stared at herself in the mirror and did not like what she saw. The bruise given to her in the boxing ring a few days earlier had all but faded, but her eyes were large and sad. There were dark circles underneath them, and her face looked strained.

He did this to me, she thought, him and his lies. Alex grabbed her room key and stuffed some Euros into her trouser pocket in case she needed them.

Just then, there was a knock at her door. She froze.

"Who is it?" she called.

Chapter 12 - De Luca

There was a pause. "Alex, it's me, Nick."

Fuck! Alex went to the door and yanked it open. Nick stood there appearing upset and sorry, but handsome. She hated that he still looked handsome. Boyish and gorgeous. Fuck, fuck, fuckity fuck.

"What do you want? And how the hell did you find me?" she demanded.

"Can I come in?" His voice was sheepish.

"No."

"Please, Alex."

She glanced at him and she felt her resolve melt. Must. Not. Let. Him. In.

"Alex, I really need to talk to you," he said. His dark eyes were sad and pleading. "You've got me all wrong. I mean… please let me in."

Alex bit her lip and with a reluctant sigh, stepped back and held the door open. He gave her a weak smile as he entered her room and turned to face her.

"So how did you find me?" she demanded, arms crossed, face like fury. He couldn't have tracked her phone; he didn't have her number. Had he followed her?

"Tracking device," he confessed, averting his eyes downward.

"What the fuck?" She stared at him. "Where did you put it?"

"In your car."

"Well, you can just go down to the car park and remove it right now!" she hissed, pointing to the door.

"I will, but I need a couple of minutes to explain myself first," he said. He took a step towards her, hand out wanting to touch her, but she shooed him away and moved to the window. Sighing, Nick sat down on a chair at the other end of the room. Alex perched on the window sill and waited.

"I am so sorry," Nick began. "I was going to tell you everything, but I didn't know how. Yes, I work for MI6, and yes, we were spying on you. I didn't mean to lie to you or to hurt you."

"No, you meant to seduce me and find out all about the Sisters so one of your lot could infiltrate it," she snapped.

"No! Well, okay, yes, but that was the plan, but that was before… before I fell in love with you," he said. Yearning filled his brown eyes from beneath an errant lock of brown hair. But Alex had been hurt badly before, and once the trust was gone, she found it difficult to get it back. She could not, would not trust him now despite the fact her heart was breaking. He was just telling her what he thought she wanted to hear. He was incorrigible. He'd do anything to infiltrate the Sisters.

"You're such a liar, Nick Walker," she snapped, making sure to place heavy emphasis on his real surname. "A big fat fucking liar and I can never trust you again." She stood up. "I think you should leave."

"But, Alex!"

"Just go." She walked to the door and opened it. "I don't

want anything to do with you ever again." She stared blankly away from him and held back the tears.

"But, Alex, I said I love you, and I know you feel the same way too!"

As much as it killed her, Alex fixed him with a deathly stare. "I don't love you, Nick. It was just a fling. You were fun, something to occupy my time, that's all. Now, leave."

Crushed, Nick nodded and slowly walked to her bedroom door. He paused, turned around and opened his mouth as if to say something then shook his head and went out.

"And make sure you take that thing off my car!" she shouted as she slammed the door behind him.

Alex waited until she was sure he was well away from her room before sliding to the floor and crying. Why was he tormenting her like this? The bastard! Did he have no heart? She couldn't believe he had had the gall to follow her to Florence to tell her more lies. And he'd put a tracker in her car to do it. Jesus! She allowed herself a few more minutes of wracking sobs before calming down and mentally picking herself up.

"Alex Grier, get a grip of yourself girl!" she scolded. "He's just a man. There will be other men!" But not like this one, her inner voice wailed.

She scrambled to her feet, brushed herself down and gave herself a good talking to in the mirror on the vanity unit. "Get a grip, woman. He's an arsehole man, and you don't need him. You have a job to do. Those diamonds won't be bought by anyone else. If you want them, you have to earn them. Get your arse out the door and do your job!"

It was dark and dry when Alex left the hotel. The warm air

had soaked up the earlier downpour leaving the streets smelling of warmth and blossoms. Her first job was to reconnoitre de Luca's main place of business to work out his habits and how best to kill him. She slipped out the rear door, making sure Nick was nowhere in sight before leaving. Keeping to the quieter streets, she made her way to a small restaurant called Delizioso that was situated on a grubby street in a less salubrious area of the city. This, she knew, was de Luca's headquarters. The mafia boss was worth millions and had fancy houses and buildings all over that area of Italy, but he seemed to like using this non-descript little café best to oversee his operations. Alex wondered if it was because it was the first business his mother had set up. She had read that in the background notes Conexus had supplied her. Italian men loved their mammas, and mafiosi bosses were no different. Alex situated herself at a pavement table of the Café Pomodorio opposite and watched the comings and goings of the Delizioso crowd.

A traditional Italian restaurant, the Delizioso had maybe ten tables inside and another five out. The tables and chairs were old, wooden, rickety with use over many years. The tables sported red and white chequered tablecloths. Old Chianti bottles acted as candlesticks, and there were at least three waiting staff. When she sat down, the restaurant had already started to fill up with locals.

"Cosa vorrebbe ordinare?" said a voice breaking into her thoughts. What would you like to order? "Ha già deciso?" Have you decided yet?

A handsome young waiter stood alongside her table. Alex picked up the menu and read it quickly.

"Cosa mi può raccomandare?" she replied. What would you recommend?

As the waiter took her through a list of dishes, Alex kept her eyes on Delizioso opposite. A large black car had drawn up and three heavies got out. Then de Luca himself emerged, arrogant and cruel. She recognised him from the photo supplied to her for the job. He was even nastier in real life. An older man, de Luca had seen some action. A large scar cut through his left cheek and he was missing a finger on his right hand. He was wearing smart, but casual clothing of good quality and around his neck was a heavy gold chain. He laughed at something one of his associates said and went in. His henchmen weren't much better. All three of them sported facial scars and were heavily tattooed. One was missing half an ear. She wondered briefly what had happened to it, but decided she didn't care

"Vorrei le lasagne," she said to the waiter. "Posso avere una bicchiere di vino bianco?" I'll have the lasagne and a glass of white wine.

She closed the menu, and the waiter nodded and disappeared inside. Alex took her time over her meal, using her vantage point to watch and learn the movements of de Luca and his men. The mafia boss spent the whole evening inside the restaurant. She could not see him or his thugs in with the customers, so guessed he must have offices around the back. She should investigate that later. She forked the last piece of lasagne into her mouth and enjoyed the garlicky taste. They might be off the tourist beaten track, but this food was delicious.

Well, there's no reason why I can't enjoy myself while I'm here, she mused.

Alex downed her wine, left some Euros for the waiter and then quickly walked across the street. Delizioso was quieter now; there were only three or four couples still eating. The candles on the tables guttered in a soft evening breeze lending the whole scene a romantic air. She quickly walked past the premises, taking in as much information as she could. The restaurant was jammed in between two other buildings with no alleyway either side. There must be a rear door, though, where staff entered and where supplies were brought in. There was a floor above with a couple of windows looking down on the street. She walked further along the road and minute later found what she was looking for: the entranceway to a dark backstreet. Checking she was not being followed, Alex slipped down the alleyway to investigate.

Lit by dull lamps over the back doors of the businesses, the alleyway smelled of trash cans and decay. She wrinkled her nose as she walked in. This was part of the job she hated. Taking her time, she carefully made her way along the dark and dingy cobbled road until she got to a door that she thought might be that of Delizioso, but how to tell? There were two large waste trucks with lids sitting close to the door and above them, a small window. Hoisting herself up on to the nearest bin, she crawled along its dirty and smelly lid until she could peep inside. The window was filthy, but there was enough clear glass left for her to make out the interior.

De Luca was sitting at a table in the restaurant's kitchen dealing cards with some of his men. They were in a jovial mood, clowning around and joking with each other unaware that death was peering in the window. As they talked, the kitchen staff, a chef and three kitchen hands worked away in the main part of the kitchen, cooking and clearing and serving. Huge pots filled with bubbling sauces and boiling pasta sat on the stove. In one corner, the chef put the final garnish on a completed dish before sending it out with a waitress. In another, an elderly man did the dishes. The air was full of delicious smells and the shouts of the kitchen staff as they worked away.

De Luca called the chef over and gave him a food order gesturing with his hands as he told him what he wanted. The chef nodded and then went back to his stove. He immediately put on the mafia boss's order and got to work, oblivious to the assassin in the window.

Alex took everything in. She had originally thought of taking de Luca out at one of his many homes, but the restaurant would be easier. He was relaxed here, he let down his guard here, he would die here.

As Alex observed the scene and thought about the task ahead, she suddenly had the creeping sensation that she was not alone, that she was being watched herself. Slowly she turned her head to see one of de Luca's henchmen staring at her from a little way down the street.

"Hey!" he shouted. He pointed at the window and drew his gun.

Alex leapt into action. She scrambled down from the garbage bin and ran past the kitchen's back door just as it flew open and two heavies poured out. They grabbed for her as she sped past, but missed. She ran for her life, leaping over piles of rubbish and negotiating the bins and boxes that had been discarded in the alley. It seemed like every piece of Italian garbage had suddenly been left there to stop her escape. Panting heavily, she dodged the first man and managed to reach the alleyway entrance. Keep going, keep going, she said as she sprinted to safety. She just turned the corner into the main street when a large shadow loomed in front of her and stopped her in her tracks. A fourth henchman was standing there holding a gun at her and grinning.

"Where do you think you're going, little lady?" he said in Italian.

Alex stared up at him and gasped. Could she take him out? Maybe. Should she try? She weighed up her options. This guy was huge, and he was armed.

"Hands up," he said using the handgun to motion to her to raise her hands. She did it slowly.

In the dull light, Alex caught the glint of a gold tooth in the grinning thug's mouth. Time to wipe that smile off your face, she thought as she launched into action. She knocked the gun out of his hand and gave him a hard punch in the solar plexus. The man went down like he had been shot. Those boxing lessons were paying off. As he slid to the ground with a grunt, Alex ran around him and out into the street, the other thugs hot in pursuit.

Running hard, she tore down the street urgently looking for a hiding spot. Behind her she could hear the heavy sounds of feet pounding on pavement. Her head was a maelstrom of thoughts. Should she try and outrun them? Or should she hide and wait until the coast was clear before making it to safety? The second option seemed the better one.

A group of people were standing at a bus stop outside a small fashion boutique. The boutique was in darkness and sported an inset door where someone of her stature could easily hide in the shadows. Now was her chance. She ran up to them and, using their bodies as cover, quickly slipped into dark doorway and crouched down, making herself as small as possible so the men would not see her.

A minute later, de Luca's men thudded past her and continued down the street. She took a breath. So far so good. She gave them a minute before coming out of her hiding place and looking to see where they had gone. They were a good bit down the street and showed no signs of turning back. She was safe. For now. Thank God.

A bus arrived, and the crowd gathered to embark. Alex joined them. She would ride it a few blocks before getting off and going back to the hotel. She was so busy checking that the thugs had not yet turned back for her that she did not notice someone big and tattooed creeping up behind her.

"Oh!" she cried as something heavy hit her over the back of her head. She fell back. The last she remembered was passing out and then nothing.

Wolter's face was pale and sweaty in the lamplight when Dominika spied him sitting alone on a bench in the middle of the park. From this distance, through her high-tech binoculars, he resembled, for all intents and purposes, an over anxious moon-faced man making an impromptu visit to the Earth. It would almost be amusing if it wasn't so pathetic. It was nearly nine, a few minutes before they were due to speak. Dominika lowered the field glasses. She sighed with frustration at the little man's suspicious behaviour. He was jumpy, nervous. Anyone looking at him would know he was up to something. She decided it was time to put him out his misery. She stepped out of the shadows and sashayed up the park's paved pathway towards him, her high-heeled boots making sharp clicking noises on the ground.

His head snapped up at her approach, relief flooding his pallid expression. He gave her an uneasy smile as she approached, moving along the bench to give her room to sit. Dominika remained standing.

"Do you have it?" she asked.

"Money first," he replied.

She sighed, slipped a hand into a pocket of her fitted leather jacket and pulled out an envelope. She offered it to Wolter who snatched it up. He slit it open and beamed when he saw the cash inside.

"Well?" She stared down at him for all the world looking like a witch, a banshee, a thing of the night standing there dressed all in black. Her long, straight black hair was worn down, her face was eerily white in the dull street light and the only bit of colour was a slash of red lipstick at her mouth. She grimaced as she waited. Wolter quickly stuffed the envelope in a jacket pocket. From another, he produced a printed sheet of paper. He offered it to her.

"It wasn't easy to get this," he said.

She took it and opened it. "I don't care," she replied, glancing at the contents and smiling. "Are you sure this is correct?"

"Yes, it's his last known address," Wolter assured her.

She folded the paper and slipped it into another pocket, leaving her hand there.

"And is there anything else you can tell me?" she asked.

"That's all I could get. The man is like a ghost," he said, getting to his feet. He looked up at her. "That's the last, you hear? I can't do any more for you. They are already getting suspicious. If I keep doing this, they'll find out. I can't afford to lost my job, my pension."

"You don't have to worry about that, Wolter," she said with an uncharacteristic smile. "I will always take care of you."

"You will? I mean…look, I can't do it again. My nerves are shot to pieces," he said. He offered her a hand. "No hard feelings, but I'm out."

She looked at his hand like he'd offered her a dead fish.

"That's such a pity," she said, "I was starting to like you."

He smiled and then frowned. Before he could react again,

she pulled a handgun with a silencer from her pocket, pointed it at Wolter and pulled the trigger. With a dull crack, the bullet hit him square in the chest, sending him flying backwards. As his body hit the ground, Dominika was over him putting a bullet right between his eyes. Wolter barely felt a thing so swift and clean was the hit.

Wolfe emerged from a group of trees nearby and walked over to his mistress.

"Want me to dispose of this?" he asked, looking down at Wolter's body.

"Throw him in the Spree. Weigh him down so his body sinks," she said, but as Wolfe bent down to lift the body, she suddenly had an idea. "No, on second thought, don't throw him in the river. I have a better idea. Pass me my cell, I have a call to make."

Dino de Luca was tucking into a plate of meatballs and spaghetti when Alex came to. She was tied to a chair at his kitchen table, the ropes wound around her hands and her arms biting into her skin. She tried to move her legs, but they, too, were held fast against the chair legs. Fuck! She opened her eyes.

"Well, well, well, our little alley cat is awake," de Luca said in Italian. "Now, why were you spying on us, little girl?"

"I don't know what you're talking about. I wasn't spying on you," Alex replied in English. "Why have you tied me up? Let me go at once!" She twisted and turned in the chair to see if she could free herself, but she was bound tight. Her protestations and attempt to free herself produced loud peals of laughter from de Luca and his gang.

"Ah, English!" he said in English. "Well, if you weren't spying, perhaps you could tell me why you were looking in that window?"

"I wasn't," she said.

"You weren't? That wasn't you? Are you saying Gio here got it wrong?" de Luca said, pointing to the massive thug standing next to her. Gio grinned and waved at her, his gold tooth flashing in the light of the kitchen.

"Yes, I was lost. I wandered into the alley and was looking for a way out," she lied. "I was not spying on you."

De Luca nodded to Gio who backhanded her across the face. He hit her so hard, Alex saw stars.

"Want to try that again? In fact, let's start by finding out your name," de Luca said his face darkening. Alex kept her mouth shut. "Well? You must have a name. What is it?"

"Mind your own business and let me go," she snarled.

"Oh, we have a feisty one here," de Luca said in Italian. His goons laughed. In English, he said, "Let's try this again: who are you and why were you spying on me?" He nodded to Gio, and Alex felt the thug's hand whack the side of her head again. Her teeth jangled in her mouth. Wow! That drew blood, she could taste it. She felt sick, but she wasn't giving in to them.

"Let me go, or you'll be sorry," she said. "I am simply a visitor to your city, and I got lost and now I just want to go back to my hotel room."

Gio thumped her again, and this time she passed out. The last she knew was hearing de Luca chastising at Gio for hitting her so hard. Then everything went black.

Chapter 13 - Partners

Alex was unsure how long she had been left tied to the chair for when she came round the entire kitchen was empty and in darkness. Although it was quite warm in there, she shivered and regretted the movement for it made her head and jaw ache. That bastard battered me, she thought. He's going to be the first one I take out. She stretched her neck this way and that to get the kinks out and surveyed the scene. Squinting, Alex peered at her blackened surroundings. A small light above the back door filtered in through the dirty window, but it wasn't enough to really make out anything she could use to free herself. Shit. She struggled against the rope binding her to the chair. It was tied tight. Fuck. Now what? She stopped struggling for a moment to think. She was well and truly caught. How could she have allowed this to happen?

"You're slipping," she whispered to herself. Bollocks!

Alex was just attempting to stand up still tied to the chair when she became aware of a small sound over at the back door. It was a scraping noise, almost imperceptible, but to a person with her training she knew exactly what was happening. Someone was picking the lock. She froze. The scraping stopped, the door handle turned, and the door swung open slowly. The beam of a pocket torch shone into the kitchen and rested on her face. Blinded by the light, she could not see who it was who had come through the door.

"Alex," a familiar voice whispered, "are you alright?"

She frowned. Was that-? No, it couldn't be. "Nick?" she said quietly.

"Yes." The light went from her face, and Nick rushed to her side. "How the hell did you get yourself into this one? You're meant to be a professional," he asked as he sought a way to untie her. "No, don't tell me just now. Save it for later. I need to get you out of here first. Are you hurt?"

"I'm fine," she said both relieved and mortified that she was being rescued by someone from MI6. She could feel him tugging on the rope and then he cursed.

"Hold on," he whispered, "while I get my knife out. I'm going to have to cut you loose."

"Are any of de Luca's men about?" she whispered; fearful they would be discovered. She could not hear them, but they were bound to be somewhere in the building.

"There's no one about. De Luca and his goons left around an hour ago. The chef lives in the flat above, but he drank a full bottle of red wine before turning in. He won't be disturbing us."

Relieved, Alex said, "Did you see where de Luca went?"

"He left in a large black car. I don't know where, but I managed to get a tracker put on the car before it left." He began to cut the ropes.

"Thanks," she said. "I owe you one. How did you know where to find me?" Her face hardened. "Oh, wait, you've put another tracker on me, haven't you?"

Nick did not answer, but the brief pause before he continued working on her binds told her all she needed to know. The bastard had tracked her again. At last, with a grunt, he cut through the last thread of rope and unwound it from her. She wriggled free and tried to stand up, but fell down immediately. Her legs, stiff, sore and numb from being in the same position for hours, would not hold her weight. Silently she cursed her own body's limitations.

"Come on," said Nick, giving her his hand. "I'll help you."

Leaning heavily on Nick, trying not to let his heavenly manly scent and the feel of his strong, muscular arm affect her, Alex hobbled out of the kitchen and along the alleyway. Dawn was starting to break over the city, the warm rays making the red rooftops glow. It would have been truly beautiful, had it not been for the fact they were escaping. Nick helped her to the main street and looked at her properly for the first time that night.

"Shit! Look at the state of you, Alex! Did someone beat you up?"

"Gio did, but don't worry. I'll get the bastard back. How bad is it?"

Nick examined her faced and sighed. "Bruising all over your left jaw, a black eye and a burst lip…You still look beautiful though." He looked away as if unsure how she would react to that and then back to her when she began laughing. He frowned.

"What's so funny?"

Alex was laughing at the absurdity of it all. Here was the man she had fallen in love with, a man who had lied about who he was, a man who had broken her heart, standing before her telling her that despite her beat up face, she was beautiful. There was nothing attractive about her then, she knew that; she was a mess of dried-on blood, bruising and cuts. It was too much.

The stress of the last couple of days evaporated as she giggled.

"What is it?" Nick asked, puzzled at her reaction.

"Nothing," she said. "I'm just so glad to see you."

"Come on, let's get you back to the hotel where I'll get you cleaned up," Nick said.

Alex did not argue, instead enjoying having his arms around her once more allowed him to lead her down the street. Nick hailed a solitary taxi and ordered the driver to take them to Alex's hotel. The driver took one look at Alex's face and began to protest, but Nick told him she had been mugged and that he was taking her back to her room where a doctor would be called.

"If you get us there quickly," he said in perfect Italian, "I will give you a handsome tip."

The driver glanced at Alex for reassurance. She gave him a half smile and a thumbs up, and that seemed to make his mind up for him. He switched off his taxi for hire sign and drove them to her hotel.

By the time they arrived, Alex had regained some feeling back in her legs and pushed Nick away when he tried to help her out of the taxi. He might have saved her, but there was no way she had forgiven him yet. With a lopsided stagger, she stumbled into the hotel by herself and, Nick at her back, made her way up to her room where she collapsed on her bed.

"Uh-uh!" Nick said. "No sleeping until we've cleaned you up. Come on, into the bathroom with you."

Alex had already unpacked a small first aid kit when she had arrived the previous day, so Nick combed through that until he found some antiseptic wipes. Forcing Alex to sit on the closed toilet, he gently washed her face with some warm water before dabbing the cut lip and other abrasions with the antiseptic. She winced with every sting of the solution, but actually felt glad

Nick was there. He made her feel safe. Damnit!

"Thank you for rescuing me," she said as Nick finished up.

"My pleasure," he replied with a tight smile. The stress of the evening was written all over his face and, for the first time, Alex knew that he truly cared about her. He threw the used wipes in the trash can and helped her to her feet. "Now, strip off and into bed with you," he ordered, ushering her out of the bathroom. "You've had a rough night."

He followed her into the bedroom and shut the curtains.

"I'm fine," she protested, turning about and making for the bathroom again. "I'll just take a quick shower and get dressed."

He ran in front of her, grabbed her gently by the shoulders and spun her. "You're not fine, you're going for a sleep," he told her, pushing her towards the bed.

"And what will you be doing while I'm sleeping?" she asked as she got down to her underwear and pulled back the covers. He was removing his trousers and t-shirt.

"I'm going to be sleeping too," he said, climbing into the bed and patting the space next to him. "I'm exhausted. I had to wait most of the night to rescue you."

Alex hesitated, unsure whether to get into bed with him or not.

"It's okay, you're safe to get in," he said with a smile. "I promise I won't touch you."

Resigned that they were going to have to share, she got in. She was too tired and too sore to argue. She would sort out the Nick problem when they had both had a good sleep and were feeling more refreshed. She turned her back to him and felt a strong, protective arm slip around her waist. He pulled her towards her so they spooned. It felt good. It felt safe. It felt right. She took a deep breath and relaxed.

Some hours later, Alex woke to the loud snores of Nick beside her. She studied his face, relaxed in sleep. Could she trust him again? Could she allow him back into her life? Did they have a future together? And how would she work around the fact he was MI6? One of them would have to think about changing career, and she was sure it wouldn't be her. Or could she? Could she give up being a Sister for a man? Could she give up all that money and all the goodies it brought? She still didn't know.

Alex slipped out of the bed and padded into the bathroom. She had no clue what time it was, but she needed to get cleaned up. It had been a warm lying there in Nick's arms and she had been sweating. She jumped in the shower and let the hot and reviving water wash away all the aches and pains she had gained from the previous night. As she washed, her mind went into overdrive. How had she managed to get herself caught? She had never been so careless as to get caught before. It wasn't like her. She was definitely slipping and she knew the cause: her mind wasn't totally on the job, and Nick Walker was to blame. Her head was full of him still, and it didn't help that he was in her bed sleeping peacefully, all warm and manly. Lust bloomed in her body and she took a deep breath to stop herself from rushing out of the shower and jumping his bones.

Stop it! she told herself. He lied to you. He's the enemy. He was using you. Then why did it not feel like that? Why did it feel like she should trust him? Why was her body gearing up for another round in the sack? Her whole being yearned for him, was desperate for him to run his hands all over her, to make her his again. Her heart told her she could trust him. But her head was saying otherwise.

"Oh, for fuck's sake!" she said aloud.

"What's the matter?" Nick was standing in the bathroom in nothing on but a pair of jockey shorts and a grin. She jumped, pulled back the shower curtain and stared at him.

"Why are you in here?"

"I was looking for you," he replied with a wicked grin. "I wondered if you were up for a bit of…"

"I'm not up for anything, thank you very much," she said, grabbing the bath towel from a wall peg and wrapping it around her dripping body. She stepped out of the shower and onto the bath mat.

"Oh," he replied. He had on his sad puppy dog eyes again. She wasn't falling for it.

"What? Did you think just because you were my knight in shining armour I'd fall straight back into your bed?" she demanded. What a cheek!

"No, of course not," he said. "It's just that we shared a bed together, and I was hoping … you had forgiven me."

"We were both exhausted. I wasn't in the mood for an argument, so I let you stay," she said. "But you're not staying tonight."

"Alex, I thought we had gone through all of this," he said exasperated. "You know I didn't mean to hurt you. I was just doing my job. When I got the assignment, never in my wildest dreams did I think I'd actually fall in love with you. I'm sorry. What can I do to make it up to you?"

"You say you love me?"

"Yes, with all my heart."

"Well, prove it!"

"How can I do that?"

She shrugged. He bit his lip and thought for a moment.

"I'm assuming de Luca is your next target?" he said. She

nodded. "Then why don't I help you take him out?"

"No."

"Why not?"

"It's not your job to murder him. It's mine"

"But I wouldn't be doing the actual murder, I'd just be helping."

"No, I can't allow it. It goes against our rules."

"Who's going to know?" he asked. "Please, Alex. Let me help."

"No."

"At least let me go with you to watch your back?"

She thought for a moment. That wasn't such a bad idea, but could she trust him not to slap a pair of handcuffs on her and drag her off to jail?

"How do I know you won't arrest me?" she asked, staring at him intently.

He held her stare then sighed. The answer took her totally by surprise. "I've been thinking a lot about that," he began. "I'm going to hand in my notice."

"What? You can't do that!"

"I can and I will," he replied. "Look, why don't we go get de Luca together, and we can talk about my job later?"

"But what I'm asking you to do is illegal. What if you're caught and get arrested?" she asked.

"I won't. Now, can I come or not?"

"Okay, but I'm running the operation. You do what I say, okay?"

"Deal."

"Now get out of here whilst I get ready," she said, shooing him with her hands.

He smirked at her. "It's not like I haven't seen it all before," he said with a wicked grin.

"Yes, but I don't want you to see it right now," she replied. Or else I might just whip those shorts off you and take you right now, she thought and then blushed. He must have seen her colour because his eyes narrowed.

"All right, but don't be long. I need to get ready too."

They breakfasted at a café near the hotel. It was situated in a small square a couple of streets away. A small, trendy business favoured by students and hip young things, the café had ten tables on the terrace outside, sectioned off with a small white picket fence, and the pair sat down on one close to the entrance. Alex, in black t-shirt and cargo trousers, ordered croissants and coffee. Nick, more casual in a light shirt and shorts, had baked egg and sausage with a glass of orange juice. As they ate, they discussed the job ahead.

"So, we know de Luca is often at his restaurant," said Nick, "but he knows we're coming now so he'll be expecting us to hit him there. Are there any other places he frequents?"

Alex opened her mobile and flicked through the de Luca file. The man was a bit of an enigma. He had his properties and a few known hang-out spots, but only a handful of close associates.

"I think we're going to have to scope him out before we go for a hit," she said, sipping her coffee. It was milky and smooth and just hit the spot.

"Do we know where he lives?"

"He's got a villa outside the city where he lives with his wife and kids. I thought about taking him out there, but it's built like Fort Knox, plus I don't want to take him out in front of his family. That's not my style," she said.

"I'll try and get more intel on him from a police source I have here," he said. "Maybe she can give us more information."

"She?"

"Just someone I came across in my career."

"Oh. Right." Was she feeling jealous? She? Alex Grier, who prided herself on having complete control of her emotions?

"Are you jealous?" Nick asked a twinkle of merriment in his eye.

"No."

"You are! You're jealous!"

"I'm not, of course, I'm not," Alex lied.

"Well," he said leaning back in his chair, "there's hope for me yet."

She made a face at him across the table, and they both laughed.

"It's nice to see you laugh again," Nick said.

"It's nice to laugh again," she conceded. "I never did thank you properly for saving me last night. I don't know what I would have done if you hadn't have traced me to that place. I'd probably be dead by now."

"It was nothing," he said.

"By the way," she added. "Where did you place that tracer on me?"

"I put it in the heel of your boots."

"How did you know I would wear that particular pair?" He looked a bit shifty. "Nick? Is there something you're not telling me?"

"I might have put a tracer in a few pairs."

Alex looked at him, aghast. "When did you do that?"

"When you went to the gym. After you had thrown me out."

"What? Why?" She didn't know whether to be furious or

grateful.

"Because I wanted to keep an eye on you," he confessed. "I was worried." He looked down at his plate and suddenly an unfinished sausage was fascinating to him.

"But, why? I had finished with you!"

He met her eyes and repeated sentiments he'd made before. "Because I love you. Because I was worried about you. Because if anything had happened to you and I wasn't there to help, I would never forgive myself."

It was Alex's turn to sit back in her chair. Her mind was a blizzard of questions and angry responses. She broke eye contact, focussing down the street. The indecency of it all was astounding.

"I can't believe you did that!" Her head snapped back to him. "Wait a minute! In order to put these devices in my boots you must have broken into my apartment!" He nodded. "Oh my God!" she said, standing up. "I can't believe you did that!"

"Alex, I'm sorry. I over-stepped the mark I know I did. But if I hadn't tracked you, I would never have found you and you'd be dead now."

"And are those the only trackers you have on me? Have you bugged my apartment too? Do you know everything that goes on in my life?" she said. She could feel the heat of her anger in her face. She resisted the urge to punch him, although it took everything she had.

"No," he replied calmly. "I didn't want to listen in on your private conversations. I just wanted to make sure I knew where you were so you would be safe."

"For fuck's sake, Nick," she snarled, throwing her napkin on the table, "this is unacceptable!"

"Alex! Please!" He stood up and held his hand out to her,

but she batted it away.

"That's the last straw, Nick. I can't believe you did that to me. It's unforgiveable!" Alex crossed her arms. "No, I don't want to take your hand. Leave me alone! Just leave me alone!"

She stormed off, not knowing which direction she was headed but only that she had to get away from him. She needed to think. This was getting creepy. Nick Walker had been stalking her. Shit, she had the boots on now. She sat down on a public bench a couple of streets away and wrenched her boots off. Examining the heels, she took off the heel cover and tapped a small device out on to her hand. Putting her boots back on, she threw the tracker on the ground and crushed it underfoot.

Fuck you, Nick Walker, she thought as she ran off towards the city centre. She couldn't deal with this right now. It was just too much. He had stepped over every single one of her boundaries.

Chapter 14 - Rescue

Nick watched her go with real regret. Why had he told her about the trackers? Why hadn't he said he had just followed her here? He should have lied. Stupid, stupid, stupid. But he knew in his heart of hearts that if he wanted her to trust him again, he would have to tell her the truth from now on. He finished his coffee, paid the bill and, heavy-hearted, strolled back towards the hotel, barely noticing the life on the streets. Tourists, workers, school kids, delivery men all went past him, but he did not see them. Head down, eyes on the road, depressed, head only full of Alex, Nick walked on oblivious to the wonderous Florentine architecture and history around him.

Maybe if he had kept more wits about him. Maybe if his head hadn't been so full of hurt, he might have seen the white van being slowly driven up beside him, the door slid open and two men jump out. It was only when the bag went on his head, and he was dragged inside the vehicle that he finally realised what was happening. He was being kidnapped. Pushed roughly to the floor, kicked inside, Nick heard the door bang shut, and the van drive off.

"Hey! What's happening?" he demanded of his kidnappers. He tried to pull the bag off his head but got a hard slap for his trouble. "Who are you, and what are you doing?"

"Shuttup!" a voice snarled.

Nick felt his hands and feet being bound. Someone went through his pockets and removed his wallet. Then he was left on the floor of the van again to feel every bump in the road on the journey to who-knew-where.

Dino de Luca was sitting at the table in the kitchen of his restaurant eating meatballs when Nick was dragged inside and the hood removed. As he blinked in the morning light, he counted the number of men inside. Four goons and de Luca, no kitchen staff. Every one of them was armed with a handgun. Every one of them looked like they wanted to kick the shit out of him right there and then.

"Sit down," de Luca demanded.

Still bound, Nick found himself roughly pushed on to a chair opposite the mafia boss who was grinning like the Cheshire cat.

"So," de Luca said, "you are the man who is friendly with the woman who tried to break into my business empire last night."

"I don't know what you're talking about," Nick replied.

"You were seen having breakfast with her this morning," he replied. "Now, let's try this again. Who are you, and what do you and your woman want with me?"

"Boss," one of the thugs said in Italian. He handed de Luca Nick's wallet. It was made of a soft, black leather and had been a birthday present from his mother. Nick flinched as de Luca went through it looking for ID. "So, you are Nick Walker of England," he said reading Nick's driving license. "Well, Nick Walker of England what are you doing in this great city of mine? And what is your interest in my business?"

"I'm here on holiday," Nick lied. "And I don't know who this woman is you are talking about."

"We caught her snooping outside these premises last night. We detained her, but somehow, she escaped. Did you have something to do with her escape, Nick Walker?"

Nick looked at de Luca. There was a globule of thick tomato sauce dripping down the man's mouth. It was all Nick could do to not stare. "Look, I don't know who you are or what you are talking about. Now, please let me go. I am an innocent tourist who has come to Florence to see the sights, that's all."

De Luca nodded to his man standing nearest to Nick and the man punched him hard on the mouth. Nick felt his head snap to the side and tasted blood. It took him a moment to regain his faculties and then he stared at de Luca again.

"Let's try that again, shall we, Mr Walker?" de Luca said. "Your lady friend said the exact same thing last night and look how that turned out for her. I'd suggest you tell me what I want to know."

Alex returned to her hotel and went to the bar. It was too early for alcohol, so she ordered a large frothy cappuccino and sat at the window staring out into the busy street. In the street, officer workers, tourists and shoppers hurried to and fro as she blindly sipped on her drink. She was not really focussing on anything, except what was going on in her mind, so she nearly jumped out of her skin when a staff member tapped her on the shoulder ten minutes later.

"Signorina Grier?" he said.

"Yes?"

"You have a telephone call at reception."

"Thank you."

Alex abandoned her half-finished coffee on the table and rose to follow the man to reception. With a quick gesture, he motioned to the upturned receiver lying on the reception counter. She nodded and lifted it to her ear.

"Hello?" She tried to keep the annoyance out of her voice as she made contact with whoever was on the other end. She had had an irritating enough experience this morning without adding another.

"Signorina Grier?" a man's voice rasped.

"Yes?"

"Alex Greir?" The voice was speaking English with a heavy Italian accent.

"Yes."

"I have someone here who wants to talk with you."

She waited whilst someone was brought to the phone.

"Alex?" It was Nick. That got her dander up right away.

"What do you want, Nick?" she snapped. "I don't have time for this. I thought I already told you…"

"Alex!" he growled and something in his voice made her pause. "I've been kidnapped. They say if you don't show up with 100,000 Euros and a truthful explanation as to why you were there last night, they'll kill me and then come after you. They want to know who sent you."

Alex's gut churned. Although she hated him, she couldn't let Nick die. "Who's got you?"

"De Luca."

"Where have I to meet him?"

"At his restaurant kitchen."

"When?"

"3pm when the restaurant is empty. Mr de Luca doesn't like

to be disturbed when he's doing business."

"Alright."

"And Alex…!"

The phone was yanked away from Nick and the first man's voice came on.

"And Signor de Luca says no funny business, you hear? Come unarmed and alone."

The receiver went down, leaving Alex only with the monotonous drone of a dead tone. She carefully replaced the hotel phone receiver back in its cradle and paused. Fuck! Now what? Think! Think! She would have to rescue him. She owed him that at least. But how?

Alex walked to the hotel elevator and pressed the button. As she heard the lift clank into action, a plan was beginning to form in her mind. She glanced at her watch just as the elevator doors swooshed open. It was coming up to noon. If she went and stormed the place now, they wouldn't be expecting her. Should she call for help from Mother or one of the Sisters? No, Sisters of Sin were not allowed to form love attachments to individuals. Besides, Nick was MI6, they would kill him as soon as look at him.

In her hotel room, she pulled her rucksack from under the bed and threw it open.. Inside, broken down, was her rifle, some rounds, a handgun and a four-inch knife. She took out the gun and knife, and left the rifle. She would be fighting hand to hand. She considered using the rifle to take out any guards, but they would kill Nick instantly if that happened. Fuck. She closed the compartment, zipped up the case and stowed it carefully under the bed again.

Then Alex went to the room's vanity unit and sat down. Taking a bundle of hair pins from her overnight bag, she laid them out in front of her. Then she carefully began to wind her hair up into a bun on top of her head. Grabbing the knife, with its ornate and beautiful handle, she placed in her hair, its haff folding down horizontally to look like a woman's hair clip. The pistol she tucked into the back of her trousers and covered it with her top. She met her worried eyes in the mirror and frowned. Her black eye was looking magnificent this morning and the burst lip had swollen to twice its size, but the steeliness in her gaze remained true and strong.

I'm going to get that bastard back for taking Nick and making me look like this, Alex promised her reflection, just see if I don't. She zipped up her bag and stood up. Alex stuffed a small leather case containing her lock-picks and her mobile into a leg pocket of her cotton cargo trousers and a half metre long thin wire in the other.

"Right," she said aloud, "time for action."

The restaurant was busy when Alex arrived. Standing behind a van across the street, she surveyed the place for a few minutes. There was one thug inside sitting in a window seat drinking coffee and reading a newspaper. The rest of the tables were packed with holiday makers and locals alike, and waiters flitted from table to table topping up drinks and taking orders. Outside, on the narrow walkway, two thugs were sitting at tables watching and waiting for her. No way in there without being seen.

Careful to not draw attention to herself, she left her hiding place and made her way to the alleyway. She walked up the side of the building and stopped at the corner. Slowly, she angled her head around the corner to see the lay of the land. Three de Luca heavies were smoking at the back of the restaurant. Standing at the doorway, they only moved when a kitchen porter came out to empty rubbish into the large industrial bins at the rear. In a room above them, a fourth goon showed himself at the window, flicking ash outside.

Alex drew back into the shade of the side of the house. Too many to take on at once. She would have to be clever about this. She glanced at her watch again. It was now 1.30pm. Less than two hours to go until they expected her to arrive. She slunk back along the wall and peered around into the street and the front of the restaurant. Just as she did this, a delivery van drew up outside and parked. The driver, a young man in his late 20s, got out and went to the back of the van where he opened the doors.

The Maître D' of the café ran out and began an animated conversation with him, arms waving as he accentuated every word. From what Alex could gather, he was shouting about the delivery being late. The driver exchanged some angry words sending the Maître D' back inside. Alex watched as the driver pulled out a large tray of fresh fish and balanced it on his shoulder. Carefully, he carried it inside, leaving the van wide open. Thinking fast, she put her plan into action. Alex stepped out on to the street, ran on to the road and hurried along the side of three parked cars. On reaching the delivery van, she straightened and waited patiently for the van driver to return.

"What are you doing there?" he demanded in Italian when he saw her.

In perfect Italian, she nodded towards the restaurant. "They've sent me out to help you bring the delivery in."

"They did, did they? Well, that's the least they could do after that rogue called me a lazy shit. You would think it was my fault the delivery was late!" he complained.

"He's always moaning," she said. "Now give me something to carry inside."

He stared at her face. "What happened to you? Did your old man beat you up?"

"I fell," she said, putting her arms out to take a load. "But never mind that. The boss is waiting."

He shrugged. "Can you carry that?" He pointed to a tray of assorted cheeses.

"Sure," she replied, praying that she could.

"Great, that'll let me get on with the rest of my deliveries," he said, lifting the cheese box and putting it into her outstretched arms. It was heavy. "What's your name, by the way?"

"Maria," she replied.

"Ciao, Maria. Maybe I'll see you around," he said with a wink.

Alex smiled and took the tray from him. "Not if I can help it," she murmured as she balanced the box on her shoulder and carried it inside. Walking as confidently as she could, the box hiding her face, she took it right up to the Maître D' and asked him where to put it.

"The driver told me to bring it in. I'm his assistant," she lied.

"Take it straight through to the kitchen," he replied, barely looking at her. He waved his hands towards the back. "You people are late, you know! You should be giving us a discount!"

"Take it up with the boss," she called as she made her way into the back. "We're just the people who deliver."

"I will!"

Alex found herself in a short corridor leading between the restaurant and the kitchen at the back. The door to the kitchen was wide open, and several workers were run back and forth as they prepared meals. She placed her box of cheeses on a low table. To her right, a door marked the entrance to the toilets. Be side it, a cupboard containing cleaning products and toilet rolls. She knew this because she opened it and loose rolls tumbled out on top of her. Quickly closing the door, Alex hoped no one had seen or heard that. A set of stairs led down into the cellar and another lead up.

Now if I had a kidnapping victim I wanted to hide where would I keep him? she wondered. The basement she decided and began to descend the creaking wooden stairs down.

The cellar ran the entire length of the restaurant and kitchen combined and was full of stock. Using the torch on her mobile, she scanned the place. Crates of beer, wine and other spirits were stacked high on the floor. A large metal shelving unit was packed full of packets of dried pasta, jars of roasted peppers and pesto, and tins of tomatoes and anchovies. Another held dry ingredients for bread and dessert making. A third had baskets of fruit, potatoes and paper napkins.

Classy joint, thought Alex as she lifted a crackling packet. No linen napkins for customers at this place. The place smelled of stale bread and rotten cabbage. She crept along, seeking signs of Nick, but could find none. Above her the floorboards creaked and groaned, and there was the muffled laughter and chat of happy patrons leaving the café.

"Yes, I'll go get it," a voice said from the top of the basement stairs.

Quickly, Alex concealed herself behind a stack of beer crates and held her breath. Peeking out behind the crate she saw a man walk down the stairs and switch on the cellar light. It gave off a dull glow and hummed. Whistling, the man searched through some shelves nearby. Muttering to himself, he grabbed three jars of anchovies and turned to leave.

In her hiding place, Alex held her breath. Please don't find me, she thought as she heard him walk to the bottom of the stairs. He paused on the bottom step and looked around. I am not here, I am invisible, thought Alex behind the crates. With a shrug, the man flicked a switch. The light went off and, still whistling, he climbed the stairs and was gone.

Alex sighed in relief. Jesus, that was a bit close for comfort. She crept out of her hiding place and gave the cellar one last scan. No Nick here. So, there was only one other way to go and that was up. As quietly as she could, Alex crept up the basement steps and paused at the landing. Seeing the way was clear, swift as a deer she ran across the hall and scuttled up the second set of stairs, pausing at the top to make sure the corridor was empty.

The corridor stretched the length of the building and had three rooms off it all marked by closed doors. The first door opened into a bathroom smelling of soap and shaving cream. The second was the bedroom of the chef who was snoozing in the warm afternoon. He snorted and shifted slightly as she peered in, but did not wake. Tip-toing along the corridor, Alex reached the third door and tried the handle. It was locked. She removed her lockpicking gear from her pocket and got to work. Taking her all of thirty seconds to pick the lock and push the door open, she gasped when she looked inside.

Nick, beaten and bloody, was lying on his back, splayed, tied to a bed in the corner of the room. Gagged and barely conscious, he heard her, opened his eyes and saw her. A look of relief washed over him as she ran to him and tried to untie the knots that bound him. Finding them stuck fast, she removed the knife from her hair and, fingers trembling, began to saw. Nick moaned.

"Shhh, they'll hear you," she whispered. But he moaned again. Alex frowned, stopped sawing and undid his gag. "What?"

"I knew you'd come for me," he said, voice croaky.

"I'm just repaying the compliment," she said, getting back

to the ropes. It took her several minutes to free each limb, and as each one was liberated, Nick flexed it to get the blood flow going again.

"Thank you for coming for me," he said when he was finally released. His voice was hoarse. He sat up and gingerly touched his face.

"That's us even now," she said. "Now, come on, we need to get out of here."

Stashing her knife in her back pocket, she retrieved the pistol from her hair and helped him to his feet. He was sore, but mobile. They crept to the door and paused. Alex inspected the corridor. It was still empty. Nick at her back, she crept out and along to the head of the stairs. Then stopped. Straining her ears for any sign of someone coming, only when she was sure the way was clear, did she start to walk again.

"Come on," Alex said as she led the way down.

Slowly, slowly, they made their way down, carefully treading on each step to make as little noise as possible. They were about halfway down and had almost reached the middle landing when one of de Luca's men suddenly appeared from nowhere. He looked shocked to see the pair of them on the stairs, but before he could open his mouth to protest, Alex shot him between the eyes.

The body fell backwards. He slammed into the floor as he fell. There was a loud crack as he hit the ground floor, and then people started shouting. Alex grabbed Nick, and they ran for it, stumbling down the remaining stairs and leaping over the body as they reached the bottom.

"Stop right there!" someone yelled in Italian.

Alex looked to see two of de Luca's men run out of the kitchen towards them. She took a shot at them before pulling

Nick through the restaurant, past fleeing waiting staff and into the startled arms of a third man. Hearing the shots, he had unholstered his gun and was going to see what the commotion was about when Alex ran into him. The man, too slow to draw his gun, received a smack on the nose with Alex's pistol. Yelling in pain, blinded by tears, he backed off allowing her and Nick to sidestep him towards the door. There was the bang of another gunshot. Alex looked around to see the kitchen goons in the restaurant. They were firing at them. There was no time to get to the exit.

"Shit!" Alex aimed her gun and fired off another couple of rounds.

The goons took cover behind the bar counter as Alex and Nick overturned two tables and hid behind them. She quickly reloaded her gun and began to return fire.

"Have you got another weapon?" Nick asked as there was a pause in the shooting.

"Only this," she said, waggling her tiny gun.

"That pea shooter won't take out anyone," he said. "Why didn't you bring something better?"

"This pea shooter has already taken out two thugs," she said.

"Hmph."

"I'm going to run out of ammo soon," she said. "We need to get out of here."

The restaurant's exit was only a few feet away, but they couldn't risk going for it, not with the hail of bullets being fired at them.

"We're going to have to make a run for it," he said. "When they reload, okay?"

There was a pause in the firing and that was their chance. Without waiting for the fire fight to start again, Alex and Nick scrambled to their feet and ran to the door. Yanking it open, they raced out of the restaurant and into the street.

"This way!" Alex yelled as they pounded along.

Her muscles were already screaming for mercy, lungs bursting for air, but she kept going. There was no way she was going to die here, not today. Putting as much space in between them and de Luca's men was her goal, and she quickly achieved it. A mile from the restaurant, once they were sure they weren't being followed, they stopped to rest. Panting, Alex stood with her back against a shop window and closed her eyes as she fought to regain control of her breathing.

"Fuck, that was close!" she said.

"Now what?" Nick said.

"Now, we regroup back at the hotel and make a plan," she said. "I'm going to take that fucker out once and for all."

"I think we should take him out at the restaurant," Alex said as she and Nick debated the best way of killing their target. "I know there could be casualties. Despite its owner, it does seem to be a popular place for Italians to eat. But my gut is saying let's get him there."

They were sitting eating room service snacks in their hotel room after first cleaning up. Nick was now as battered and bruised as she was. He was lying on the bed, propped up by pillows, whilst she sat on the chair.

"Well, it's going to have to be tonight," Nick said. "If we leave it any later, he'll be able to get more men in and strike first."

"Agreed," she said. "Plus, he'll not be expecting us back so soon. Here's what I think we should do."

Nick lay on the flat roof of the garage overlooking the rear of the restaurant and sighed. This was not quite what he'd had in mind when he had followed Alex to Florence. Still, there were worst ways to spend an evening. It was 1am and he was lying with Alex's sniper rifle pointed at the back of the de Luca restaurant. Their plan was simple. He was to take out the guards whilst Alex killed de Luca. Well, it had sounded simple when they had talked about it earlier. Now he was getting leg cramps and his face ached.

Alex snuck back into the alleyway and hid behind an industrial bin. From her position she could see the figures of two guards in the dull light of the restaurant's overhead light. One was smoking a cigarette while the other was taking a piss.

Dirty bastard, she thought, there's toilets inside. She glanced at the illuminated face of her watch. Any time now, Nick. She glanced up at the roof, but could not see her accomplice hidden there. Suddenly, there was a whooshing sound followed by another and both guards crumpled to the ground. Nick, a sniper almost as skilled as she was, had brought down the pair with barely a whimper. Impressed with his shots, Alex snuck up to the back of the kitchen and went to the door. Slowly, she opened it and slipped inside.

The kitchen was empty, the staff having cleared up and gone home for the night. Alex was surprised not to see any signs of police having been there to investigate their escape, but she supposed de Luca must have paid them to turn a blind eye to the earlier shit show. She tip toed through to the corridor connect ing the kitchen with the restaurant and stopped. Voices could be heard within.

"I want you to get that bitch and take her out," de Luca said. "Find out where she's staying and put a bullet in her head."

"What about him?"

"Him as well."

"Sure, boss. What if they've already left Florence?"

"They're still here. They came for a reason and haven't finished with me yet. And I haven't finished with them. Get on with it and take Gio with you. She's a slippery bitch. Make sure you get her."

There was the sound of footsteps, and the restaurant's street door opened and closed.

"What do you think this woman wants, Rico?" de Luca said. "Who do you think sent her?"

"Could be anyone," Rico said. "You've pissed off a lot of people lately, boss."

"Meh! Comes with the territory."

In the shadows, Alex crept closer to the door.

"Go get me a glass of red, will you, Rico?"

"Sure boss."

She was almost at the door.

"And make it the nice one, the one I like."

"Sure, boss."

Alex stilled as Rico walked past the door to the bar of the restaurant. His back to her, he was busy pulling an expensive bottle of wine down from a shelf and uncorking it. She took a quick peek at de Luca. He was sitting at the other end of the restaurant which had been cleaned up since her earlier visit. The only signs there had been a gun fight were the pockmarks on the walls behind him. The mob boss was counting a large amount of cash on a table at the other end of the restaurant. It was all in notes and he was engrossed in what he was doing.

No time like the present. Alex pulled out her gun and aimed it at Rico. The sound smothered by a silencer, the gun only made a phhht sound as it released the bullet from its barrel. It caught Rico on the right temple and he teetered for a brief moment before slumping forward. Alex ran out of her hiding spot and caught the big guy before he could make a sound. With great effort, she guided the body to the floor and pulled it further behind the bar so that de Luca couldn't see what had happened. She returned to her hiding place in the shadows of the restaurant corridor.

At the other end of the restaurant, de Luca lit another cigarette and took a puff. "Hey, Rico, what's happening with that drink?... Rico?"

De Luca rose, searching for his man. From his viewpoint he could not see the dead body behind the bar, but could see the bottle sitting waiting to be poured.

"Rico, where are you, you idiot? A man could die of thirst here!" Getting no reply, de Luca stood up and sighed. "Jesus, have I got to pour my own?"

He stomped down the length of his café and made for the bar. In the shadows, ready to pounce, Alex waited. The mob boss muttered to himself as he arrived at the bar and made to go around behind it. It was then she moved. As silent as a cat, she sprang at him and landed on his back. Wrapping her legs around his torso and her arms around his shoulders, she pinned the mafioso long enough to draw her dagger across his neck.

De Luca barely had any time to react as the knife sliced open his carotid arteries and jugular veins. Alex slid off him just as he dropped like a stone, hitting his head on the way down. Blood spurted everywhere and Alex grimaced. That was the only thing she didn't like about this way of killing, the blood. She wiped her knife on de Luca's buttocks and stowed it away in a pocket. Job done.

On the garage roof, Nick waited nervously for her to reappear. The minutes ticked by, and it was all he could do to prevent himself from running in there to help. Where was she? Had she been captured again? What if she had been killed? The questions rattled about in his brain like hungry birds at a free-for-all. Where was she? At last, the back door opened and a blood-drenched Alex stood at the door. Through the sight of his rifle, he could see her gingerly pick her way across the dead guards he had taken out earlier and run down the alleyway. Quick as a flash, he was up and folding down the rifle, which he stashed in a bag. Then he climbed down from the garage and ran to meet her at their arranged place two streets down.

Alex was trying to wipe the blood from her t-shirt when he arrived at the alleyway rendezvous.

"I'm glad I wore black tonight," she said, "that de Luca spurted blood like a fountain."

"Have you cleaned up?"

"There's not a trace of me in there," she said.

"Good." He looked at her. Blood spattered her face. "You could have wiped your face before you came out."

"I was busy escaping," she said. Then they both burst out laughing.

"Here, hold this," he said, handing her the rifle bag. She took it without questions and watched as he took off his own zippered hoodie. He handed it to her. "Put this on. It'll draw less attention to your bloody look. And wipe your face."

"What with?" she said, placing the bag on the floor and slipping into the hoodie.

"There's wipes in the pockets," he said.

"You think of everything," she said with a smile.

"Just as well one of us does."

They had booked out of the hotel room earlier that day and stowed their baggage in Alex's car, which was parked in the same alleyway. As they approached the Aston Martin, Alex pulled her keys out of her pocket.

"Want me to drive?" Nick asked.

"No chance," she said. "This is my baby."

Stashing her weapons on the back seat, she slipped behind the wheel and started the engine. The car roared into life. Nick got in beside her and put on his seatbelt, rightly assuming that if she drove anywhere like she lived, this was going to be a fast ride.

"Are we heading back to Berlin?" he asked as the car moved off.

"No," she said, "I'm going down to our HQ in Rome. I need to speak to Mother about what happened there. And about Dominika."

"Dominika?"

"She's another story."

Nick's cell rang. He pulled it out of his jacket pocket and looked to see who the caller was. He switched his cell off and returned it to his pocket.

"Who was that?" Alex wanted to know.

"No-one," he replied. He looked at her, seeing her frowning. "It was my office. I should check in."

"I thought you were done with all that."

"I was… I am…I just need to let them know that so they

don't send anyone after me."

She bit her lip and nodded. That made sense.

"Seeing as how you're driving," Nick said, "I'll choose the music."

"Over my dead body," she joked.

Nine hundred miles away, deep in the offices of Britain's Secret Service HQ at Vauxhall, Ben Littlejohn put down his telephone receiver and frowned. Was Nick ghosting him? They had arranged this call time only last week. He was supposed to check in every day. He hadn't heard from Nick for two days and now this. Why hadn't he picked up? Why had he switched his cell off? Was it him who had done it or someone else? He leaned back in his seat thinking. The click-clack of high heels on tiles woke him from his reflecting, and he turned around to see Lettis, in a pencil skirt suit and stilettos, approaching. She saw his face.

"Everything okay, Ben?" she asked.

"I'm not sure," he replied. "I've lost contact with Nick." Ben didn't want to admit it, but he was worried his old friend was in trouble.

"How long?"

"Forty-eight hours."

"Well, that's no issue. This isn't the first time an agent has gone silent for this length of time. He's probably deeply in with Miss Grier and is unable to contact us."

"It's not like him, though," Ben replied.

"Give him another day to make contact, and if he doesn't, come and see me." she said. "I'm sure he's fine. It's not like he's done this before."

"Yes, but this feels different."

"Okay, we'll give him the 24 hours and then start to worry." She began walking away.

"Actually, I have another idea."

Lettis turned and gave him a quizzical look. "Alright, I'm listening."

Chapter 15 - Rome

As the car sped out of Florence, Alex called Mother to request a meet. Mother sounded harassed, and Alex couldn't help but feel her handler was desperate to get her off the phone.

"Is it important?" Mother snapped. There was the sound of drilling going on in the background. Of course, work would have already begun to put the Conexus HQ back together.

"Very. There's something going on with Dominika. I don't know exactly, but I need to speak to you about her."

"I don't know," came the reply. Mother was never normally indecisive, and it worried Alex. "No…you over there…that doesn't go there! Do I have to do everything myself!" She returned her attention back to Alex. "Sorry about that, workmen."

"What's wrong?" Alex asked. "You sound stressed."

"I am stressed," Mother snapped. "You would be too if you had to deal with everything I'm dealing with right now."

"I'm sorry."

"No, look, I'm sorry," Mother said. "I shouldn't have barked at you. Alright, come down to Rome. The headquarters building is still in disarray, but I actually could use you right now. I may have a small job for you."

"Alright, we're heading over now. We'll see you soon."

"Wait a minute! We?" Mother said, but Alex had already rung off.

Alex and Nick arrived in Rome around three hours later. They booked into a small hotel in the city centre, parking Alex's car in a private garage she had rented. Alex got changed. It was still hot outside, so she forewent her usual black trousers and vest for a loose pale-yellow mini-dress and ballet pumps. She could do nothing about her injuries, which were still emblazoned brightly across her face, but she did her best to cover the bruising with some light make-up. She didn't want to draw attention to them as they walked the few streets between the hotel and Conexus' HQ.

The Conexus building in Via della Conciliazion was still standing in its usual place when she arrived and, from a distance, did not look like the site of a bomb blast. However, as they walked nearer, she could see that the windows had been blown out, and black soot had flamed up the exterior showed the ferocity of the blast. The glass had been cleared from the street below, but that didn't stop her feeling horrified by what she saw. She paused outside. It was a miracle that anyone had gotten out alive. She felt Nick take her hand and give it a squeeze.

"Are you alright?" he asked, his brown eyes full of concern.

"It's just… taken me by surprise," she said, giving him a weak smile. "I hadn't expected it to be so bad."

He put his arm around her shoulder and pulled her in. "We don't have to go in, if you don't want to," he said, giving her a warm hug.

Alex laid her head against his chest for a moment and closed her eyes. If only she could stay like this forever, safe and not having to deal with the bad things in life. She smiled. What a weird thing for a kick-ass assassin to think. She took a deep breath and got herself together. Gently pulling away from Nick, she took his hand.

"I'm fine," she said. "It was just a bit of a shock, that's all. This place has been like a second home to me. People I know died."

He squeezed her hand again.

"I'm sorry," he said.

"So am I," she replied. "For the person who did this." Cause I'm going fuck that person up, she thought. "Come on, let's go. I need to speak to Mother."

Mother was standing on the steps leading up to the HQ entrance wearing a white hard hat and a high vis vest over a beautifully tailored Italian suit and high-heeled pumps. Clipboard in hand, she was talking to an Italian contractor about the clear-up and did not appear to notice them approach. But, of course, she knew they were there. This was Mother, after all.

Elizabeth Danvers, codename Mother, was an older woman of high intelligence and amazing style. Tall, slim, white-haired, she was the coordinator of the Sisters of Sin, a kind of Bosley to their Charlie's Angels. She recruited the girls, handed out the jobs, ensured they had the right equipment and generally looked after them. If they had a problem, they went to her for she was Mother and she would sort it out.

"How are you, Greed?" she asked, without looking up as Alex and Nick arrived. She turned and her pale blue eyes rested on Nick. "Who is this?" she asked, voice emotionless.

"Mother, this is Nick," Alex said. "He's been helping me."

"What is Nick?" asked Mother, still staring at Nick, but ignoring him as he offered his hand for a handshake.

"He's my… friend," Alex said. "You can trust him. I'll vouch for him. He saved my life, that's all you need to know."

"And are you lovers?"

Alex visibly started. "Of course not," she said, but she could feel the blush spread quickly from her toes to the top of her head.

Mother did not look convinced, but said nothing, instead she returned her attention to the contractor, and after saying a few more words in Italian to him, dismissed him with a wave of her perfectly manicured hand. As she clipped her pen to her clipboard, Alex took a step forward.

"Mother, we came to offer our help," she said. "You said you had a job for me."

"Yes," Mother replied looking up. "And you want to discuss Aggravate?" Aggravate was Dominika's code name, although Mother was the only person to use it.

"Yes."

Mother's ice-cold eyes bored into Alex making the young assassin feel uncomfortable, like Mother was blaming her for the blast. "Come," Mother said curtly. She led them towards a basement entrance. "We've managed to make safe the basement rooms so we can use them again." At the top of some stone steps, she stopped and pointed at Nick. "Not him." Nick stepped back abruptly.

"But he needs to come," Alex said. "Please, Mother."

Mother looked him up and down, stripping him apart with her piercing eyes. He looked awkward.

"Alright, but if I find he has breathed a word about what he sees down there I will personally take him out," Mother replied, "and it will be slow and painful." She turned to Nick. "Got it?"

"I won't say a word, ma'am," Nick said.

"You'd better not."

As they followed her down the staircase, Nick leaned over to Alex and whispered, "Is she always this warm?"

Alex threw him a look and did not answer. The staircase led down to a metal door on which was placed a grey metal box of about a foot square. As Mother approached, an inside panel suddenly lit up showing a hand scanner. She placed her right hand on the panel, waited until it scanned her hand before dropping it to wait until the beep sounded to indicate they could enter. The door then clicked open, and she yanked it towards her. Although of normal size, the door was made of bomb-blast proof metal and was heavy to move.

"We're having to use the fire exits just now," she explained as she entered. "The ground floor is totally unusable at the moment, which is why we're going via the basement. We have people in to fix it, as you can see, but it's going to be some weeks before we can move back in or use it again."

Mother stepped into the dark corridor beyond and the lights flickered on. Alex followed closely behind and then Nick. There was an audible click and the entranceway locked behind them. They followed her down the corridor until they reached a second metal door. Again, Mother used a scanner to open it using her hand as the software recognition tool. It opened allowing the three inside into a second corridor with several rooms leading off. Mother led them to one at the far end, her personal office, a lovely and welcoming the underground room.

Mother had installed large screens resembling floor to ceiling windows on three of the walls, making it look like the office was above ground overlooking a beautiful lake. The sky was blue, there was hardly a cloud in the sky and somewhere birds were chirping. The scene gave the office a weirdly joyful air despite its large size. As big as a standard boardroom, at one end was an enormous desk with two desktop computers and several gadgets. A high-backed leather chair sat behind it underneath a portrait in oil of Mother as a younger woman.

Before the desk were two leather chairs for guests. A printer sat off to one side with a photocopier. A table on the other side of the desk held tea and coffee making things and sported a large bowl of fresh fruit. On the other side of the room was a three-piece suite consisting of a four-seater sofa and two two-seater ones in matching leather to the rest of the office chairs. A large smoked glass coffee table sat in the middle of them looking like a prop from the 1970s. The entire office smelled of new leather and had a fresh, grassy smell. Mother showed them to the three-piece suite. The couple sat close together on the four-seater.

"Do you want a drink? Coffee? Tea? Something stronger? I have nice bottle of red wine somewhere."

"No, thank you," Alex said. Alcohol could wait. She wanted to find out what was going on.

"Suit yourself. Nick?"

Nick also shook his head. "I'm fine, thank you."

"Is that a Cornwall accent I hear, Nick?" Mother asked as she found the wine and poured herself a glass. She took it with her and sat on one of the other seats.

"Nearly. I'm from Devon originally," Nick said.

"I've been out of the UK for so long now, I'm losing my skill at being able to accurately guess an accent," she said sadly. She took a sip of her wine and savoured the taste. "So, why did you want to talk to me, Alex?"

Alex explained about the strange visits by Dominika, and her peer's desperate desire to know what was going on with the

SOS.

"I can't put my finger on it, but she's acting strange," Alex said. "I mean, she was supposed to be in South America when she was actually in Berlin."

"And?" Mother asked. "What does that tell us?"

"I don't know," Alex admitted, "but I thought I should tell you my suspicions anyway. I don't know what's going on with her. I don't have any evidence that she's up to something, but my gut is telling me Dominika is up to something. She's acting strangely, well, more strangely than usual. I'm sorry, but I can't be any more specific than that."

"Could it be that she's just upset about the bombing?" Mother said. "I'm sure all you girls are acting a little out of sorts because of it."

"No, I think it's more than that," Alex said.

"And what do you think, Nick?"

"I don't know this Dominika, so I can't really say," he replied. "Sorry."

Mother watched him closely over the top of her glass as she took another sip. "And what is it you do, Nick?" she wanted to know.

"I work for…" he began.

"He's a computer analysist for private business," Alex said quickly.

Mother's eyes narrowed. "And how did you two meet?"

"We met at a nightclub in Berlin," Nick said.

"Hmmmm."

Alex could see that Mother was sizing up Nick and, not wanting her to ask another question that could lead Nick to admit who he really was, she changed the subject.

"So, you said you had a job you wanted me to do?"

Mother turned her razor-like attention to Alex. "Yes." She rose and went to her desk. Placing her glass down, she picked up a small cardboard box from in front of one of the monitors. She brought it back to them and handed the box to Alex. Alex opened it and found a mangled piece of metal inside.

"What is it?" she asked.

"That," said Mother, sitting down again, "is a piece of the bomb that nearly destroyed us. It's yielded us our first clue to whoever set it."

Alex read a serial number emblazoned on one side.

"That was bought at an electronics store in the city centre."

"It was made here?" Nick gasped.

"Don't look so surprised, Nick," said Mother with a coolness that froze the air. "Italians make bombs too, you know." She turned back to Alex. "Finn had a look at it. He says there are only three people in the city who could have made them. I'll send you their contact details."

"Who's Finn?" Nick wanted to know.

"He's one of our…managers," Alex replied.

"I want you to find out which one of them created the bomb and for whom," Mother said. "Then take them out."

"Okay," Alex said. This was an important job; she would not let Mother down.

"I'll help," Nick offered.

"You will not," Mother replied. "This is our business, not yours, so keep your nose out."

Nick looked offended, but said nothing. Alex nodded and stood up. "I'll get whoever it was," she promised. "Come on, Nick."

Mother watched as the pair exited her office and disappeared outside. Who is this Nick and what is he to Greed? She wondered. Mother always discouraged her girls from forming attachments, she didn't need them distracted and it was in the rules: no love affairs whilst working for the Sisters. Although Alex claimed Nick was only a friend, Mother could see that her Greed was falling for him. That would not do. She picked up her phone and dialled. Aggravate picked up.

"It's Mother. I have a job for you. I need you to find out about someone for me and then take him out."

It took one police officer five tries of the battering ram before Alex's apartment door burst open. With shouts of 'Polizei' the Berlin armed police streamed into her home, tactical weapons raised. As colleagues searched each room, Detective Inspector Gerhard Struber of the Berlin Kriminalpolizei examined the body that had been left in the living room. It was a middle-aged man who had been shot in the chest and head. He searched the body's jacket, found the wallet and opened it. An ID card identified the dead man as Wolter Kraus, an analyst for Interpol.

A constable approached. "No sign of Miss Grier," he said.

Struber got to his feet and examined Wolter's body. Whomever had done this was a professional. Alex Grier had been a skilled marksman in the British Army, that much he had been told. He thought back to the mysterious call he had taken only half an hour before. It had been a woman, her voice muffled to disguise it, on a burner phone. She had said there was a body at this address, and she was right.

"Frank," Struber called to his Detective Constable. The younger man was at his side in an instant. "Put an APB out on Miss Grier. She has some explaining to do."

"Yes, sir."

"Any luck in tracing the call?"

"No, sir. We couldn't track it."

At Berlin Airport, Ben Littlejohn was waiting for a large German family to alight from the plane. It had been a quick flight, but a stressful one. The children – five in total – were all under the age of 12 and bent on making as much noise as possible causing as much annoyance as they possibly could. By the time they had landed at Berlin, Ben had a pounding headache and desperately wanted a whisky. That would have to wait, though.

Half an hour later, he was through Customs and standing outside the airport, where he hailed a taxi. He gave the driver instructions for it to take him to Nick's hotel and sat back. His gut was telling him something was wrong with his friend, and he had to go see for himself. Sure, he could have got some local people to check up on Nick, but he had to see for himself. They had known each other since they had trained together. He had to make sure he was alright. Lettis had been understanding, but she couldn't let him go on official business. He had to go in his own time. So, he had quickly booked a couple of days off and stepped onto the first plane he could. He hoped he was wrong, he hoped Nick was alright, but Nick would never have left him hanging like this. No way.

Chapter 16 - Bomber

Dominika in her signature leather trousers and wearing a loose, bell-sleeved blouse listened to her instructions from Mother and agreed to do it. She closed the call down and looked around her. She was standing in the courtyard of a set of apartments in Rome where she knew Arman Adontz, local bomb-maker and Armenian national, lived. She stowed her phone away in her oversized leather shoulder bag and climbed the stairs to his dwelling.

Arman lived on the second floor in a small, dingy flat that needed the help of a good decorator. Dominika was always surprised where incendiary makers created their masterpieces. It was always in their own homes. What idiot would make explosives on their own dining room table? And those homes were never what she would call smart, despite the maker charging such high prices for their wares. Arman could live somewhere better, but chose to remain in this slum. There was no accounting for taste.

It was now early evening in the Italian capital, but it was still warm, and she was beginning to regret wearing the leather. Still, animal skin made her feel powerful, which was perfect for what she had in mind for Arman.

Arman paled when he saw the gorgeous Russian at his door. "Miss Gagolin," he stuttered, "what brings you to my door? Are you here to order another?"

Dominika smiled. It was the type of smile a cat would give before it killed – if cats could smile. It was warm at the mouth, but glacial in the eyes.

"Arman, my dear," she replied sweetly. "May I come in? I do indeed have some more business to discuss with you."

Arman's eyes lit up. Dominika knew he was thinking of the money she could bring him through another commission. Greedy little man. He opened the door wide and beckoned her inside. "Of course, come in, come in," he said, rubbing his hands together.

Dominika stepped inside the dull apartment and could not stop the look of disgust from flickering over her face. She followed him down the passageway. Arman was a bachelor, and it showed in his hygiene and choice of decoration. The place hadn't been decorated for years, nor cleaned, and it smelled of sour bodies and rotten food. Dominika walked down the hallway, and they paused outside a closed door at the end which she knew led into Arman's living room. He opened the door and stepped inside beckoning her to follow.

A used pizza box was strewn on the sofa. A television was on, the sound turned down to a murmur, and a Tabby cat sat in the windowsill next to a pot of dead herbs. On a small table near the window were Arman's tools of the trade: solders, wires, screwdrivers and a half-made device. A chair was half pulled out as if he had only just vacated it. The shabby curtains at the window were drawn, but enough light was still coming through for her to see perfectly.

"Come in, make yourself at home," Arman said, picking up the pizza box and closing it. He placed it carefully back on the sofa.

As if that would make a difference to this pigsty, Dominika thought.

"Have a seat," he said with a sweep of his hand.

Dominika wrinkled her nose to where he was motioning. The sofa. "I'll stand," she said coolly.

"Now, what brings you to Arman's house?" Arman always referred to himself in the third person, a habit Dominika found intensely irritating. "Do you want another bomb made? I'm working on something spectacular." He moved over to the window where the unfinished bomb lay. He gently picked it up like it was a new-born kitten and held it in his hands.

Dominika smiled. "Yes, that's what I'm here for, Arman," she said putting her hands behind her back as she slowly walked towards him. "Well? Show me."

Arman, eyes glittering, placed the bomb down and began to explain the components. Dominika, feigning interest, stood behind him, leaning over the enthusiastic maker as if to get a better look. Her long hair brushed his cheek, causing him to shiver, and she made sounds of approval as he took her through his latest – and best - make.

Unbeknownst to Arman, as Dominika used her raw sexuality to distract him, she was removing a long thin steel chain from the back pocket of her trousers. Slowly, she brought it round to her front and got it read. As Arman was explaining about how much Semtex he was going to place in the bomb, Dominika quickly brought the ligature up and looped it around his neck, pulling tight.

Before he could properly react, the Armenian was fighting

for his life. Eyes bulging, choking and gasping, Arman clawed at his neck in a futile attempt to remove whatever it was that was throttling the life out of him. His legs thrashed under the table, but Dominika pulled all the tighter until, at last, she felt his body jerk one last time before it relaxed. She removed the chain and carefully rolled it up as Arman's body slowly fell forward. His head hit the table, scattering tools and his precious unfinished bomb to the floor.

"Just as well that wasn't armed," Dominika said ruefully. She stood back and took a moment. It never got old, this killing people. She would like to say she enjoyed it, but the truth was she liked it far more than that. She loved the killing. It made her feel powerful. Like a Goddess. She surveyed his nasty apartment a final time. Dirty fucker, she thought as she walked towards the door.

Just then, there came an urgent knocking on the front door. Fuck! Who was that? She crept along the corridor and put an ear to the door. It sounded like there were at least two people outside.

"Arman Adontz?" someone called. That voice was familiar. More knocking. A polite, English voice. "Arman, may we please speak with you?"

Fuck. Greed was here. And I bet she's trailing that MI6 guy too, thought Dominika. She mused with opening the door and letting them in. The look on their faces would be worth it. But, no, that wouldn't do. She opted instead to seek out an escape route and hurried back into the living room. She drew back the curtains and looked out the open window hoping for a fire escape or balcony on which she could make her getaway, but there was none.

Fuck, Arman, why did you have to live in such a stinking

fleapit?

There was an urgent knocking at the door. So, Dominika did the only thing she could do in the circumstances. She glided down the corridor again and opened the door to an astonished Alex and Nick.

"Dominika? What are you doing here?" Alex wanted to know.

"Probably the same as you," Dominika said with a smoothness that belied the annoyance she felt inside. She hated being caught in a scene of her crime. "You'd better come in."

Alex and Nick entered the flat and followed the willowy Russian to the living room. Alex cursed when she saw Arman's body slumped over the table.

"I've just found him like this," Dominika claimed. "It's a pity because I'm sure he was the one who supplied the bomb that took out our HQ."

"Damnit!" Alex said. She looked at Nick.

"How did you find him, Dominika?" Alex wanted to know. She walked over to the body and began to examine it. He was still warm, which meant he had only just been killed. He smelled fresh. No rigor mortis. Ligature marks around his neck.

"Like you, I was horrified about the bombing, and I decided to do a little bit of detective work," Dominika replied.

"How did you know the bomb was from Rome?" This was all too much of a coincidence for Alex. Did Mother task Dominika with finding the bomb maker too? That didn't seem right.

"I didn't," the Russian replied breezily. "But I thought Arman here might be a good place to start. I've used him in the past, and he knows people."

"So, you came to ask him about it and just found him like this?" Alex was having a hard time believing anything her Sister said. Dominika's answers were too quick, too smooth and there was a self-satisfied air about her…like she was enjoying this.

"Yes."

"And did you see anyone suspicious when you arrived?" Alex asked.

"No. I did not." Dominika moved towards the door. She gave them a smile. "Well, if that's all, I'd better be off," she said. "I have a job that needs doing quickly," she added, looking pointedly at Nick. "I'll see you both later. Ciao."

"Well, that was strange," Nick said to Alex after Dominika left the apartment and slammed the door behind her.

"It was, wasn't it?" Alex replied. She examined the dead man more closely. "Arman's been strangled. With a thin ligature, probably a thin steel chain."

"How can you be sure? It could be anything."

"Because that's one of her signature ways of killing," Alex said, gazing off towards the door. She was as certain as she could be that Dominika had killed the bomb maker.

"Who's?"

"Dominika's." She glanced at Nick. "I'm pretty sure she killed Arman."

"But why?"

"Because she didn't want us finding him and interrogating him. I think he knew too much about something shady she's involved in and she killed him to cover it up. Which leads me to think that she or someone she's close to is somehow involved."

"In thc bombing? But I thought she was one of you."

Alex exhaled heavily. "She is, but it's the only thing that makes sense," she said. But why would Dominika do it?

They took a look around the apartment, carefully examining Arman's life. He didn't have a lot of possessions and what he did was old. Alex did find a photo of him, a woman and three kids in a small wooden frame and wondered if they were his family. Apart from the half-made bomb and a small tin of money they found under his un-made bed, Arman's apartment gave them no clues. Then, in the distance, came the sound of Italian police sirens. Alex was on alert immediately. With every moment they were in this apartment, they were closer to getting caught and blamed for the murder. How had they found out so quickly? Shit. Had Dominika called the cops? They needed to leave. Now.

"We have to get out of here," Alex said grabbing Nick by the arm.

"Agreed."

Alex and Nick left the apartment quietly and carefully. Satisfied there was no one about, they quickly walked down the stairs and were just making their way towards the courtyard entrance when two police officers appeared. Nick grabbed Alex's hand and pulled her behind a pillar as the two cops got closer. Putting his finger to his lips to quieten her protest, he kept a firm hold of her hand until the two officers had walked by. They disappeared into the stairwell and began to climb up towards Arman's apartment.

"Come on," Nick whispered. He led Alex by the hand out of the courtyard and into the street. They walked smartly away, acting as if nothing extraordinary had happened. Confident and happy looking, they were just like any other couple in love in the city of Rome. At least, that was the plan.

A few streets away, Alex stopped in her tracks.

"Can I have my hand back now?" she said, struggling to

loosen his grip. He let go. "That's better. You were holding it so tightly you were cutting off the circulation." She opened and closed her hand to get the blood flowing again.

"Where to now?"

"We need to tell Mother about our findings," she said. "She needs to know she can't trust Dominika anymore. I'm sure she was the one who murdered Arman Adontz. She may even have been behind the bombing. I can't believe this is happening. Why would she do it?"

The pair walked back to the HQ each deep in their own thoughts. Alex was troubled the most. Although she had never warmed to Dominika, she couldn't believe that the Russian was somehow involved in the bombing of Conexus. It just didn't make sense. Conexus' Chief Executive, Jeff Lynsey, had brought her out of Russia, given her a job, found her an apartment and taken care of her for years. Why would she turn on them now? Maybe I've got this all wrong, Alex thought. Maybe Dominika really didn't kill Arman and someone else had. But who? And why?

She thought through what they knew already: the bomb had been made in Rome, Arman Adontz had been a bomb maker and he could have made the bomb that brought down Conexus. However, there were at least two other bomb makers in the city that they had yet to check out, so she couldn't rule out one of them had created it.

They turned a corner into Via della Conciliazion and began to walk towards the large 200-year-old building that housed SOS. It was beginning to get dark, and the street lighting had just come on illuminating the tops of the many cars parked on either side of the street. The empty upper carcass of the HQ building was in darkness, the builders having gone home for the night.

But, even so, it wa still an impressive building. The outside was an architect's dream of classical design, built with Travertine, a local pale yellow coloured limestone that had been carved into a beautiful façade of columns and statues. All was quiet except for the sounds of cars and vans driving through the city's street.

"Are you alright?" Nick asked. "You've hardly said a word since we left that apartment."

"I'm just thinking about things," she said. "Weighing stuff up."

The words were barely out of her mouth when a shot rang out. Alex dived for cover, dragging Nick down with her. They hid behind an expensive sports car as a second bullet whizzed past.

"What the fuck?" Nick gasped.

"Did you see where it came from?" she asked.

"The building directly across the street, I think," he replied. He sat on the ground with his back against the car and his right hand strayed to his shoulder. Alex removed her gun from its holster and, sitting on her haunches, peered up through the car's windows to see if she could get a better look at the shooter.

"Alex?" Nick said. His voice was quiet, weak.

"Shhh," she replied, peering up into the darkness of the old building across the street. She stared hard at the windows, willing the gunman to show himself or give away his position. There was an eerie silence as she waited for the shooter and the shooter waited for her.

"Alex," Nick gasped again.

"What?" She turned to face him and started. In the dull light of the overhead lamps, she could see that his face had turned a ghastly grey colour. He was holding his shoulder, and blood was oozing out between his fingers. "Nick?"

"I've been shot." His body began to slide towards the ground and Alex helped it go. She gently placed his head on the pavement and got out her phone. She rang Mother.

"Greed," Mother said.

"Are you still at the HQ?" Alex asked.

"Yes, why…?"

"I need you to send out some help. We're outside. Someone is shooting at us from across the road. Nick has been shot. He needs medical assistance now." Before Mother could answer, Alex hung up. "Now, you mother fucker," she said under her breath, "let's see if I can draw your fire and smoke you out." She poked her head above the car and held her breath. The gunman did not fire at her. Slowly, she stood up and gazed at the building across the way. Where are you? Come and get me, bitch. Nothing. Alex knew better than to trust that the gunman had gone, but she braved it anyway. She walked out into the open, gun in hand.

"I'm here!" she shouted. "Take your best shot."

"It's not you I'm after," a familiar voice shouted back. "Just give me the MI6 agent and we'll call it quits."

"Fuck! Dominika, is that you?"

"The one and only!"

"What the fuck are you firing at us for?"

"I'm not firing at you, darling!"

Alex frowned. Then it dawned on her what her trigger-happy Sister meant.

"Nick? You're shooting at Nick? Why?"

"You know very well why, Greed," Dominika said. "It's against the rules to take a lover. Besides he's the enemy. He needs to be… removed."

"Nick is not my lover," Alex lied, "and he saved my life.

Surely that stands for something, Dom?"

"The name's Dominika, as you well know," the Russian shouted back. "And it's not my call."

"What do you mean?"

"If I were you, I'd ask Mother why she wants rid of him."

Alex was so stunned by the revelation that she did not see Conexus body guards, big burly men of six foot and over, come streaming out of the HQ building and run towards her. Following on their heels came the familiar figure of Mother. As her handler walked towards her, Alex ran back to where Nick lay and raised her gun.

"Don't come any closer!" she growled at the nearest man. He stopped dead in his tracks at the car bonnet and looked back at Mother for guidance. She nodded to him to move back and stepped towards Alex. "Don't come any closer, Mother," Alex warned. "You're not getting anywhere near Nick. He's done nothing wrong."

"But, Alex, he's MI6," Mother said. "He's dangerous to us. We don't know what he knows or who he'll tell about us. Conexus will be compromised."

"It's already compromised," Alex said. "No, don't take another step. I will shoot you."

"Alex, let's talk about this," Mother said.

"Let's not," she replied. "Now, I need to get Nick to a hospital before he bleeds out. Anyone getting in my way will be shot."

And then someone hit her from behind. She felt herself blacking out and then nothing.

Chapter 17 - Assassin

Alex slowly opened her eyes and winced. Her head felt like it had been crushed by giant gorilla. It ached, especially at the back. She carefully looked around her. It wouldn't do to let whomever knocked her out know she was awake. She was lying on her side on an examination bed in the medical room of the Conexus building. She recognised it right away. Pushing herself up, she tried to remember what had happened. They had been outside the building, and Dominika had been trying to kill Nick…Nick!

"He's in surgery," a voice said. Mother stood behind her.

Alex turned around and immediately regretted it, her head spun. She clutched it and waited until the dizziness passed.

"Don't worry, he's in good hands."

"But you were trying to kill him," Alex said. "Why are you trying to save him now?"

"Let's just say, I had second thoughts," Mother replied. She walked around the bed and stood beside Alex.

"That doesn't make sense."

Mother smiled and fidgeted with some gauze lying on a table next to the bed. "I didn't know how much Nick meant to you,

Alex, until I saw you defend him out there. I thought he was just another agent trying to infiltrate the Sisters, someone who needed to be got rid of." She paused and looked directly at her. "But I can see I was wrong about that. You love him, don't you?"

"I…"

"Don't try and deny it. I can see it in your eyes," Mother said.

Alex said nothing and looked away.

"Just as a I thought."

"Mother, I'm sorry, I didn't mean to…"

Mother held up a hand. "Don't," she said. "I don't need to an explanation. We've all been there."

Alex looked at Mother quizzically. Had Mother been in love? Her boss did not elaborate.

"Anyway, in these strange times, strange decisions have to be made, and I've decided to let him live…on condition you leave the SOS."

"But - !"

"No arguments. He's a liability, Greed, you know that. In order to be with him, you can no longer be a Sister. I'm sorry, but the rules are there for a reason," said Mother.

"I understand," Alex replied. She now had a big decision to make: did she remain an assassin with the Sisters of Sin with all the lovely money that brought? Or give it up for love? "What about Dominika?"

"I've called her off."

Alex was relieved. "Can I see him?"

"Soon."

Alex nodded and then winced. Her hand went up to the back of her head.

"Ah, yes, your head injury. I'm afraid one of the boys was a bit over enthusiastic with you," Mother said. "I'm sorry about that. He was only supposed to disarm you."

Alex gave Mother a look that said 'really?' and Mother shrugged.

"So, what happens next?" Alex wanted to know.

"Well, once Nick is well enough to travel, I would suggest you both disappear," Mother said. "I believe the police in Germany want to speak to you about a body they found in your apartment."

"What? What body?" Alex was sure she was suffering from hallucinations because she could have sworn Mother had just said there was a body in her apartment.

"It's all over the news. The police have put out a red alert on you across Europe. You're quite the wanted person," Mother said with a wry smile.

"I don't know anything about a body," Alex protested.

"I know," Mother said.

Alex threw her a quizzical look.

"It's not your style. You're a professional. You'd never shit on your own doorstep. But why would anyone else do it?"

"I don't know…No-one knows what I do for a living. I have no enemies that I know of, so why…?" And then Alex stopped and an idea popped into her head that made so much sense she could only gasp. "Dominika!" Mother frowned. Alex continued, "She's done it. No, don't start to protest her innocence, I know it was her. She was Berlin last week, and she's been acting odd. She knew I was suspicious of her, so she's planted the body to take me out of the picture."

Mother tried to speak but Alex was on a roll.

"She was also in Arman Adontz's apartment moments after he was murdered. She claimed it wasn't her, but the death had all her trademarks. Now why would she do that unless she was trying to stop him telling us who hired him to blow up Conexus?"

"Well, I…" Mother began.

"Why would she cover that up? Unless she was behind the bomb. Yes, it's all beginning to make sense now." She looked at Mother triumphantly. "Was Dominika here the day the bomb went off?"

"Yes, she was." Worry crossed Mother's polished features. Alex gave her a triumphant look. "But it couldn't have been her, could it?" Now Mother was deep in thought.

Alex frowned. "The body in my apartment? Do you know who it was?"

"A man called Wolter Kraus. My sources say he was an analyst for Interpol. Did you know him?"

"No, but I'm now wondering if he had a connection to Dominika?"

"I don't know, but I'll make sure we find out," Mother replied.

"But, why would she do it?"

"That, I don't know, but I'm going to keep Dominika under surveillance until we know more," her handler replied. "Now that you are awake, shall we see if Nick is ready for visitors?"

Alex nodded.

In a hotel somewhere in Rome, Dominika was listening. Praising herself for having the foresight to bug Mother's phone, she heard every conversation her great leader had on the phone and in person. Damn that Alex! She's going to spoil everything. I'll get that bitch back! So, Mother is going to keep an eye on me, is she? Well, we'll see about that.

Nick was lying bare-chested in a hospital bed, his shoulder

bandaged and his eyes closed. He opened them as soon as he became aware there was someone in the room. He smiled when he saw Alex, and her heart melted to see him. She ran to him and gave him a gentle hug that still made him wince. At the door, Mother smiled to see them reunited.

"How are you feeling?"

"Better," he replied. "Did you get the shooter?"

"No," she said. "You know it was Dominika who shot you… on the orders of Mother?"

Nick looked to Mother who shrugged. "Yes, I'm rather sorry about that," she said sheepishly.

"Why? What did I do?" he wanted to know.

"Well, there's a small matter of you being MI6," she pointed out.

Ah. "I'm handing in my notice as soon as I can," he said. Then he looked at Alex. "I love you Alex, and I want to be with you. If that means changing careers, so be it."

"Let's get you better first," Alex said kissing him lightly on the forehead. "Now, I have a few things to discuss with Mother, so you get some rest and I'll be back soon," she added.

In Berlin, Ben was exploring Nick's hotel room. MI6 was still paying for the room, so no-one had touched it since Nick had left. The bed had been made, the sheets changed, that was it. Nick had left nothing to chance. There was not even a razor in the bathroom. He had taken all his things, so that mean he had left of his own accord. His eyes rested on a small notepad and pencil lying next to the telephone. He sat down on the bed, lifted the notebook and looked at it. There were some indentations of letters. He used the pencil to colour over the words and the name of Alex's hotel in Florence revealed itself to him.

Well, I suppose I'm going to Florence now, he thought, ripping the sheet off and placing it in his pocket.

In Mother's office, Alex offered to find Dominika and bring her in, but Mother would hear none of it. She wanted to find out what Dominika's motivations were and whether or not someone else was behind the bombing. There was to be no 'bringing in' until Mother had concrete proof that Dominika knew something about it or was directly involved.

"We don't have any solid evidence," she told Alex. She sat down behind her desk and switched her computer on.

"But I've told you everything we know. Shouldn't you at least speak to her?" Alex was exasperated. This day had gone from bad to worse within minutes. She took a seat opposite and glared at Mother.

"I will. In my own time," Mother replied. She read something on screen. "Oh good," she said. "About time."

"What?"

"Finn's doing a sweep of the building checking for…" She mouthed the last part: bugs. Alex looked horrified and mimed 'in here?'. Mother nodded, her arms making a circular motion to say that they were doing the whole building.

'Why?' mouthed Alex. She looked around the desk for paper and a pen and found both. She quickly scribbled: Have we been compromised?"

Mother wrote back: 'Possibly'.

"So," said her leader matter-of-factly, "what do you plan to do with yourself whilst Nick is recovering?"

That question floored Alex because she hadn't had time to think about it. "I don't know," she said.

"Well, Rome has many beautiful shops that would be right up your street: designer, expensive, glamorous," Mother said.

Alex shook her head. "I would prefer to stay here… with Nick."

"So be it."

The door opened and handsome American in his 50s walked in carrying some sort of detecting device. He was tall with short, salt and pepper hair that suited the sophisticated air about him.

"Hi, Greed, long time no see," he said, and he began scanning the office. "Elizabeth." He was the only person who could get away with calling Mother by her real name. They had known each other for years.

"Finn."

Finn Rogers slowly and carefully began to scan the office. "How are you ladies today? I hear we have a visitor in the infirmary?" he said jovially.

"Yes," Alex replied. She stood up. "And I'd best be getting back to him. I'll speak to you later."

Mother returned to her computer screen as Alex left for the hospital rooms. She had a lot on her mind and needed to get on with work. As she read her emails, Finn continued to scan the room. He slowly worked his way around until he was standing at her desk. Mother, who had always been fond of the big New Yorker, smiled as he carefully scanned her desk.

"Do you wish to scan me as well?" she said with a grin.

"Maybe," he replied with a wink and then he frowned. He was scanning close to where she was sitting and had picked something up. "Hold still," he instructed her as he scanned along her arm and down to her chair. Something beeped as scanned the seat. "Could you stand for a minute?" She got out of the way as he scanned the seat again. Nothing. His frown deepened. "C'mere a minute," he said. "Turn around for me, will ya?"

Mother turned around so that her back was to him, and he scanned her body. The scanner beeped just as he ran it over the back pocket of her highly tailored trousers.

"Excuse me," he said. Before she could object, he put his hand in her pocket and fished out her mobile phone. He laid it on the desk and scanned it. Again, the beep. They looked at each other in shock. Someone had been listening in.

Nick was sleeping soundly when Alex arrived at his room. A nurse was taking his blood pressure and checking his vitals. Things looked good, she told Alex as the assassin entered and sat down next to Nick's bed. Thank God, Alex thought as she took his hand. It was warm and she lifted it to her lips and kissed it. Please get better soon.

"We'll soon have him back on his feet," the nurse said. She was a pretty Italian girl with bobbed blonde hair and a name-tag with the name Celine printed on it. "I'll check on him again later."

"Thank you," Alex said, relieved he was going to be okay.

"Alex," Nick whispered. He was parched and his lips were dry.

"Nick, how are you feeling?" she said a little too loudly, for he winced. "Sorry," she said more softly.

"I feel like I've been run over by a steam roller," he said. He tried to sit up, but winced in pain.

"Don't," she said as she gently guided him back down. "You're not fit enough to sit up."

"But we have to get out of here," he said.

"All in good time," Alex said.

"It's not safe for us here," he said. "Mother, was it? She wants us dead."

"She wants you dead," Alex reminded him.

"Whatever," he replied. "Anyway, we have to leave. Now."

"Calm down. I've sorted everything with Mother. You're safe now. She's called off the hit and apologised."

"Well, that's all right then," he said sarcastically.

"Trust me, we're safe here," Alex reassured him.

"How can we trust her?"

"We can. Do you trust me?" He nodded. "Then trust that I know Mother and I know she would never hurt you." Truth be told, Alex did not know whether she could trust Mother anymore. Or any of her sisters. Mother and Dominika had tried to kill the man she loved and… Shit. She loved him. She loved Nick. A large grin formed on her lips. Nick frowned.

"What? Why have you got that big goofy look on your face?" he asked. "It's weird."

"I just realised something."

"What?"

"I love you, Nick Walker."

"I know that. I could have told you that. I did tell you that, remember?"

"Yes, but I've only just realised it myself."

"Jesus, Alex, if you take this long to make up your mind what are you going to be like when I ask you to marry me?"

But Alex didn't have time to respond for their conversation was interrupted by the arrival of a doctor. Alexandro Lorenzo was tall, slim and attractive, and highly skilled.

"How's the patient?" he asked checking Nick's chart.

"Better," Nick said. "I can't actually feel anything right now and my head is a bit woozy."

"That'll be the morphine," the doctor said.

"When can I leave?" Nick wanted to know.

"Well, you were lucky the bullet went right through your shoulder and missed anything vital. However, you've still been shot, so you'll need several weeks to recuperate." Dr Lorenzo flipped the chart closed.

"I can't stay here for several weeks," Nick said.

"You won't need to," the doctor said. "All going well, you could be out of here in a week, so long as you promise to take it easy at home."

Nick looked uncomfortable. Alex jumped in. "That's great news," she said. "Isn't it?"

When the doctor left, taking the nurse with him, Nick repeated to Alex, "I can't stay here a week."

"Well, you're going to have to."

"They want to kill me."

"They wanted to, past tense," she replied, although she didn't really believe it herself. "They don't now."

"So, you say. I still don't trust them. I think we need to leave as soon as we can."

In her heart, Alex knew Nick was right. She couldn't risk leaving him in here any longer than they had to. She hoped that Mother had been speaking the truth when she said she didn't want to kill Nick anymore. She had called off the hit after all. But Dominika? She wasn't sure someone like her could be called off a hit. It had never happened before.

"Don't worry," she said, taking a handgun from its place down the back waistband of her trousers. She put it on his bed. "I'll make sure nothing happens to us."

"Where did you get that?"

"I work here, remember? I just went to the armoury and got one," she said with a smile. Inside, though, Alex wasn't smiling at all.

Nick spent a quiet night in the infirmary with Alex sleeping at his side. It wasn't such a comfortable night for her, curled up as she was in a chair, but it was better than being away from him, fretting that his life was in danger. She was woken only twice during the night: once when a nurse came to check on the patient and a second time by someone walking past the doorway. Both times she jerked into alertness and immediately held the gun up. The nurse, used to working there, smiled and reassured her she was only there to tend to Nick. The second time, Alex had no idea who was there, but the person came and went and did not disturb them. At 6am, a second nurse appeared and shook her awake.

"What?" Alex mumbled as she came to. She rubbed her eyes.

"I'm just going to administer more pain relief to Mr Walker," the nurse said. "Perhaps you might want to go and get tidied up or get yourself a coffee?"

"No, I'm fine." Alex narrowed her eyes at the nurse. "Are you new here?"

"Started a couple of months ago," the nurse said with a smile.

"Really? I didn't know," Alex said, looking at her closely. The nurse was fiddling around with some tubes that fed morphine from a machine into an IV line on the back of his hand. "What's your name?"

"Nancy," said the nurse, taking out a syringe.

"What are you doing with that?"

"Doctor wants me to administer some anti-blood clotting drugs," the nurse explained. Averting her eyes, she carried on with her task.

Alex frowned and raised the gun. "Step away from Nick,"

she said. "Now!"

The nurse jumped and stepped back, terrified.

"What are you really putting in his line?"

"Anti-blood clotting drugs," she squealed holding her hands up. "I promise."

Still holding the gun on the nurse, Alex leant over Nick and pushed the Nurse Call button. "We'll soon see about that," Alex said, "when the doctor comes."

Before she had even finished her sentence, Nancy picked up an empty bed pan and threw it at Alex. It hit the assassin in the head, sending her hurtling backwards. The nurse fled the room, leaving Alex in a tangled heap. She scrambled to her feet and pursued her, but the nurse was quick and was out one of the fire-exits of the building before Alex could catch her. "Damnit!"

She returned to the infirmary just as another nurse, one Alex knew this time, and a doctor walked in Nick's room. Nick was now awake and attempting to sit up.

"What happened?" he said when she entered. "I woke up to a commotion, and you running out of this room with a gun in your hand."

"I think a bogus nurse tried to poison you," she said. She searched for the syringe Nancy had been holding and found it lying under his bed. She knelt down, picked it up and presented it to the doctor. "Can you find out what this is?" she asked.

"Yes, of course," said the doctor.

Alex waited until the nurse had performed her duties and checked on Nick's vitals. He was doing well. Then she sat down, gun still in hand, and stroked his arm. She was exhausted.

"Shit!" she said. "That was a close one."

"Are you sure she was trying to kill me?" Nick asked.

"Why else would she run?" Alex glanced nervously toward

Chapter 18 - Fleeing

the door, then back to Nick. "Anyway, we'll soon find out when the tests come back on the syringe."

Concern was evident on Mother's face when Alex told her about the attack. They were sitting on the three-piece-suite in her office. Mother on the sofa and Alex directly opposite. The young assassin demanded to know what had happened. And so did Mother. It wasn't just that someone had tried to kill Nick, but that they had got through their tight security. She summoned her chief of security, Valentina Gotti, and bawled her out, demanding to know what went wrong and why. After she had finished, she instructed the diminutive Italian to tighten all security and to find out how the bogus nurse had entered the building. The only entry points had biometric security using handprint, so whomever had opened the doors must have been the person responsible, and that meant it was a member of staff.

"We'll soon find out who it was and take care of them," Mother promised Alex as Valentina left the office. "In the meantime, I've put security on Nick. All staff will be checked going in."

Her mobile phone rang, and she picked it up. "Yes? Hmm, huh-huh…hmph…okay, thanks for telling me." She hung up and looked at Alex. "You were right to suspect the nurse. The syringe contained a lethal dose of adrenaline. Had it got into Nick's bloodstream he would be dead by now. You saved his life."

"Fuck," Alex said. We need to get out of here, she thought. "Look, I know you've increased security, but I really think I should take Nick away from here to a safe house."

"He's not strong enough to be moved right now," Mother said.

"I can't leave him here!" Alex wailed. "It's not safe. You can't protect him."

"And it's not safe to move him. At best, you could set his recovery back by weeks, at worst, you could kill him."

"Well, I can't leave him in here!" Alex shouted. The stress of the last few days was finally getting to her. She needed to let off steam. She needed her gym. She needed to give a pounding in the ring and take one back. She took a deep breath and let the air circulate down to her lungs. "Look, I'm sorry," she said. "I'm just a bit stressed."

"It's all right," replied Mother, "we all are stressed right now. These are unprecedented times. It would take an extraordinary person not to feel tense." Her eyes softened as she attempted to reassure Alex. "I promise you we are taking the very best care of Nick. We'll keep him safe. You have my word."

"Okay," Alex said, but did not really believe her. In her mind she was already working out how she was going to sneak Nick out to safety. Her thoughts were broken by the sound of Mother's phone going again.

"What have you got for me?" Mother said into the mobile. There was a pause whilst Mother listened to whomever was on the other end of the call. She nodded. "Find her." The phone-call ended. Mother turned to Alex. "It seems it one was of the other nurses who let the nurse in. Valentina and her men are just searching for her now. She's traced her mobile, and she's still in the building. It won't be long until we find her and we get this all sorted out. In the meantime, why don't you go and get yourself something to eat in the staff canteen? You must be famished."

"I'm fine," Alex replied. She couldn't face eating right then, which was not like her. Her stomach was churning and her throat felt constricted.

"Alex, you're no use to anyone if your energy levels have dipped so low you are catatonic," Mother said. "Go get some food, and we'll look after your Nick. I promise."

The staff canteen was more like a Michelin star restaurant than a traditional eating place for staff. Located in the centre of the underground complex, the restaurant had enough tables and chairs to comfortably sit 100 diners at one time. Although, like most staff canteens, you had to queue at a serving desk for your food, this food was like nothing Alex had ever tasted in an employee café. Using nothing but the best quality fare, under the management of chef, Nero Caballi, the canteen staff produced amazing food on a daily basis all day, every day. The décor was beautiful too. The tables and chairs were antiques, white linen tablecloths adorned the wooden tables, and the whole place was lit by three huge crystal chandeliers. Oil paintings of various mythical people and creatures adorned the walls.

Alex walked up to the service desk and ordered a coffee and a pastry. She did not feel like eating, but forced herself to swallow it. She needed the energy. The coffee was easier going down, and she savoured its bitter taste. She closed her eyes as a sudden exhaustion overtook her. I need a holiday, she thought as she drained her cup.

Nick was awake and cheerful when she arrived at his room. He had just eaten a breakfast and was finishing a glass of orange juice when she walked in.

"Hey, beautiful," he said. "I hear you saved my life again this morning."

"Something like that," she said, sitting down beside his bed.

"Thank you," he said with a grin. "Are you alright? You look a bit peaky."

"I just need to get you out of here," she replied in hushed tones. "It's not safe."

"The doctor said I can try getting out of bed for a while today," he said. "Will you stay with me while I do it?"

"Of course."

There was a knock on the door that put Alex on to immediate alert. She pulled her handgun from where it had been tucked into the waistband of her trousers and held it up.

"Come in," Nick said.

Mother put her head around the door and smiled. "How's the patient?" she asked.

"I'm feeling better," Nick replied.

Mother entered the room, and in a rare conciliatory form, said, "I'm sorry that you ended up being shot."

"No thanks to you," Nick said.

"Yes, well, I believed you were a threat to Alex, and I always look out for my girls," she said, giving Alex a motherly smile.

"I'm not a threat to her or you."

"So, Alex assures me." Mother shifted her gaze between Alex and Nick. "Anyway, I will leave you in peace. I have some insurance forms to fill in regarding the bombing."

After they were sure she had left, Alex looked at Nick wondering if he was well enough to move. He frowned.

"What's going on in that head of yours?"

"Do you think you could walk out of here?" she asked.

"With help, probably," he said. "I know it's the morphine, but I feel pretty good, considering what's happened. Why?"

"I think we should make a break for it and go into hiding. I know somewhere we can go." Alex waited for a response.

"I'm not sure that's such a good idea. The doctor said…"

"I know what the doctor said, but if you stay here you are going to get killed. Please, Nick, for me!"

"Why the sudden interest in my welfare?" he said with a smile playing about his lips. "Have you got feelings for me, Miss Grier?" She blushed. "My goodness," he quipped, "I do believe you do!"

"I just don't want to see you killed, not because of me," she said quickly.

"Alright, I'll go," he said, "but on one condition: tell me how you really feel about me or I won't go. The truth, mind, not something made up."

Staring down into his eyes, Alex could have melted into their chocolate depths right then and there. Who was she kidding? This man before her, this clever, handsome man, made her heart sing. Despite her better judgement, despite vowing never to be tied down ever again, she loved him. And she loved him with all her heart.

"I love you," she said after a few moments of torturing herself over whether to tell him or not.

"Sorry, I didn't quite catch that," Nick joked. "Did you just say you love me?"

She nodded. "Yes."

"Well, about bloody time," he replied. "Come here. I want to kiss you." He opened his good arm, and she went to him. Sitting on the bed, she allowed him to stroke her face. "I love you too," he whispered and leaned in for a kiss.

His lips were warm and soft and, although he smelled of iodine, it wasn't an unpleasant scent, but was clean and medical. She smiled as she drew back from him, and for a few moments, it felt like they were the only two people on the Earth and that nothing but being together mattered. She took a deep breath.

"We need to go," she said.

"I know."

"I'll help you."

Nick's blood-stained shirt had been discarded by medical staff and his shorts were nowhere to be seen, so Alex entered the Conexus gym and training area and snagged him a pair of men's clean sweatpants and a sweatshirt. She found a pair of pool shoes next to a locker and added it to her cache. She hoped everything would fit and that none of her colleagues would mind.

She found Nick sitting up on the edge of the bed in his underwear, ready to remove his line and heart monitor. They would have to be quick, for as soon as he took them off, the alarms would sound and medical staff would come running. She helped him into the sweatpants and slipped the pool shoes on his feet. They were a little big, but they would do.

Nick quickly removed the morphine line and ripped the heart monitor off his chest. Wincing as it stung, he threw the line and monitor sensor on the bed. Alex helped him to his feet and threw the sweatshirt over his head. A moment went by as they fumbled to get his arm through the sleeve. His injured side, they left tucked up inside the shirt. Just then a loud beeping sang from the heart monitor in the corner. Shit, it had begun. Then the morphine line began to squeal too.

Slipping her arm under his good shoulder, Alex helped Nick to the door. A quick look out to check the coast was clear, and she walked him out into the corridor. They had only gone a few paces when they heard shouts from the nurses' station. Alex pulled him along to the nearest fire exit and yanked it open. She rushed him outside and into a small alleyway at the back of Conexus. The alley was empty, save for a number of industrial bins and a small, disused building that had once housed a security guard whose job it had been to check deliveries being made to the rear of the building.

They stopped for a few minutes to catch their breath before resuming their flight.

"Are you okay?" Alex wanted to know. She gazed up at Nick and was shocked to see how white he had become.

"I'll be fine after a few moments rest," he said.

From within the building, Alex heard running feet and shouts of security staff directing a search for them. Alex, after a second check on Nick, realised he could go no further, not right now.

"Come on," she said, pushing open the door of the small building. "Let's hide in here for half an hour until the search dies down a bit, and then we'll make our escape."

"Sounds good to me."

The building was tiny, no more than the size of a covered bus stop, and the only light came from the dirty window in the door. Still, it would keep them hidden until Nick was able to move again. Alex was already planning how she would get him out. She manoeuvred him inside and sat him down on an old chair that had been abandoned there. They waited.

There was the sound of the fire exit opening and the heavy boots of security staff, men and women, rushing outside. Shouting at each other in animated Italian, the security staff searched the alley. Someone tried the door of their hiding place, but Alex held it shut. The rattling continued, and then the seeker gave up and walked away. The footsteps and the shouting became faint, and soon, they were alone again.

"Alex," Nick whispered.

"Shhh, they'll hear us," she scolded.

"But, Alex, I think there's someone in here with us," he said.

"Don't be daft, it's an abandoned building," she said.

"I can feel a foot on the floor," he said gingerly moving his own foot. "Yup, there's the leg."

"What are you talking about?" she whispered.

"There's a body in here."

"What?"

"There's a…"

"I heard what you said. I just don't believe it," she said. "Can you stand by yourself?"

"Yes."

She extricated herself from Nick's arms and fished her cell phone out of her pocket. Putting it on as a flashlight, she scanned the floor of the cupboard. Sure enough, there was a foot and a leg sticking out from under a dirty old tarpaulin.

Fuck, she mouthed to herself and she bent down and pulled the tarpaulin off the body. She gasped.

Lying there, eyes open and blood dripping from her mouth, was Celine, Nick's nurse from the previous night. As Alex examined the body, she gasped again. Celine was missing her right hand. Someone had cut it off. The wound at her wrist was ragged and badly done. Whoever had done had not taken the hand cleanly, it had been hacked off.

"Shit!" Nick said, seeing everything Alex did. "She was really nice. Why would anyone do that?"

"To gain access to the building. They used her hand in the biometrics machine," Alex said.

The police arrived at the Grand Hotel, Florence just as Ben was leaving. He had slipped the receptionist a few Euros for information about where Nick might have gone. The man had been very animated about the pretty woman Nick had had with him and when Ben showed him an image of Alex on his cell, had confirmed that that was who it was.

"Do you know where they went?" he asked. The man shrugged and Ben offered him a few more hundred Euros. That loosened his tongue.

"My sister, she's a maid here, said she overheard them talking about Rome. That's all I know," he replied, stuffing the money into his inside jacket pocket.

"Thank you."

As Ben left, two Polizia officers entered. The policemen barely gave Ben as glance as the MI6 operative exited the hotel. Ben paused on the street to think about where to go next. MI6 had always suspected that SOS had a base in Rome, could that be where the pair were going? He called in.

"Lettis, I've come up a blank here in Florence," he told his superior over his cell. "Nick is definitely with Alex Grier, and they seem to be making their way to Rome. I'm due back at my desk tomorrow, do you want me to come in or can I pursue?"

"Is Nick in danger?"

"I don't know."

"Do you think he's following another lead?"

"That seems likely, but why not call it in?"

"So, maybe he's gone rogue?"

Ben thought for a moment. "No, that's not like Nick. He'd never do that."

"My sensible head is telling me to call you back in, but my gut is saying something's going on. I'm giving you permission to pursue them. I'll authorise a hotel and funds in Rome. Can you get there today?"

"Yes."

"Do it."

Chapter 19 - Corfu

It didn't feel right leaving Celine there to rot under the tarpaulin so Alex and Nick went back inside the building to report what they found. They told Valentina they had just stepped out for air and were curious as to what the tiny building, the shed as Alex put it, held. They were horrified to find Celine's body and reported it right away. Valentina did not look convinced, but Alex didn't care. That was the story, and she was sticking to it.

"We found Celine's right hand," Valentina said. "One of the dogs discovered it in a waste bin in the hospital wing. I was just taking it to Mother when you two took your walk. In future, if you leave the building, please alert someone."

"Sorry," said Alex, but not feeling it.

The women were standing in the corridor outside Nick's hospital room. Nick, exhausted from their aborted flight, was back in his bed sleeping. Alex insisted Valentina interview him later after he had rested (and she had got her story straight with him).

Nick awoke two hours later, refreshed and feeling better.

Alex, cup of coffee in hand, was reading a magazine at his side.

"Hey, gorgeous," he said sleepily.

"Hey," she replied.

"Did I miss anything?"

"Only me getting bolloxed out by Valentina for our escapade," she said. She filled him in and schooled him on what he was to say to the diminutive head of security.

"So, what happens next?"

"Next, I'm going to get you out of here," she replied. "I've arranged to have a meeting with Mother in half an hour. I'm going to insist we leave today. I can't risk someone trying to kill you again."

Deep in a plush apartment in Rome, Dominika was having a meltdown about her bug being found.

"Bloody Finn," she muttered as she carried her laptop to a small window seat. She sat down and opened it to see what the chat was on the SOS dark site. Mother was suspicious of her, but had no proof so she had two options: act as if she was innocent and continue to work for SOS or break out on her own. She wasn't quite ready to do the latter. She still had work to do to avenge the death of her parents, so she would have to suck up to the boss. She made a face. She hated sucking up to people, particularly people like Mother. She was just so pleasant, so nice, so holier than thou. There was nothing on the site, so she shut the laptop down, lay it beside her on the seat and picked up her mobile. She crossed her legs and dialled a number.

"Hello? Mother? How are you after the bombing? How is the rebuilding going?" she said. She chewed on her lip waiting.

"Aggravate, I've been hoping you'd call," Mother replied.

"Oh, yes? And why is that?" Dominika was as cool as a cu-

cumber as always. Her training had been thorough, and she never showed emotion, even in her voice. She smoothed her hair with her free hand.

"I want to make sure that you understand the bounty on Nick Walker is off," she said.

"Yes, I know. You already told me that."

"Someone tried to kill him this morning."

"Oh? What a shame." The words came out, but she didn't mean them.

"Do you know anything about it?" Mother sounded suspicious.

"Of course, I don't," snapped Dominika. "You told me not to kill him, and I complied. I don't know anything about this latest attempt."

"Someone killed one of the nurses and used her hand to get access to the building," Mother said.

"How clever." My plan worked then. I must remember that for future missions.

"She posed as a nurse and tried to kill Nick with adrenaline," Mother continued.

"That would work," replied Dominika. She examined the finger nails of her free hand.

"But she didn't succeed. Greed was too quick. She realised what she was doing and stopped her."

"Good for Greed." Damn Greed. Her face contorted into a scowl.

"Nick is still recovering from that gunshot wound you gave him," Mother continued, "but we've moved him to a more secure site." That last part was a lie.

"And where would that be?" Dominika uncrossed her legs and sat up.

"Our safe house in San Marino," Mother said. "He and Greed should be arriving there in a few hours."

"Ah, good. San Marino is so lovely this time of year. It's the perfect spot for him to recover in peace," Dominika said, her voice smooth as honey. "I hope they enjoy their stay."

"Anyway," Mother continued. "I just wanted to make sure you weren't involved and that you were safe. If someone can get into HQ that easily, then someone can get to you girls. We all need to be on high alert now until we find out who is behind these attacks."

"I'm always on alert," Dominika assured her. "Nothing gets past me." She pursed her lips. Now she knew where Nick and Greed were going. Perfect.

"I know, but I needed to say it," Mother replied. "I must go, I have a meeting to attend. I'll speak to you soon."

"Alright, ciao!" Dominika ended the call and tapped her mobile off her lips.

Mother hung up and turned to the woman sitting before her.

"Did you get all that?" she asked Alex.

"Yes."

"If Dominika really is behind today's attack, we'll soon know. She will either go to San Marino herself or send someone else to take Nick out," Mother said.

"And if it wasn't her?"

"Then we have a big problem."

Back in Dominika's apartment, she was dialling another number. It rang several times before a woman picked up and answered.

"Hello?"

"Cora, it's Dominika," the assassin said. "I need you to go to San Marino and kill that MI6 agent you were supposed to kill this morning. And take out the woman too… I don't care if she'll recognise you. It was you who fucked it up, so you can sort it… What? They are in a safe house in the Principality. I'll text you the address… Just do it. I don't give a fuck how it's done I just need the pair of them taken out pronto, go it?...Okay, speak soon. Ciao!"

Two bullet proof limousines were sitting in the Conexus underground garage when Mother, Alex and Nick, in a wheelchair, arrived. One was to drive to San Marino—empty, save for the driver—the other was to take Nick and Alex to safety. Away from Dominika and away from the prying eyes of the police. The TV bulletins were now showing an image of Alex, and they couldn't risk her being seen in Rome. Mother insisted both she and Nick go into hiding, somewhere far away from Conexus and Alex's former life. Alex, she said, would have to give up her life as an assassin. Although Alex protested, she knew that Mother was right. Her identity had been compromised. She was on the radar of Interpol now, and she could never work for Conexus as a hired killer again. It was too risky. She acquiesced.

The first car departed, and they made their way over to the second. The driver was loading Alex and Nick's bags into the boot.

"I've arranged for you to pick up a car in Turin. From there, it's up to you where you go," Mother said as they stood at the open rear door. She put a hand on Alex's cheek. It was soft and warm. "Take care of yourself, Alex," she said. To Nick, she said, "Be good to her."

"I will."

Alex helped Nick into the back of the limousine, pausing before getting in herself.

"Will I ever see you again?" Alex asked Mother.

"I hope so," she replied, "I'm very fond of you, Alex. You are like a daughter to me. But we must say our farewells for now. I want you two to go and lead a peaceful life somewhere safe. I had Finn put a case full of weapons in the boot. Your passports are here."

She handed Alex the books and a new mobile phone. Alex frowned.

"I've destroyed your phones. It's for your own safety. I don't want anyone tracing you that way." She paused. "I nearly forgot, I had Nero make you up a basket of food car for lunch, the driver has his own. I think that's about it."

Good old Lorenzo, Alex thought as she wondered what the Conexus chef had given them. Then it was back to reality. Alex, tears in her eyes, looked up at Mother. Then, without warning, she flung herself into Mother's arms and gave the startled woman a hug.

"Thanks for everything," she said. Before Mother could answer, Alex took got into the car and shut the door. She put down the window, waved. "Bye."

Mother watched the car leave with some regret. She sighed. Alex had indeed been a good assassin. It was a shame to lose her. Still, she was too much a liability for Conexus what with the police after her and whoever it was who was trying to kill Nick. She was sure it was Dominika, but why hadn't she stopped the hit when she had been instructed to? Why was she still after Nick? It wasn't like the tall Russian to disobey orders. She hoped in her heart that Dominika hadn't been behind the bombing, but it was certainly beginning to look that way. She turned and went back inside. She had work to do. No rest for the wicked.

Alex and Nick arrived in the northern Italian city of Turin eight hours later, exhausted but very glad to be away from Rome and from Conexus. It was early evening, and the sky was just beginning to darken. The car Alex was to pick up had been arranged for her by Mother through a contact she had there. Teddy Markham was an English expat who worked as a professor of Cultural Heritage. He had known Mother since childhood and was only too happy to arrange to quickly purchase a small car for her friends. They were to meet him close to the Turin Egyptian Museum on the Via Maria Vittoria. The chauffeur-driven limousine slid along the street, the driver slowing down so they could see the museum. A large sandstone building of impressive dimensions, the museum was not hard to spot and neither was the older white-haired man standing outside it.

"There he is," Alex said to the driver. "Can you pull over somewhere?"

"Yes, ma'am," the driver replied.

The car pulled over as close to Teddy Markham as the chauffeur could get it and Alex got out. Teddy Markham was in his 50s, a little overweight, but still young looking. He wore a stylish linen suit and white shirt. A Panama hat adorned his head and he had a leather case tucked under one arm. One his feet were beautifully hand-made Italian leather shoes. Alex spotted those right away.

"Mr Markham?" she shouted as she hurried over to him.

"The very same," he said, "and you must be Miss Grier?"

"Yes," she replied, shaking his hand. "Have you been waiting long?"

"Not very," he replied with a smile that lit up his face. He got down to business straight away. "Now, I have something to give you," he added, rummaging in his case. He frowned. Then he felt in his jacket pockets, and he smiled. He pulled out a set of car keys and handed them to her. "The car is in the underground car park across the road." He handed her a slip of paper. "Here's the make, model and registration number. It's parked on the first floor down."

"Thank you," Alex said.

"And Mother wanted you to have this," he added, pulling a wad of Euros out of his case and handing it to her. "Go on, take it. She said you might refuse, but I've to tell you to look on it as a bonus for all the good work you've done over the years."

Alex smiled and accepted the gift. "Thank you, Mr Markham," she said.

"Don't thank me, thank Lizzie," he said eyes twinkling. "She's very fond of you, you know, Alex. She's fond of all her girls, but you're particularly special to her."

He zipped up his case. "Well, now that I've done my part, it's up to you," he said. "Take care of yourself, my dear."

"Thank you."

Alex went back to the limousine and instructed Nick to stay inside whilst she got the car. She asked the chauffeur to get their luggage out and guard it and Nick until she came back. Then she fetched the car from the underground. She went inside the building and hurried down the stairwell to the first floor down. Under the strip lighting, she opened the note and read: Sorry, but this was the only make I could get at such short notice. She looked at the car make and sighed. It was a Fiat SUV.

"I fucking hate Fiats," she muttered to herself and she sought the car. She found it in a corner at the other end of the car park. It was silver and second-hand, but in good condition.

"It's better than nothing," she said as she slid behind the wheel.

Nick and their luggage were on the pavement at the museum when she drove out of the car park. He was shaking the hand of the chauffeur and offering him a tip. The man declined. Alex tooted the horn of the Fiat, causing Nick to turn around. He grimaced when he saw the car, but waved none-the-less. She drove it close to him, double parked, got out and started to lug their luggage into the boot aided by the chauffeur. Nick, still in pain and weak from his injury, went to wait in the passenger seat.

"Thank you," Alex said to the chauffeur handing him one hundred Euros.

"You're very welcome, ma'am," he said. He shook his head, refusing to take the money, and then returned to his own car.

As the limousine drove off, Alex got into the car and helped Nick on with his seatbelt. He was pale and in obvious pain, but they couldn't afford to stop to rest. She gave his hand a gentle squeeze, then started the car. She drove down to the next road junction and stopped.

"Where to?" she said to Nick.

"I was thinking about that," he said. "I think we should head east to Venice and then get a ferry from there to mainland Greece. We can catch another ferry from there to Kerkyra on Corfu. I have a mate there who might be able to put us up for a little while. He's got a couple of holiday homes that may be free. We could work on our suntans whilst I recuperate. What do you think?"

"I think it sounds like the best thing I've heard all day," she said, "but I'm hungry. Let's drive to Milan—it's not that far—and see if we can get something to eat there. I think we should stay the night and then move on in the morning."

Nick nodded. He was tired and could do with a bed for the night. Alex handed him her cell which displayed a map of northern Italy she had already looked up. "You map read, and I'll drive."

They found a small family run hotel on the outskirts of Milan. Their room was small, but clean and comfortable, and the welcome they got from the family was warm and friendly. The Milanese put on a delicious Northern Italian meal for them and offered them wine, which neither took. Nick was still on painkillers, and Alex wanted a clear head for the drive in the morning. They went to bed early, Alex changing Nick's dressings before they settled down. Neither slept well and tossed and turned the night away.

Alex rose early the next morning, breakfasted with Nick and then slipped out to drive to the nearest Tourist Information Office in the city. There she queried about the best way to get to mainland Greece. She was not relishing the drive across the north of Italy, through Slovenia, Croatia, Serbia and North Macedonia so was delighted when the man behind the desk told her she got get a car ferry from Venice to Igoumounitsa on Greece's western coast. If they could get to Venice by noon that day, they could arrive in Igoumounitsa by 3.30pm the following day. Alex looked at her watch. It was 9am. The man told her it would take around two-and-a-half hours to drive to Venice from there. It would be tight but manageable. She thanked him and rushed back to Nick whom she found in the foyer of the hotel paying their hosts.

"You should have waited for me?" she said, giving him a kiss.

"I figured we'd probably need to leave quickly, so I thought

I'd get a head start," he replied. "Did you get what you needed?"

She nodded.

Waving goodbye to the family, Nick and Alex got into the Fiat and drove east through Milan and out into the Italian countryside. It was a typically warm and sunny day, and for the first time in ages, Alex relaxed. Here she was, running from the law and a would-be killer, but she was with a man she loved heading for a new life on a beautiful Greek island. She smiled.

"What are you so happy about?" Nick asked, then winced as the car hit a pothole in the road.

"It's a lovely day, we're in Italy, and we're heading to Greece. What can be more perfect?"

"Well, I can think of something," he said with a mischievous grin, "but this shoulder puts that out of the question for a while."

"If you're talking about sex, that's a definite no until I am sure you are back to full health," she chided.

"Spoilsport," he said and laughed.

For the first time in forever, Alex was truly happy. She felt free, like some great weight had been lifted from her shoulders. She thought about her past life, where all she could think about was buying expensive jewellery and clothes. How shallow that life had been. There was so much more fun to be had living a simpler life with the man she loved. Nick was staring out of the window, smiling to himself, and she felt her heart would burst with joy. If only I could bottle this feeling and keep it forever, she thought as she turned right to drive towards the road to Venice.

Ben set up watch on Conexus from an office building across the road. He enjoyed being back in Rome. It was one of his favourite cities. Pity he was here for work. He set up his binoculars on a stand facing the SOS headquarters and waited. The floor he was on was disused, and the air conditioning switched off, so his vigil was hot and wearying.

After a couple of days, it became evident that neither Nick nor Alex was in the building. Ben had been so sure that was where they had been going, but there was no sign of them. He thought about where he could go next. He didn't want to return to London with nothing. He had to keep going. He knew that a watch alert had been put on all airports in Europe for the pair, so they couldn't fly anywhere, so where would they go? More importantly, where would Nick go? Were they hiding out somewhere in Rome? His gut told him they were not in the city. The television was still running with the story about Alex being wanted for murder, so they would have to go underground. But where? He took his eyes from the binoculars and stared out the window. If I were Nick Walker, where would I hide? And then he remembered Nick's stories about his childhood holidays in the Med.

Chapter 20 - Safety

They arrived in Venice a little after 11.30am. Alex found the port road and drove them straight down to the ferry terminal. The ferry was already in port when the car arrived, and she parked near the terminal building in order to buy their tickets. Returning to the car ten minutes later, Alex stopped off at a mobile food van for coffee and pastries before re-joining Nick. She handed him the goodies as she switched on the car and drove it into the queue for the ferry. They ate the delicious fare as they waited to get on. Nick wolfed his down like a starving dog. He been a little pale just before they arrived, but the coffee and pastry restored him. He had more colour about his face and seemed brighter, two signs that Alex was pleased to see. Twenty minutes later, the ferry began accepting passengers and vehicles. They drove aboard and finally began to properly relax.

The journey took more than 30 hours, and Alex was pleased she had booked them a tiny cabin. Although dark and the size of a hamster cage, the cabin gave them enough privacy to see to Nick's wounds and to hide away from others who might recognise them. Disguised with a wig and glasses, Alex fetched food for them from the canteen at lunch and dinner to be eaten in the cabin. She allowed only them to surface and take some air when the sun went down. It was a pretty long and boring time, but she couldn't risk them being caught.

The following afternoon the ferry arrived at Igoumounitsa on mainland Greece. A busy little port town, they had no time to explore the noisy, dusty place for they had to disembark the larger ship and then embark on the Corfu ferry within an hour-and-a-half. It was a case of waiting to get off one ferry and then waiting to get on another.

But it was worth it. By 7pm, they had arrived. The sun was setting over the island, glittering like jewels on the dark turquoise Ionian Sea. It was warm, but there was a slight breeze that was so welcome to the exhausted travellers after their mammoth journey. It washed away the tiredness just long enough for them to take in the loveliness of the island and of Corfu town (Kerkyra) itself.

An ancient port town, Corfu was a mix of old-style elegant mansions and palaces, and more modern buildings. French-style squares bloomed with flowers, courtyards offered travellers welcome shade, and stunning churches dotted the streets, standing proud against the early evening sky. The couple took a room at a hotel overlooking the sea. They ate Greek kebabs in the hotel restaurant and were in bed by 9pm local time. Exhausted by the stress of the long journey, no sooner had she turned out the light than Alex was asleep, lulled into her dreams by the soothing swish of the sea outside. It was heaven.

The following morning, after breakfasting on bread, Greek cheese and yoghurt on their balcony, Nick made a call.

"Gregory," he said into the hotel room phone. "It's Nick. I have a favour to ask."

Alex smiled as she watched him speak to his friend. Nick was looking so much better. The pinched, drawn expression of his face was gone and he seemed in less pain. His shoulder still hurt, there was no doubt about that, but it was healing. She wandered out on to their balcony and gazed out at the beautiful blue of the Mediterranean Sea. The sun's warmth glittered on the calm of the water.

On the small beach, tourists were wandering along the sand enjoying the heat of the morning. Locals wandered up and down the seafront heading for work or to shop. Somewhere, someone was baking bread, she could smell its delicious aroma from where she was. A bakery must be nearby, she thought, promising herself to visit before they left the town. The baking smell mingled with the fresh saltiness of the sea air and something else. What was it? Pine trees. It reminded her of home. Home. When would she ever go there again? She thought about her family and the place where she grew up, and there was real regret in her heart. When she could go back and forth as she pleased, she never gave the place much thought. Now she and Nick were fugitives of sorts and could not go home to Britain, she longed for it. She gave herself a mental shake. This situation wouldn't last forever. Mother would see to it.

"Everything okay?" Nick asked as he joined her on the balcony.

"Yes. Does he have one?"

"The perfect one. It's a romantic getaway in the north-east of the island near Afion. It's quite remote, but it'll be perfect for us. He's given me directions, and we've to meet him there in a couple of hours."

"Perfect. That gives us time to relax for a bit before we have to join him."

Gregory Galani was standing at the wooden front door of the Village Persephone when Alex's Fiat drove through the double gates. A tall bearded Greek, he was a handsome man with a smiling face. Nick grinned when he saw his friend and waved. He had known Gregory for a long time. Both Nick and Gregory's fathers had been business partners, and the families had holidayed on and off for years. The sons had met as infants and been friends ever since.

"Hallo!" the big Greek shouted as Alex parked in front of the villa. She released Nick from his seatbelt and he got out. "How are you, my friend?" Gregory said, walking towards them. He held out a hand to shake, then withdrew it when he saw Nick's arm sling. "What the hell happened to you?"

"It's a long story, Gregory," Nick said. "Good to see you. May I introduce my girlfriend, Alex?"

Alex was a little taken aback by being introduced that way. She had not really thought about her status in their relationship, but it pleased her that Nick thought of her as his girlfriend.

"Nice to meet you," she said, shaking Gregory's massive hand.

"Alex? From Alexandra?" Gregory asked. Alex nodded. "Good Greek name," he said with a grin. "Now, come in, and I will show you around."

Persephone Villa was a huge old house about five miles north of Afion. It was perched on top of massive cliffs overlooking the sea and surrounded by a large, well-established garden of fir trees and other Greek flora. Two peacocks roamed the grounds calling for a mate and a ginger cat lay sunning itself on stone steps that led up to the wooden entranceway. Alex looked at the house in awe. It was crumbling in places, but was still magnificent. Built over three storeys, she counted at least 14 shuttered windows on that side of the house alone.

"Come inside," Gregory said. "I show you around."

The downstairs consisted of a large modern kitchen with all the mod cons; a huge reception room filled with comfortable sofas and coffee tables; a downstairs toilet that was bigger than Alex's whole bathroom in Berlin; a study cum library that was packed full of old books in both Greek and English. A marble staircase in the hall led up to the first floor which had five spacious bedrooms decorated in sumptuous antique furniture and a huge bathroom. Each room had its name painted on gold on the doors and they were called after Greek heroes: Hercules, Prometheus, Perseus. The second floor also had five bedrooms, one of which had been converted into a child's playroom.

"You can take any bedroom you want," Gregory said as they descended the stairwell, "but I would recommend the Hercules room on the first floor. It is the biggest and has the four-poster bed, which is great for a little romance, yes?"

He waggled his eyebrows at Alex, who blushed.

"Now," he said, "allow me to take you for lunch so you can tell me why you needed to come here and how you got that arm."

Over lunch of Stifado, a Greek stew, and vegetables at taverna nearby, Nick told Gregory all that had happened to them over the past few weeks. The Greek sat there, mouth open, as he told him about Alex being set up for murder and someone trying to kill him.

"It seems my boss took out a contract on Nick," Alex explained, "because she thought Nick was hassling me, that he was only with me because he wanted an in to my organisation. She didn't realise we had…feelings for one another."

"Tough boss," said Gregory.

"She's actually very nice," Alex said. "She took the contract off as soon as I explained that we are together. However, not everyone seems to have got the message."

"So now you hide, yes?"

"For a little while," Alex replied.

"Well, there is nowhere nicer on Earth than this paradise that is Corfu," said Gregory with a grin.

"It is beautiful," Nick agreed.

They settled into the villa quickly and enjoyed the peaceful life it gave them. Nick continued to heal well and within a couple of weeks was joining Alex on her walks along the clifftop and to shopping trips to Corfu town where she picked up fresh produce. The town was bustling with tourists drawn there by the beauty of the old Venetian buildings, its warren of winding lanes and alleyways, its bustling restaurants and bars, and its fine collection of shops.

Above the town, looming over it like sleeping sentries, were the fortresses on the town's twin hills. Built to ward off Ottoman sieges, they were now invaded by other, less violent, visitors. Alex, always one for quality and beauty, explored the town's museums and the Liston shopping area. She dragged Nick along as she visited Corfu's ancient churches, and together, they explored the countryside and beaches around the town.

Back at the villa, Alex became well acquainted with the locale, making friends with the shopkeepers of Afion, walking along the shoreline and taking Nick on voyages of discovery as they drove along the winding roads to new horizons. She had never felt so free, so loved, being here with the man of her dreams on a fantasy island. It was almost too perfect. She knew some time this paradise would all come crashing down about her ears, but she didn't expect it to happen so soon.

They had been at the market in Corfu Town, around three weeks after they had arrived, enjoying strolling along inspecting the goods offered by the many stalls. A spot of lunch at a favourite taverna followed, and all would have been perfect had Nick not suddenly stiffened mid-sentence.

"What's the matter?" Alex said, worried.

"See that man over there?" Nick said. Alex slowly and carefully glanced over her left shoulder. There was a dark-haired man sitting a few metres away drinking coffee and pretending to read a copy of a British newspaper.

"Yes?"

"He's British intelligence," Nick said

"How do you know?"

"He was on my team. His name is Ben Littlejohn."

"Shit. Do you think he's seen us?"

"He's seen us alright."

"What are we going to do?"

Nick's face grew tight and emotionless. "I need to speak to him. Stay here."

Before she could object, Nick was on his feet and striding towards his colleague.

Ben Littlejohn looked up and smiled. "Nick Walker," he said. "At last!"

Alex knew their idyll was going to end at some point, but had hoped they would at least have had a few months on Corfu before having to move on again. As she drove their car back to Villa Persephone, her head was a whirl of thoughts about where they could go now that their hiding place had been compromised. Nick was strangely quiet on the way home, and nothing Alex said would bring him out of the torpor that he seemed to be in. It wasn't until they were sitting on the terrace having a glass of wine later that he shared his thoughts with her. They were sitting close together at a large wooden table. He put his good arm around her.

"I'm going to have to go back," he said.

Her stomach lurched. "What? Why?"

"MI6 want to talk to me."

"What about?"

"Well, I did disappear on them without a single word about where I was or what I was doing. They believed I'd been murdered or gone rogue. Now they know different, they want a debrief."

"But what if you get there and you can never come back again? They will arrest you and put you in jail," Alex warned. Inside, her whole being was screaming, "No!"

"No, they won't. I'll get a reprimand. Of course, I'll come back," he reassured her. He leant over and took her hand. He gave it a squeeze. "There's something else."

Alex took a sip of her wine before responding. "What?"

"They want you to give yourself up."

"But I did not murder that man."

"I know that and you know that," he said, "but the German authorities need to eliminate you from their enquiries."

There was a strained silence whilst each thought about the situation. Then Alex spoke. "How did they find us?"

"Ben's been on our tail since Berlin. He said the trail went cold in Rome, but then he remembered my stories about going to Corfu, and he thought it was worth a try. He got the first ferry here. It's taken him a couple of weeks to track us down."

"You've got to be kidding me."

He put his hands up. "These things happen. I should have kept my big mouth shut." He leant in and gave her a sweet kiss on the lips.

"How long do we have?" she asked after a moment.

"Ben said he'll give us until the end of the week, and then we need to go in."

She put her glass on the table and turned to face him. "What if we run? We could go anywhere. Start again."

Nick sighed and brought her hand to his lips. "No, my love," he said. "It's time to face the music. We must go back, clear our names, and only then can we live the lives we want."

"What do you mean 'clear OUR names'?"

"MI6 want to talk to me about the murder too."

"Oh, Nick!"

"It's going to alright," he said. His voice was reassuring, but his face was strained. "I promise."

"You can't promise me that," she said, extracting her hand from his and standing up.

"Where are you going?"

"I've got a headache. I'm going to lie down."

Alex hurried upstairs to the large bedroom they shared and sat down on the bed. Her heart was racing, her mind a blizzard of thoughts, and she felt sick. If she and Nick returned to Berlin and London respectively, the person who was trying to kill them would know where they were. Person? Let's face it—it was Dominika who was trying to take them out. The minute they showed their faces in their old haunts, Dominika was sure to know about it.

Alex let out a long breath and tried to calm down. Panicking about this was only making her situation worse. No, she had to calm down and think things through calmly and methodically. She cursed for allowing herself to relax. Why did I get comfortable? I should have known better.

She looked at the telephone sitting on a bedside table and thought about phoning Mother for advice. She knew the number by heart, it would take only a moment. No, best to do it at a payphone somewhere off island, she decided. She couldn't risk Dominika finding out where they were now, not when they had plans to make.

Fuck! I hate my life, she thought. Fuck, fuck, fuck.

If they didn't go back and face the music, they would never be free. They would be running forever. And she did so want to be free right now. Living with Nick these past few weeks, caring for him, loving him, had been amazing, and she knew she wanted to spend the rest of her life with him. But that dream could only come true if they went back and faced their accusers. They were both innocent, and they needed to prove that. By hiding away, they only looked guilty and that would deflect law enforcement from looking for someone else for the crime.

Fuck. Nick was right: they would have to go back.

Chapter 21 - Interrogation

Alex's apartment building looked benign. The curtains were open on all the apartment windows, except for hers. The security door was still securely shut. Her neighbours went about their daily business in the same quiet manner. There was no sign of police. No sign of anyone. She paid the taxi driver and got out of the cab towing her small suitcase and bag. She had been forced to leave her weapons in Corfu in order to fly back to Berlin. Gregory had locked them away in the Villa Persephone safe and promised they would be secure. She felt naked without them, vulnerable. She walked up the pathway to the front door and put her key in the lock. She turned it. The door opened as it always had. So far, so good, she thought as she hauled the suitcase inside and began to climb the stairs to her flat above.

Alex saw no one going up to the apartment. She heard no sign of life except for the barking of a neighbour's dog above. The familiar high-pitched barks were comforting to her as she unlocked the apartment door. Yes, she was home.

The flat was in darkness, and she put her suitcase down to switch on the overhead light. She paused and looked around her.

The apartment was a mess: furniture and ornaments had been moved and dusted for fingerprints, a chair lay overturned on the floor its base ripped open as if someone had been searching for something inside. Yellow and black police tape was strewn over the entranceway as if it had been hastily torn aside and discarded. A plant pot with her favourite yucca was smashed.

"Bastards," she muttered under her breath as she closed the door and went to rescue the plant. "They could have at least tidied up after themselves." Finding the plant dead, she went to her kitchen to retrieve some binbags. "I suppose I'd better do it myself."

An hour later, the flat was back to normal and a washing was on. Alex made herself a cup of tea as she thought about her next move. She knew she had to give herself up, but was reluctant to do it just yet. She wanted to savour being in the apartment again, to enjoy the peaceful familiarity of her home. But fate had other ideas. There was a loud knocking on the door.

"Open up! Police!" a woman shouted.

"Fuck," said Alex, discarding the tea and going to open the door. And so, it begins.

The police station was a modern monstrosity that was built to intimidate and depress. It was a stark, serious building with nothing going for it externally, at least in Alex's eyes. In handcuffs she was led inside to a modern, bright office space. The police officer who had arrested her booked her in and then handed her over to the head of the local murder squad.

Detective Inspector Gerhard Struber was sitting behind a table in an interview room going through a file. He was a thin, humourless man who barely looked at her as Alex was handcuffed to a ring on the table and told to sit down. Only then did he look up and acknowledge her. He switched on video recording equipment and checked Alex's name and address before launching into his investigation.

"Miss Grier, can you tell me please why the body of Wolter Kraus was found at your apartment on the 13th of last month?"

"I have no idea," she replied. "I don't know him. Did you say the 13th? I wasn't even in the country on that date ... Do you think I could get a cup of tea? I'm parched. I've only just arrived back in Berlin and haven't had anything to eat or drink for hours."

"We can arrange that… in good time," he replied. He glanced back down at the file before him and pulled out some photographs of the murdered man. He placed them in front of her and pointed at the images so she would look. "So, you don't know what Herr Kraus was doing in your apartment on that date?"

"No, "she said, picking up a photograph and studying it. Wolter Kraus had been shot twice, once in the chest and once in the head, a vicious way to die. An assassin's way to die. Dominika. She did it to frame me, she thought. It all makes sense. She put the image back down and looked straight at Struber. "I've never even met him and I have no clue as to why he was there. Who is he anyway?"

"He was an analyst with Interpol," Struber replied. He glanced down at his notes and changed tack. "You were a sniper with the British Army?"

"Yes, that's correct, but I left the army a couple of years ago."

"And what do you do now?" He took up a pen and help it, poised to take down her answer.

"I'm a business consultant," she replied smoothly.

"So, you're not an assassin for hire?" he asked, his eyes boring into hers.

"Of course not," she scoffed. He was making her feel uncomfortable, but she couldn't show it.

"So, if you didn't murder Herr Kraus at your apartment on the 13th, who did?"

"I have no idea," she replied.

"Why do you think he was at your apartment?"

"I really don't know. Like I said, I don't know this man. I've never met him."

"So, if you weren't there, where were you that evening?"

"I was en route to Italy for a few days away with my boyfriend."

"Who is this boyfriend?"

Alex let out a sigh. She was reluctant to give over any information alluding to Nick, but she had to prove her innocence so she told him. Struber questioned her as to why she had not come forward sooner, and she claimed she did not know she was wanted. She had been on holiday; they had been avoiding the news. They wanted to relax.

"So, you can imagine my surprise to find out I was a wanted woman," she said. "I came back to Berlin straight away."

Struber looked up from his note-taking and did not look impressed.

Two hours of continual questioning passed in that small room, and Alex was beginning to flag. Her wrist still chained to the table ached, but she did not let down her guard for one moment. Then, at last, he said, "That will be all for today, Miss Grier."

"Okay," she replied, "so, am I free to go?"

"I'm afraid not," he said, "our investigations are continuing, and I may have some further questions. You'll be comfortable in one of our cells for the night."

As he said it, the door to the room opened and a police constable walked in. He went to Struber's side and whispered something in his ear. Struber glanced at Alex and nodded. He stood up.

"It seems your lawyer has arrived," he said.

Finally, Alex thought. She had called Mother when the police arrived and asked her to arrange legal representation. "That's good," she said.

Across the English Channel, sitting in another interview room in an office in the middle of London, Nick, in a smart suit and open-necked shirt, was idly pulling apart a used paper drinks cup as he waited for his bosses to arrive. He had been fed and given copious cups of coffee, but so far no one had come to speak to him. They were letting him sweat. He knew it, they knew he knew it, but they still were trying to freak him out. So, he went AWOL from the service? So what? He was sure he wasn't the only one to have ever gone this way. It's not as if he had defected to Russia or North Korea. He had done it for love.

Nick looked around. It was a modern room in a modern office block. The walls were plain, the table he was sitting at was about the size of a family kitchen table and the chairs were metal-framed with black fabric seat covering. They were comfortable enough. Against one wall was a sideboard containing tea and coffee making facilities and a tin of biscuits. The last time he had been in this particular room in MI6 headquarters he had been on the other side of the table as the interviewer. Now he was the interviewee, and he already wasn't enjoying it.

At last, the door opened and his immediate superior, Len Ross, and the woman above him, Lettis Green, entered. Len was a man in his 50s with white hair and a fit, slim body. Lettis, 42 with blonde curly hair, was also looking good. Slim and smart in a pencil skirt and blouse, she would have been attractive had it not been for the ridiculously grim expression on her face. She was carrying a leather conference folder which she threw down on the table. She took a seat opposite Nick. Len sat beside her. Nick didn't say a word, but instead waited for them.

"Nick," Len said by way of greeting.

"Len," he replied.

"Lettis Green, you know," Len said, turning to his superior.

"Yes, hello, Lettis," Nick said looking Lettis directly in her frosty green eyes.

"Good of you to finally join us Nick," she replied. Nick did not rise to the barb, but gave her a smile instead.

Introductions and greetings over, Lettis launched right into it. She opened her conference folder and pulled out some paperwork.

"Right," she said, "you've got some explaining to do."

"I know, but…"

"Please remain quiet. I haven't finished," she snapped as she glared at him. She returned to her file. "On the 13th of July, you disappeared, allegedly running off with a Miss Alex Grier whom you had been sent to gather intelligence on. Is that correct?"

"Yes."

"Where did you go to?"

"I followed her to Italy," he replied, "to Florence."

"For what reason?"

Nick paused. "I believed she had been hired for a job so I followed her there hoping to stop her."

"And had she? Been hired for a job that is? And what was the nature of the job? A hit?"

Fuck, do I lie, do I tell the truth? A vision of Alex's lovely face swam in his mind and that made it up for him.

"No, she was there taking a break," he replied. "Apparently Florence has some of the best designer shops in Europe, according to Miss Grier."

"And yet the very same weekend you and she were there, a mob boss called Dino de Luca was assassinated along with several of his men. Do you know anything about that?" Lettis continued.

"Nope. Alex and I were too busy. You see, we became very…close on that trip, and we spent a lot of time indoors," he lied. "I had been tasked with romancing her by MI6, so I was actually just carrying out my job," he added with a smirk.

"Hmmm."

"I thought if I could get close to her, she might give me information about the Sisters of Sin," Nick said.

"And did she?"

More memories of their time in Rome and his being looked after in the SOS headquarters came sharply to mind. "No," he replied. "I believe Alex Grier is not an assassin."

"How can you be sure?"

"She's not like that."

Lettis frowned, then scribbled something down in a notebook and then looked up at Nick. "Where did you go to after Florence?"

"We spent a few days in Rome before…"

"Before what?"

He looked at Lettis and then at Len. Fuck, this was hard to admit.

"Before I decided I was in love with her," he said. "And she's in love with me. So, we decided to go away together for a little while."

"And that was when you met Agent Littlejohn in Corfu?"

"Yes."

"Did he persuade you to hand yourself in?"

"No, I was already thinking I'd have to get back in touch. Then after I spoke with him, I realised I would have to do it now," he replied. He put his hand into his jacket pocket and pulled out a folded piece of white paper. He put it down on the table and slid it over to Lettis. "Here."

"What's that?" she said, looking at the paper like it was a steaming dog turd.

"My letter of resignation, I quit," he said.

"You can't just quit." Lettis's face belied sheer shock.

"I just have." He stood up. "Now, are there any more questions?"

"Just a minute," Len said also rising, "you can't just leave. We haven't finished questioning you yet."

"I can, and I will," Nick said. "I've told you everything I found out, which is nothing, and I've officially handed in my resignation. So, I'm going."

He strode to the door, pressed the lock and the door clicked open. He turned. "Alex and I are going to go away together," he said. "You'll not see or hear from us again. I hope I'll not see or hear from this agency either."

Neither Len nor Lettis spoke but stood there, open-mouthed.

"Good," he said and went out.

In Berlin, Detective Inspector Gerhard Struber was finding it hard to find any evidence Alex Grier had murdered Wolter

Kraus. Forensics proved the Interpol analyst had not been killed in her apartment and checks on her story showed she had been nowhere near the place on that night. He had to let her go. He had nothing to keep her on.

Alex smiled when he gave her the news. "I hope you find whoever killed Herr Kraus," she said as she picked up her jacket and put it on.

"Don't leave the country, fraulein," he said. "We may have more questions for you."

Alex smiled. "Of course," she replied sweetly.

With her stern-faced solicitor at her side, Alex left the police buildings. She paused outside, thanked the lawyer for his good work and shook the man's hand. Wishing him a safe journey home, she jumped in the first taxi she could find and headed home. She had some packing to do.

Once out into the busy London city streets, Nick finally felt able to sigh with relief. He hadn't been sure how things would have gone and felt he had got away too easily. He would need to get Alex quickly and the two of them go into hiding. He fetched his mobile from his pocket—it was a burner cell, one that couldn't easily be traced, and called Alex.

"Hi, everything okay? Good."

Nick knew there would be a tail on him as soon as he left MI6's imposing modern building in the Vauxhall area of London. He quickly walked along Albert Embankment and down into the Vauxhall Railway Station. Always glancing behind him, he knew there were at least two men following him. He hurried down the moving staircase, cursing the city for being so populated and the station being so crowded. Slipping his Oyster travel card from his jacket pocket, he used it to gain access to the platform and was relieved to see a train had just arrived. He pushed past commuters and jumped on board, then turned around to see the two men stuck at the barrier. Giving them a cheeky wave, he stood with his back against a partition and relaxed a little.

It took only 22 minutes for the train to make its way north from the south bank of the River Thames, where Vauxhall was, to Victoria Railway Station. Hurrying out of the 19th century building, he didn't have time to admire the Victorian architecture of the old building. Instead, he exited through its main entrance finding himself in Belgrave Road. Taking a right, he hurried up the street, turning left into Buckingham Palace Road where he could see the corner of Victoria Coach Station just ahead. Nearly there.

Nick crossed the road and turned right into Elizabeth Street where the bus station was situated. Built in 1932, this stunning station has a distinctive white Art Deco design and was a beautiful building but for its ugly sliding doors at the entranceway. They looked like they had been added sometime in the 1970s, but Nick had no time to muse on it, for he had a bus to catch. He had already bought his ticket the day before and it, some money and his passport were lying snug in his inside jacket pocket. He fetched the ticket out and handed it to the bus driver as he approached the Dover bus.

"Any luggage, mate?" the driver, a small wiry man with a strong London accent, asked.

"No."

"Just going down for the day, are you?"

"Something like that." Nick smiled as the driver punched and handed back the ticket.

Nick got on board and chose a seat near the back of the bus. He settled down, concentrating on bringing his breathing into check and his heart rate down. Ever since he had come back to London, his anxiety levels had been through the roof. He had no idea what, if any, evidence his former bosses back in Vauxhall had on himself or what the Berlin Police had on Alex. He did not know if he would have been arrested or let go. He was glad that the evidence against Alex had been sketchy. That way, they could neither pin anything on her or on himself. He thought about her, and his groin quickened. He could not wait to be back in her arms again.

It won't be long now, he told himself as the bus doors swooshed shut and the driver started the engine.

In San Marino, a woman with dark curly, bobbed hair was enjoying a refreshing beer at a café across the road from the safe house. Cora was a short, stocky woman in her late 20s who had been working for Dominika for three years and was totally loyal to her boss. Dominika had tasked her to kill the man and woman who were to be hiding out there. So far, there had been no sign of them. A bullet proof limousine had drawn up some days earlier, but that was it. She checked the images of Alex and Nick that Dominika had sent her. Nope, there had been no sightings of either one. She closed down the pictures and called Dominika to tell her so. The Russian was furious, and after a tirade of swear words, calmed down and told her employee to return immediately to Rome. As soon as the call ended, Cora paid her café bill and left. There was nothing for her to do here.

Unbeknownst to either Cora nor Dominika, a second person was watching that day. Isabella Starr, the assassin known as Envy, watched Cora with great interest from her hiding place in an apartment across the road. So, Mother was right. Dominika was behind the second attempt on Nick Walker's life. Cora being at the safe-house, watching for him and Alex, was proof of that. She was a known associate of Dominika's. They had worked together before. And Dominika was the only person Mother had told. There was no question of the Russian's guilt now.

Chapter 22 - Freedom

Alex was waiting for Nick at a small, two-person table inside Café Claudette on Calais' main street. There was a large coffee and a croissant on the table in front of her and she was reading a book. Despite being tired, her face brightened when she looked up as he approached. Alex put the book down, stood up and, arms open, ran to him. Showering his face with kisses, she hugged him tight.

"I wasn't sure you were going to make it," she said. "I thought they might have arrested you or kept you for questioning some more. I was worried I'd never see you again."

"I wondered the same," Nick admitted, "but I'm here now and I'm starving."

"I'll order you something."

As Alex went to the café counter to order him some food, Nick sat down at their table.

"Jesus it's been a long day," he said when she plonked a latte in front of him a few minutes later, "and it was a ropey crossing from Dover to Calais. I'm just relieved to be back on terra firma."

A shuttle bus had taken him from the port to the town, he

told her, and it was only now, when he was with her, that he could finally truly relax.

"So, how was it?" she asked anxious that he had not undergone too much of an interrogation.

He leaned forward. "They've got nothing on you or me," he said a low voice. "I tendered my resignation and I'm a free man."

"That's so good," she said, grinning from ear to ear. "So, what now?"

"Now we need to decide what we're doing next," he replied.

"Well," she said, giving a large rucksack under the table a kick. He stooped down to look. When he straightened again he was grinning. "I collected a few things when I was in Berlin, so we should be good for a while."

"A few things?"

Now it was her turn to lean forward and whisper, grinning, "Three million Euros of things."

"How did you…?"

"Better not to ask," she said. "Let's just say that my way in my previous job was very good and leave it at that."

He grinned and took a sip of his coffee. "Oh, I nearly forgot," he said, pulling his passport from his pocket and throwing it down on the table. "This worked brilliantly. I don't know who your forger is, but even I wouldn't have guessed that was fake."

"Shhhh, keep your voice down." She pushed it back to him. "Well, we couldn't have MI6 being alerted when you left the country. Put it away for now. You're going to need it again."

"Oh? And where is madam thinking of taking me?" he asked with a grin.

"Well, I thought before we decided where we were going to live permanently that we might want to move around the world a bit and see what's on offer. I hear Peru is nice this time of year, and I've always wanted to see Machu Picchu."

"I could do that," he said with a smile.

"Good."

The flights were booked, clothes bought and cases packed. They flew out to South America a week later, beginning their journey in the Peruvian capital of Lima. From there, they explored the country, taking in Lake Titicaca and Machu Picchu. Alex, a history lover, insisted they also take in the city of Cusco while they were there. The former capital of the Incan world, the city is now a World Heritage Site and home to the Incan fortress of Sacsayhuaman.

Exhausting all the tourist sites in Peru, they hopped on to a plane to Buenos Aires in Argentina. They spent two weeks exploring the city before heading south flying from Buenos Aires to the town of El Calafate on the banks of Lake Argentino in Argentina's south-east. It was a popular entry point into the Patagonian region, and whilst there, they took the opportunity of visiting the Perito Moreno Glacier.

Using local transport, they made their way south to the Ushuaia, the world's most southernmost city. Surrounded by snow-capped mountains, sitting on the edge of the ocean, the city was the perfect spot for a question Nick had to ask. They walked hand in hand along the water's edge, and it was there that Nick went down on one knee. Alex giggled when he took her hand. His face had such a grim expression on it, she just had to laugh.

"Stop it," he said, "this is serious!"

"Okay." She composed herself.

Nick took a breath. "Alex Grier," he began, "will you do me the honour of becoming my wife?"

Alex paused. Then she giggled.

“Is that a yes?” he asked anxiously.

She nodded. “Yes,” she replied, “that’s a very big yes!”

He got to his feet, took her in his arms and kissed her passionately on the lips. As his lips touched hers, she could feel her body melt into his, and she knew they would never be apart. He released her and put his arm around her so they could both enjoy to the stunning view of the sea. She snuggled into his shoulder. And then a thought came to her.

“I can’t wait to marry you, Nick Walker,” she said, “but where shall we live? What shall we do?”

“It doesn’t matter,” replied Nick, gazing out at Navarino Island across the strait, “so long as we’re together.”

And now I am very pleased to bring you the first chapter of the next book in the series: Pride by Sofia Aves.

I always get what I want. And I get it without a fuss.

My life consists of rigid structure. I work my job, I stay clean in every sense.

Remove the pests who darken our society. Dress, assassinate, resonate. Celebrate with platinum and champagne. Rinse & repeat.

As an assassin with a knife fetish and a penchant for wearing white, that's not anywhere as easy as it sounds.

Until a long-haired Aussie surfer walks into my happy little bubble and pops my sand-covered cherry with his personal brand of uncouth.

Who just happens to be a spy.

Who just happens to have a brilliant mind.

Who just happens to be sexy as sin.

And that's my department.

I can't fall for a man who plays for the other team.

...Right?

PRIDE is a femme fatale novel set in the stunning Sisters of Sin world.

Book three of the series, Pride, releases on August 5, 2022.

Order yours: https://books2read.com/sos3/

Pride

A SISTERS OF SIN NOVEL EXCERPT

SOFIA AVES

Chapter 1 - Catherine

Air conditioning hit me with a cool relief as I passed through Trilogy's sliding glass doors without a glance at security either side, glad to escape Cairns' saturating heat. The urge to check my deodorant remained strong, haunting me as I slipped be-tween the stoic underpaid sentinels at their posts of a haze-filled den overpopulated with wankers and addicts.

Cigarette smoke wafted past my nostrils and I swear I could feel its tarry little tendrils imbuing my sheath of pristine platinum hair with sin—and not the sort I liked, either. A smile played at the corners of my vibrant red lips. Cardinal. My favourite colour. It went well with sin, which was the entire purpose for my visit.

Of a sort.

My sort.

I skirted Trilogy's gaming tables, unable to prevent the shudder that rippled over me at the thought of pressing the heels of my brand new Monaco wrap-around pumps into the nineties-esque carpet that covered the gaming floor for what looks like acres. A girl always needs new shoes for a new job and the retro white patent leather matched my one piece, white off-the-shoulder catsuit that suited the occasion to perfection.

For this particular job, today was my first day.

And my last.

My walk ended at a pair of opulent gold doors—well, they would be opulent, if the paint hadn't been peeling off them. They had probably been hung around the same time as the carpet had been laid…and hence the aversion to sullying brand new shoes on its squishy surface.

My closed fist raised to knock, knuckles facing outward—germaphobe alert. Who needs to touch a surface more than is absolutely necessary?—my attention drawn to the cowboy-cum-surfer leaning precariously against the entryway to the pri-vate rooms. Or gaming hells, though the occupants never seemed to think of them in that way.

His fingers tapped blindly at his phone as I watched him list sideways to slide down the wall a little. One shoulder slumped into a position that had to give him a cramp, but the bastard was obviously so far gone that nothing would rouse him, not even an uncomfortable passing-out position in the worst gaming den in Northern Australia.

Bile rose in my throat as I took in the mid twenty-something young man who had thrown his lot in life away already. Given up. Sandy blond hair flopped boyishly to one side, obscuring the rest of his face. Just because I couldn't see the de-feat he'd sugar coated with blind bliss didn't mean it wasn't there.

The young man shifted again. His dozy, heavy-lidded gaze flicked up to freeze me in a sea of true ocean blue. Not the tropical sort, but the deep blue that only comes from hours of cruising in the middle of the ocean with no land to see. That sort of ocean blue. The sort I could be lost in for hours. Days.

What a bloody pathetic waste.

Blue hiccuped, slumping deeper as his phone tumbled from inert fingers.

Is he drunk at ten in the morning?

More likely still harbouring last night's party in his blood-stream.

Mind, what I was about to do could be considered a whole lot worse, but pride is a double edged blade.

An edge I dance on with a deadly grace .

I inhaled a long breath, filling my lungs with the stench of stale whiskey and body odour I could have well done without and knocked on the tarnished gilded doors.

Those golden doors allowed my entry as my not-so-compatriot slithered to the floor in a pitiful little heap.

I sighed and focussed on my task, my blades grazing my wrists inside my sleeves.

"Senora Letherna, it has been too long!" The maitre de swaggered from the short bar embedded in the back of the room toward me, his rotund body swaying in rhythm to music only he could hear. "Tell me you are here for pleasure." He drew out the last syllable, stopping a good foot below my shoulder.

Cairns attracted a plethora of cultures that seemed to stick, and Manuel had seen his share of entertainment at the small, privately owned casino.

Bonus, no one cared, provided I put enough money on the table for clean up.

"Not today, mio amico." I offered a tight-lipped smile that might have passed as either move or please hurry up.

"Apenado." The small man gave me a small glance and retreated behind the bar, jabbering at the bartender who knew better than to look my way.

Around the room, faceless men rose, their collective female company slithering to the floor. I gritted my teeth. Women weren't on my agenda, but if I could throw a few dollars down first…

"Ladies, a private dance. Anonymous audience. Who would like to go first?" Manuel smoothly emptied the room as hookers fled the proverbial coop, leaving me a clean slate.

The girls that a certain someone in the room had paid to ship to Australia in a very illegal, and unsanitary fashion.

Manuel would look after them. Give them real beds and a place to start fresh. New girls had a lot of opportunities, especially ones as pretty as they all were.

Still fresh, no scars.

Not yct.

Manuel would help them because I paid him for the privilege. But more than that, his wife had been my very first conquest. My rescue mission.

Personal note: tip heavily later.

Manuel had earned his fee in a moment's work.

A gent—the stained shirt that stretched over his bulging belly removed the salutation from my mind—stepped forward, his attention on the piece of ass in front of him that had escaped his attentions as I strode forward.

Should have kept your head down, sweetheart.

Though he wasn't a sweetheart, not when he saw my blade.

They rarely were.

I swept through the room on a regular current, a white blur amongst a cloudy sea of sin.

My favourite colour.

A ding in my ear halted my stride. I watched a single drop of blood descend in slow motion to the bent knee of my white jumpsuit, my perfectly applied lipstick raised in a sneer.

Not today.

I had never been covered in bodily fluids before and I refused to start with anything as innocuous as red.

I shifted in a mark-hitting pirouette as my earpiece bleeped a second time.

"Yes," I murmured, completing the revolution, my slim blades at full stretch.

The blades Wolfe made for me, and only me.

I must remember to provide him with a birthday present.

If the generations-old gent remembered it. Regardless of his memory problems, his craftsmanship allowed me to work with a smooth flow, uninterrupted with hitches such as an embedded blade that so often ended in splatter marks and DNA left at a scene.

A girl had to have the perfect blade and his were more than just a stiletto. Curved and minimalist, the blades Wolfe made were slimline works of art made for a select collection.

Mine.

No, Wolfe, like Manuel, was worth every penny.

"Are you busy right now?" Crave's voice echoed tinily in my ear over the strained reception within the casino, though the line was blessedly static free.

"Just a bit." I turned again.

Swipe.

Flick.

Slice.

"I think we need to have a chat." She sighed dramatically in my ear as one of the bastards pulled his own blade.

The thing was big enough to be a butcher's knife in the shape of a machete.

Where were you hiding that, big boy?

I let a dead smile split my lips as I passed him, sliding beneath the silver arc that flashed where my throat should have been. He missed.

I didn't.

"What about?"

Thud.

I stepped over the puddle, allowing momentum to turn me toward my next target.

"There's some things—well. I'm going to come right out and say it. You need to be in Rome more."

Slice.

"No, I don't."

"Yes, you do. You're missing things, Catherine. And I miss pasta nights." A pause. For dramatics or emphasis, I couldn't tell. "With you."

Spin.

"You mean you miss me picking the wines to go with the squid ink special."

Thud.

"That too."

My earpiece bleeped again. I inhaled sharply as a fist thrust at my abdomen. I pulled back, breath exploding between my lips.

"Catherine, what are you doing?"

Bleep.

"Wait one."

"No, don't—"

"Hold line one. Connect."

"Catherine. I thought you were coming to see me again."

"Mother." Not of the biological sort, just the one who had inducted me into the assassins hall of fame —he gallery that held all our pictures, past and present. Those images would last longer than any of us, as the Sisters of Sin had a remarkably short lifespan.

"Why does everyone want me in Rome?"

A little fancy footwork got me out of a corner. The damned conversations were screwing with my focus.

A hand grabbed my hair and pulled.

I halted, swallowed, and threw an elbow back just as he leaned forward with a king hit to the back of my head that never connected.

Funny thing, mine did.

"Who else wants you here?" Mother asked, not bothering to disguise the sharp tone that had me fangirling.

"Apparently I'm missing girl's night."

"What you're missing is a job."

Thud.

"Fine. Please send it through."

Slap.

I miss timed the punch and bitch slapped the bastard's bodyguard instead. He stared at me with narrowed eyes and I pretended to simper for a moment.

A girl needed a hobby, right?

"I will speak to you about it now—what on earth are you doing?"

The thug tried to move fast and failed. His blood decorated the wall.

Okay, so I'd been leaving a very hefty tip.

Thud.

"My job." I stood before the man I had come to find, my true target.

Small, rotund and balding, the bore evidence of tatty hair extensions at the sides of his reflective dome.

Short and shiny. Underwhelming.

The worst always were.

"I need you to—"

Bleep.

"Wait one." I let out a last breath, claiming my senses from distraction and focussing.

"Don't' you dare—"

"Hold." The line cleared. "Line one."

I flicked my wrist and the final body hit the floor. Blood pooled from the man's small frame. I stepped away from his excess of bodily fluids, their stink filling the room, though not a spot had touched my white catsuit.

Avoiding splatter was my superpower.

"Did you just ghost Mother?"

"Maybe?" I cleaned my blade on a bar rag and dropped it on the floor. That's what you did when you wanted hotel staff to tidy the room, right?

"That's not a good idea, Catherine."

I gave a faint smile she couldn't see. "Good night, Crave."

She huffed a half-laugh on the other end as I strode across the room and used the back of my hand to push the door ajar, just enough to slip through.

I checked my phone. Just under four minutes since I'd entered the casino. Not bad, but I could be faster. There was a lot of room for error and I couldn't let my streak be broken by a simple thing like the police. I sent through the tip for Manuel and the bartender while I was at it, leaving myself shy of a good four figures for less than five minute's work.

Mother would compensate me later.

Using the app was as safe as I could make it. No matter what I did, it would look like an international transfer. The dif-ference was that the money left an account that wasn't mine and passed through an dizzying array of porn portals to get to its intended target.

Porn might be more profitable, but it carried a much lesser penalty than murder in most places.

Not that I ever intended to get caught.

Smiling, I pocketed my phone, and aimed toward the exit.

The floppy haired surfer stood next to the door where I had left him, though he had straightened somewhat and looked a little more aware. "Bar open?"

He leaned forward but I closed the door firmly behind me, satisfied when I heard the lock snick. Manuel was speedy for a little man.

"I wouldn't. It needs staff attention. That one might be more your style." I pointed to the punter's bar across the spongy carpet.

He nodded, gave me a wobbly smile, and tottered back the way he had presumably come, though he managed to flick a hooded glance over his shoulder and wink.

Those stunning cerulean blue eyes held me for a moment, and my world shrunk.

He stumbled a little, breaking the connection as he weaved his way toward the bar. A ruined laugh rose in my throat.

Classy, Catherine.

My taste in men clearly hadn't improved since my last fling, which was why I hadn't bothered with another. I shook my head, letting my hair snake down my back and made the return journey home in record time.

https://books2read.com/sos3/

Read the first book in the series, Vanity by T Wells Brown:

My name is Catalina Willow, aka Vanity. Two items you should know about me; I'm an elite assassin, and I like nice things.

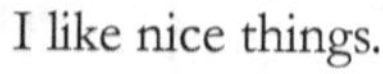

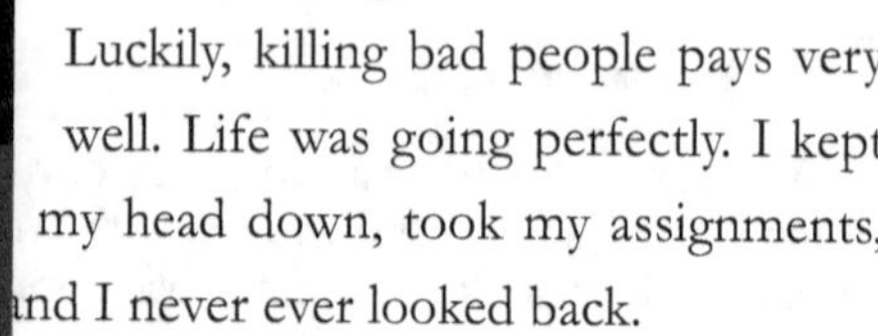

Luckily, killing bad people pays very well. Life was going perfectly. I kept my head down, took my assignments, and I never ever looked back.

That is, until I'm asked to remove an influential head of state. Apparently, my assignment's secu-rity team didn't appreciate how good I was at my job and decided to hunt me down.

Commander Juan Carlos Cortez, was the baddest of the bad, and he was hot on my stiletto stud-ded trail. But I didn't become one of the best assassins in my sisterhood by being soppy… or weak. I decided it was time for a change and believed I'd outwitted him… until he arrived on the small tropical island where I happened to be executing my newest assignment.

I don't believe in coincidences, so I took my wins, and hightailed it off the island. Now, I'm on the run of my life … and enjoying every moment of it. ??

Men. Sex. Sin.

We ruin the rules, and revel in it.

We are the Sisters of Sin.

Join me, as I dive into an elite assassin organization. One dedicated to bringing justice to the world, one kill at a time.

http://mybook.to/Vanitysistersofsin

Alex

SISTERS OF SIN:
A FEMME FATALE ORIGIN STORY

D A NELSON

THE END

Lance Corporal Alex Grier, 22, looked through the scope and lined her rifle up with the target. She closed her eyes and took a deep breath. Hitting bullseye would mean taking gold in the competition and keeping up the reputation of her unit. Missing was not an option. Besides, she couldn't bear the thought of the teasing she would have to undergo back in the mess if she failed. Nope, she would not become the butt of the jokes of her mates back in the Parachute Regiment. They would be unrelenting, and she'd never live it down.

Alex was lying on her front in an army rifle range in Hertfordshire, England. One of two from her sniper platoon taking part in the inter-military competition, she was the army's hope of gold. Her opponents were the best rifle shooters from the Royal Navy and Royal Air Force, and she was not about to let them win. She took another deep breath and opened one eye, resting it back on the scope. She lined up the crosshairs with the target and, keeping her other eye closed, gently squeezed the trigger. The bullet shot out. She felt the rifle recoil and the dull doof as the projectile hit the target. She looked up. The flagman was holding up a flag. She had hit the bullseye. Relief washed over her. Yes!! I've won! I've won! She thought as she scrambled to her feet to a round of applause and cheering from her competition buddy, platoon colleague and best friend, Stevie. As she carefully placed her rifle back in its case, he ran up to her and hugged her so tightly her blonde hair was nearly pulled out of its neat bun.

"I knew you could do it!" he said in a hoarse whisper. "I just knew it!"

He released her from his embrace. A tall, skinny man of 23, Stevie Puth had been Alex's bestie ever since they had gone through basic training. They were inseparable and were mistakenly coupled together by those not in the know. There had never been anything romantic between them, for Stevie was not a lover of the ladies. No, he was gay and proud of it.

"I can't wait until we get back to the garrison and dump all this lot," he said, looking at her case lying on the table next to them. His rifle had already been put away and was in the rifle case slung over his shoulder. "I'm going to get blinged up and take you out partying!"

"Sounds great," she said, grinning.

Their enjoyment of Alex's win was disturbed when their senior officer approached to congratulate her. Major John Hampton, 36 and devilishly handsome, grinned at his prodigy.

"Alex, you did a splendid job," he said, shaking her hand. "Well done. You're the pride of the regiment." Then he looked around him, saw that no one was watching, and leaned over to her. He said: "I'm going to take you somewhere to show you just how proud I am of you!"

"I'd love that," she replied, eyes gleaming with happiness. She had been dating Major Hampton for three months now. It was still in the 'don't tell anyone stage' as they both didn't know how it would work out. So far, so good. She was falling in love with him, and he seemed to feel the same for her. She bit her lip. "Where are you going to take me?"

He looked amused. "I was thinking somewhere romantic, like Paris."

"Oh, John, that would be amazing!" she replied.

"Shhhh! Keep your voice down, we don't want anyone overhearing," he said, looking around once more.

"I know, but it's just so exciting," she replied. "When?"

"What?"

"When are we going?" She looked up at him, eyes full of excitement. "This weekend?"

"No, not this weekend," he said. "I've got something else on, but soon. I promise." He wiggled his eyebrows. "Then I'm going to rip the knickers off you and show you a fantastic time."

"I can't wait!" she said breathlessly.

"Me either. Catch you later."

He walked away to join other uniformed officers in the refreshment tent whilst Alex finished putting her rifle away. In ten minutes, they would be presenting the prizes and she couldn't wait to get a hold of hers. It was a gold cup for keeping and a large plaque containing all the names of previous sharpshooting winners.

"What do you see in that creep?" Stevie asked, watching the Major laugh at someone's joke.

"He's not a creep, he's lovely," she said, zipping her gun case closed.

"He's not, you know," replied her friend. "Be careful with that one."

"What do you mean?" She was concerned. Stevie was her closest friend and confidante. If he knew something about John, he should say.

Stevie shook his head. "Nothing, it's nothing. I'm just jealous you've got a guy and I haven't." He gave her a weak smile, but there was a sadness in his eyes that concerned her.

"Well, maybe tonight will be your lucky night!" she said. "I hear Tony at The Flying Horse has a bit of a thing for you." She slung her rifle case across her shoulder and stuck her arm around through his. He smiled.

"Do you think so?"

"I know so!"

"Oh! Tell me more!"

*****

Back at the garrison, Alex stood in front of her full-length mirror and held a red dress up to her body. She looked at her reflection and grimaced. No, this dress was too fancy for drinks with the boys at the Flying Horse. She threw her dress on her bed and pulled a pair of black jeans and a pale cream silk blouse from her wardrobe. The blouse was her best. It was vintage Chanel and her pride and joy. Normally her British army salary would not stretch to such fancy clothing, but she had treated herself and it had paid for itself. Dressed down with jeans and boots, it was great for a night out. Dressed up with a skirt and heels, and she felt a million dollars. Yes, this would do nicely. She quickly slipped the jeans on and was just buttoning the last button of the blouse when she overheard an almighty ruckus coming from the corridor outside her shared room. She opened her door to see John holding Stevie up against the wall by his throat. His face was red with anger and placed just inches from her friend's.

"John?" she said in disbelief. What could Stevie have done to deserve this?

John let go of Stevie and stepped backwards.

"What are you doing?" she asked.

"That's between this man and me," John snapped. His face was red with anger. "A question of discipline." He looked at Stevie and grimaced. "I'll speak to you about this later," he snarled and without saying another word, turned about heel and walked smartly down the corridor.

Alex went to Stevie's side. "What was that all about?" she asked.

"It's nothing," Stevie said. "Just a disagreement about something stupid."

"Are you okay though? Want me to speak to him about this?"

"No, leave it, Alex," Stevie replied, putting his hand on her arm. "Please. Promise me you'll leave it." He looked almost… fearful.

"But he shouldn't have been treating you like that," she said.

"It was my fault," her friend replied. He looked away. "Just leave it be."

"Is there something you're not telling me?" she asked.

Stevie looked at her and shook his head. Although he seemed alright, Alex could see something was bothering him.

"No," he said. "Everything's hunky dory."

"Sure you want to go out tonight? Not fancy a takeaway and a couple of beers here?" she asked.

"No, a night out is just what we both need," he said, giving her a smile. "Besides, we have to celebrate your win."

"We sure do!" she replied. "Look, stay here and I'll got an get my bag. I'll just be a minute."

He stopped her. "You go on ahead and I'll catch up. I've got something I need to do and then I'll meet you in the pub."

"I'll just be a minute."

"I'll meet you there." His tone was one of don't argue with me. "I'm… eh… just going to change this shirt. Your boyfriend's big meaty fists have crushed it at the front."

Alex knew Stevie was always picky about his appearance, so she said nothing more, but nodded. She gave him a kiss and watched as he walked away towards his own accommodation.

"See you at the pub later?" she called.

Stevie did not stop, nor did he reply. He just waved his hand and disappeared outside.

Alex always felt guilty after that night. Had she known it would be the last time she saw her friend alive, she would have stayed with him, prevented him from walking out of the garrison and into nearby woods. She would have taken the rope from him; she would have stopped him tying it to a tree branch and she would have prevented him from hanging himself. Instead, she had gone to the Flying Horse, where she and her colleagues got blind drunk, celebrating her win. Okay, so she hadn't gotten drunk right away. Stevie was her friend, and she had left several messages on his cell phone, demanding to know why he hadn't yet joined them. He never got her messages. He never answered her calls. It wasn't until the following morning when, nursing an enormous hangover, Alex was told the devastating news that Stevie had taken his own life. A dog walker had found his body.

John had been the one to break the news. He came to her room and shut the door. "I'm so sorry, Alex," he said, and he held her in his arms as she sobbed hysterically. "I really am."

"Why would he do it? Why?" she asked.

"I don't know," he replied. "He must have been incredibly depressed to take such action."

She looked up at him through tear-stained eyes. "He wasn't depressed. He wasn't. I would know."

"You might not have. Many people with depression are very good at hiding it," he said pulling her closer again. She rested her head against his strong manly chest and felt safe. "Besides, he left a note."

Alex pulled away from him. "What does it say? Does it say why he did it?"

"I don't know, I haven't read it yet," John replied. He slipped a hand into his uniform pocket and pulled out a white envelope. Alex looked at it, aghast.

"Is that it? Why haven't you read it?" she demanded.

John looked grim. "That's because it's addressed… to you." He handed her the note. She snatched it out of his hand and tore it open. There was a single sheet of perfectly white paper inside with Stevie's distinctly messy handwriting on it. It said: My dearest girl, please forgive me. Life has gotten too difficult for me lately and I can't take it anymore. The pain is unbearable. There is no way out that I can see. Please remember me with love. Your Stevie.

As she read it, Alex felt a darkness crawl up her body and before she knew it, she was on the floor with John kneeling beside her. His handsome face was a picture of concern.

"What happened?" she asked. Her voice seemed far away and groggy.

"You fainted," he replied, "but it's okay. I caught you before your head hit the floor. No, don't sit up. Just lie there for a minute until you have recovered."

But Alex was having none of it. Slowly, she sat up and looked around her. Stevie's last letter was lying on the floor beside her. She picked it up and waved it at John.

"Stevie would never have taken his life," she began. John tried to interrupt. "No, let me finish. He was happy, full of life.

Something must have happened to him to make him do this."

"Alex…"

"No, John, you didn't know him the way I did. I know he would never do this," she said. "Something has happened and I want you to find out what it was. I need to know what drove Stevie to take his own life."

John sighed.

"Please, John, for me," she pleaded. He looked down at her and recognised the pain in her eyes. He nodded.

"Alright, I'll look into it," he said. Alex smiled, but tears fell down her face again. He pulled a clean handkerchief from his pocket and handed it to her. "But I might not find anything useful."

"I know," she sobbed, "but at least you will have tried."

****

It was raining the day of Stevie's funeral and Alex, in dress uniform, sat with the other squaddies at the back of the packed church. Following a brief service and an even shorter prayer at the freshly dug graveside, she followed the rest of them back to a local hotel where Stevie's devastated family had put on some food for the mourners. Laid out buffet style, there was a selection of finger foods, cold meats, sandwiches, and sausage rolls. Alex placed a couple of egg mayonnaise sandwiches on her plate and grabbed a glass of fresh orange juice. She was just about to make her way over to a table where her colleagues were sitting when she almost ran into Stevie's younger brother, Craig. Two years younger than Stevie, Craig was tall and skinny like his brother, but favoured his mother's genes whilst Stevie had looked more like his father.

"Alex, how are you?" he said. His face was pinched and his eyes were red.

"I'm okay," she replied. "More importantly, how are all of you? How's your parents coping?"

"Their devastated," he said, looking around to where his white-haired parents were sitting talking to a family member. "They're putting on a brave face for today, but they've taken his death really badly." He turned back to look at her. "Do you have any idea why he did it?"

She shook her head. "No. He had been a bit down that week, but nothing serious… or so I thought. Did he say anything to you?"

"I'd spoken to him the day before and the only thing he said was he was having a bit of trouble with an officer, but he was dealing with it."

"Do you know who?" This was new. Stevie had said nothing to her about having trouble with an officer. She needed to know who it was.

"Nope, he just said that he was going to put in a complaint, that was all."

****

Alex paid the taxi fare and got out of the black cab. She should have gone back to base to change out of her dress uniform, but this new information was too important. She needed to talk to John immediately. So, she had taken a taxi to his private apartment that was in a modern block of flats close to her garrison. She walked up to the security door of John's building and pressed his buzzer. A few minutes later a crackly voice said: "Hello?"

"John, it's me. Can I come up?"

John was standing barefoot at the door of his flat when the elevator door opened and Alex stepped out. Dressed in a pair of grey jogging trousers and a white t-shirt, and carrying a half-drunk mug of coffee, he appeared boyish with his ruffled hair and a look of curiosity.

"What's the matter?" he asked as she ran up to him, put her arms around his neck and kissed him. He kissed her back.

"It was Stevie's funeral today," she replied. "It was bloody awful. I just had to see you. You don't mind, do you?"

"No, of course not. Are you okay?"

She pushed past him and walked into his pristine apartment. It was a modern, two-bedroomed second-floor flat in a swanky part of the garrison town. Alex had been there only once before, when the pair of them had first hooked up, and had fallen in love with its loft apartment feel and modern clean lines.

"Do you want a coffee?" John asked. She looked at his coffee mug and shook her head.

"Got anything stronger?" she asked.

Whilst John went into his kitchen to get her a glass of wine, Alex took off her jacket and cap and sat them on a Hermes armchair. She shrugged her shoulders, easing the stress of the day out of them, and then sat down on the matching sofa. She thought about what she had learned at Stevie's funeral. It was making sense now. If Stevie was having trouble with a senior officer, then things must have been so bad for him he felt he had no other choice than to take his own life. But who was the officer and what did he or she have on Stevie to push him to kill himself? She shared her thoughts with John when he joined her.

"So, you think Stevie was getting blackmailed by this person?" John said.

"I don't know… or bullied. Stevie had seemed a bit down before he… you know," she said. She took a sip of wine. It was ice cold Chardonnay, her favourite.

"Did his brother say who it was?" John asked.

"He didn't know. Stevie didn't say."

"Well, there's really not that much we can do about it," he said, relaxing back into the sofa, his own glass of white in one hand as he stroked her back with the other. "Not without a name or proof."

She looked round at him. "You were speaking to him the other day," she said. "Was that what you were talking about?"

John screwed up his face. "No, I was just pulling him up for his top button being undone and he gave me a bit of backchat."

Alex chewed her bottom lip. "That doesn't sound like him," she said thoughtfully.

"Well, I can assure you it happened," John said. "Maybe he was feeling stressed and was acting out of character."

"Hmmm, maybe," she replied. "Anyway, I need you to follow this up. I need to find out who it was and what they did." She felt John's hand travel up her back and he stroked the back of her neck. She sighed with pleasure. He always knew how to touch her to make her feel nice. He put his glass down on the coffee table and moved closer to her, kissing her neck and nuzzling her ear. She relaxed into his caresses.

"Do you fancy… going into the bedroom?" he whispered.

Taking her hand, John led her into his bedroom where, with expert precision, he quickly undressed her and slipped out of his own clothes. Standing naked before her, Alex's heart skipped a beat as he walked towards her and took her in his arms. Kissing her passionately, he gently pushed her on to the bed and climbed on top of her. John was an experienced lover and Alex responded to his every touch, his every kiss, his every lick with increasingly louder moans. Pleasure washed over her and Alex shuddered as his hand slide down her body. Don't stop, she thought, as her skin tingled under his touch. Then without any warning and not giving her body much time to ready itself, he pushed himself inside and began to thrust. She gasped. He smiled and thrust a little harder.

"Oh, John!" she said, eyes closed as he continued.

She felt his cock begin to rhythmically slide up and down. Again and again, he thrust into her, making every nerve ending in her body sing. The thrusting grew in intensity till at last they were working as one. Alex felt like she was going to burst as she reached the sweet spot and felt her body gush and vibrate. John came, he climaxed and collapsed on top of her, sweating and out of breath. Exhausted and happy, he kissed her face and whispered words of love. Underneath him, wondering why he had stopped before she had reached orgasm, a disappointed Alex tried not to cry.

****

Two days later, Alex popped into John's office to see if he had gotten anywhere in his search for the elusive officer. He was on a telephone call when she arrived, so she stood in front of his desk and waited until he had finished.

"Okay, yes… right, I need to go now. Someone's come in," he said to the caller before hanging up. He smiled at Alex. "Official business or pleasure?" he asked with a wink.

She blushed. "Unfortunately official," she replied. "I've just come to see if you're any further with your investigation."

"What investigation?"

"Into the mystery officer, the one who was behind Stevie's suicide," she said.

"Oh that! Yes, I've asked around and none of the officers know anything about it," he said.

"What about the squaddies? Did you speak to any of them?"

"Of course, I did, but again I drew a blank. I'm afraid we've hit a brick wall with this one," he said. The words were regretful, but his tone wasn't.

"So…?"

"What?"

"Well, you can't just leave it there. Someone in this garrison is responsible for Stevie's death," she said. She felt anger rising within her. "You need to find that person and bring him or her to justice."

"Look, Alex," John said, rising from his seat and walking towards her. "I know Stevie and you were very close, and no one wants to find the person responsible more than I do, but there's not much else I can do. My hands are tied."

He put out a hand and touched her shoulder, and she batted it away. He frowned.

"So, that's it? You're not doing anything else?" She couldn't believe what she was hearing.

"Well, what else can I do?" He looked exasperated.

"I don't know… something!" she yelled and ran out of his office.

Well, if John would not track down the officer, she would. She ran across the training ground and made a beeline for the Royal Military Police office on the other side. It was a longshot. They had already investigated Stevie's death and ruled a suicide, but with this new information, perhaps they would reopen his case.

RMP officer, Rory McKee, was pouring himself a coffee in the office's small galley kitchen when she burst in. He put his mug down and went to greet her. Tall, dark and handsome, he had intelligent dark brown eyes and a body for sin. Alex flushed when she laid eyes on him. Damnit! She thought as feelings of attraction zipped through her. That's not what I'm here for.

"Can I help you?" he asked in a soft Scottish accent.

"I'm here to report new information about Lance Corporal Puth's death," she said.

"Well, you'd better come into my office then," Rory said.

****

It was well into an hour when Alex finally stopped talking and Rory could get a word in edge-wise. He had diligently noted down everything she told him about Stevie and the mysterious officer.

"Look, I don't know what was going on between them, but don't you think we should seriously investigate it?" she said.

"And you say Major Hampton has already been asking questions and gotten nowhere?"

"Yes."

"So, what makes you think I can do any better?"

"Well… you're a Police officer. This is what you do," she replied.

He chewed on his pen and reread his notes.

"There's certainly an issue here. If Lance Corporal Puth was the victim of bullying, we certainly need to find the perpetrator," he said.

Alex smiled. Relief washed over her. At last, someone was taking her seriously.

"Thank you," she said.

"Leave it with me and I'll see what I can do," he said.

****

Over the next few days, Rory interviewed several of Stevie and Alex's colleagues, and several senior officers, none of whom could spread any light on Stevie's tormentor. It wasn't until he looked into his personal life that he uncovered something startling. Alex had told him Stevie was a regular at a gay bar in the town, so that was where he went.

The Bravo Pink bar was quiet during the day, with only a handful of punters sipping pints and eating lunch on the outside terrace. Inside, a single barman, Mark Cookson, small, slim and immaculately dressed in vest and jeans, stood washing glasses. His eyes lit up when the handsome military police officer entered.

"Well, well, well, this must be my lucky day," he said as Rory approached. "I do love a man in uniform. What can I get you, officer? A pint? Tea? Me?"

Rory smiled. "Not today, thanks," he said with a smile. "I'm here investigating the death of one of your regulars, a Lance Corporal Stevie Puth."

Mark's face fell. "Oh, Stevie, yes, that was all so sad. I can't believe he took his own life," he said. "I can't believe it. He was a lovely guy. He was in here only two days before, drowning his sorrows in vodka."

"Did he talk to anyone while he was here?" Rory asked, taking out his notebook and pen. "Did he say anything about why he might take his own life?"

"No, he was in a funny mood and pretty much kept himself to himself. He did chat with me a couple of times though," he said. He put down the glass he was drying and thought for a moment. "Come to think of it, he said something was bothering him. He said he was being bullied by a senior officer, but he couldn't do anything about it because the officer was involved with his best friend. He wanted to report him, but he didn't want his friend to be hurt…or something like that."

"Did he say who the best friend was?" Rory wanted to know.

"No, but he must think a lot of him if he was putting up with being bullied like that." Mark took up another glass and polished it. "Poor guy. Such a horrible thing to have happened."

"Thank you. You've been really helpful," Rory said.

****

Alex sat opposite Rory in his office and looked aghast at what he told her. Holding back the tears, she listened as he explained what Mark had said.

"Do you know who Stevie's best friend is?" he asked.

She nodded. Tears slid down her face, and she wiped them with a hand. "Me. It was me."

"And you're involved with an officer, correct?"

"Yes."

"This officer's name?"

"It's Major John Hampton," she said in a whisper.

****

Despite Rory and Alex's best efforts, they could not find John in the garrison or get him on his mobile. They searched everywhere: his office, the gym, the officer's mess, but there was no sign of him. Rory tried to call him several times at both his home and on his cell, but nothing. It wasn't until they ran into Captain Claire Wilks that they found out where he was.

"Major Hampton has taken some emergency leave to visit his family," she said. "I think they have a house about an hour's drive away. Out in the country. One of his daughters is ill, apparently."

Alex looked at her, horrified. "One of his daughters?" she said, her voice shaky. She felt sick. And weak.

"Yes, he has three. His wife phoned him earlier to tell him about it and he left immediately. He'll be halfway there by now."

"His wife?" Alex repeated.

Claire looked at Alex, puzzled. Rory, seeing Alex struggling with this new information, quickly thanked the Captain, and led

Alex back to his office, where he furnished her with a brandy. She took it gratefully.

"I've been such a fool," she said. Her face was chalk white, and she felt faint. "He said he loved me, but he's been using me the whole time. And as for poor Stevie… John must have been the senior officer who was bullying him." She took a sip of her drink. "It all fits now." She looked up at Rory, who was perched on his desk in front of her. "Why didn't I see it? I should have known. If I had known, I could have stopped him and Stevie would be alive today."

"Look, you've had a bit of a shock," Rory said. "Is there anyone I can call for you? You know, for some support?"

She shook her head. Stevie had been her closest friend at the garrison, and her family was too far away.

"Why don't I walk you back to your room so you can have a lie down?" he suggested.

She looked up at him and shook her head. "No," she said. "I just need another drink." She held up her glass. "Pour," she said.

****

The following morning, tender-headed and feeling sick, Alex rose from her bed and chugged down a pint of water that had been left on the nightstand. She sat back down on her bed and tried to remember the night before. She had been with Rory. They had both been drinking his brandy. The thought of brandy made her stomach heave. They had been talking and then…it was a blank. She looked down at her body. She was wearing her pyjamas. She picked up her mobile phone. There was a message from Rory. Hope you're feeling okay this morning, she read. You did have rather a lot last night. Don't worry, when Major Hampton returns to the garrison, he'll have some questions to answer. Speak soon. Rory. PS, in case you don't remember, it was me who walked you back to your room. Don't worry, nothing happened.

"Of course, it didn't," she muttered as she replaced the phone on the nightstand. Although I kind of wish it had, she thought. Despite being broken-hearted over John, working with Rory these last few days had been restorative. The handsome Scot was good-natured and kind. He had comforted her over Stevie's death and listened, actually listened, to her. If things were different, maybe she and he could…

"What am I thinking?" she said. "I've just found out my boyfriend is married and bullied my best friend to death. I don't need the complications another relationship might bring." She stood up. "Nope, it's not for me. From now on, I'll concentrate on being single."

****

After eating breakfast in the mess, Alex found herself with plenty of time on her hands. It was Saturday morning, and she had nothing to occupy herself with. She went to Stevie's room to see if there was anything that needed done there. She knew that someone had tasked a couple of younger soldiers with packing up his things to send to his parents, and she needed to know they had done properly it. She didn't trust anyone with Stevie's things.

Stevie's room was eerily quiet when she entered. All his posters and pictures had been taken down and carefully placed in a cardboard box. His clothes had been removed from his wardrobe and packed into his suitcase. His toiletries in a toiletry bag on top. His books were in a long-life plastic shopping bag. His bed was bare. There was no trace of him left in the room. She sat down on the bed and looked around her. It was so sad that all that was left of such a vibrant life, such a vibrant man, were these bags of stuff. She glanced at the bag of books. Stevie had always had such eclectic taste in literature, and it amused her to look through his collection. Apart from classics such as Treasure Island, there were a few racy books featuring gay couples, a couple of Harry Potters, and a copy of Simon Armitage's translation of Sir Gawain and the Green Knight. Hiding underneath was an A5 sized notebook, which, on looking at it, Alex found was Stevie's diary. She shut it immediately, embarrassed and ashamed to be looking at such a private, personal thing. She looked at its navy faux leather cover for a few moments, reopened it, and read. It was hard going. Stevie had recorded every incident of bullying carried out on him by John. The bullying had been brutal; everything from verbal abuse to actual assault. He had been intending to report it, but when Alex had confessed she'd fallen for his oppressor, he had found himself a quandary. Should he tell Alex and risk her not believing him and their relationship falling apart? He loved her too much to lose her. The final entry was the most harrowing. In it, he had jotted down exactly what had happened the day Alex had seen John tormenting him in the corridor. Stevie had threatened to tell Alex everything, and the Major had told him he was already in the process of transferring Stevie to another unit that was currently based in the Middle East. The last words written by Stevie would haunt Alex for years to come: I can't face another tour out there. Apart from the heat and the mozzies, which are enough to drive any sane man mad, being gay is illegal out there. I can't be my true self. I'll have to hide it. I've had enough of hiding it. And what about Alex? She's my best friend. I can't bear being away from her. I just can't.

And there it ended.

Alex shut the book and took her mobile from her pocket.

She dialled.

"Rory, it's Alex," she said when her call was picked up. "I've just found some damning new evidence. Stevie's diary. It lists everything John did to him…Yes, I'll bring it to your office now. Okay, I'll meet you there."

En route across the courtyard, diary in hand, Alex felt her mobile phone vibrate in her pocket. She fetched it out and opened it. It was a text from John: Sorry, can't be with you this weekend. Visiting my sick father. Be back on Monday. I miss you, sexy.

She grimaced and wrote back: I know about your wife and kids. I know you bullied Stevie. I have proof.

She turned her phone off and put it back in her pocket.

****

Rory was pleased with the diary. That would make his job easier and it would be harder for Major Hampton to deny his actions. Over coffee in his office, they discussed what was going to happen next.

"Good find," he said, sitting back in his office chair. "He'll not wriggle out of this one."

"I want you to throw the book at him," Alex said. "He needs to pay for what he's done to Stevie."

"And to you," Rory said, then regretted it when he saw her flinch.

"I don't matter in this," she said. "Only Stevie does, and he deserves justice."

"He'll get it, I promise you," Rory said. He closed the diary and stood up. "I'll just put this in the evidence room for safe-keeping," he said, walking towards the door. "Then maybe, if you're feeling up to it, we could go out for some lunch?"

"I'd love that," she said with a smile. She too rose.

"Stay here. I'll only be a minute," he said.

"I'm just going to get my bag and give my hair a quick brush," she said. "Meet you back here in about fifteen minutes?"

"Sure."

Alex hurried across the courtyard to her room. She unlocked her door and went inside, leaving the door ajar. Grabbing her handbag, she placed it on her bed whilst she searched through it for her brush. Her hand had just located the brush when she was aware that she was not alone. Someone was standing in the doorway. She turned and jumped in fright. It was John, and he looked angry.

"I've come to speak to you," he said. "About your text. What was that all about?"

"I've got nothing to say to you," she replied. "Get out of my room." He looked shocked.

"Alex, what's going on? What have I done?"

"What did your wife think when you suddenly had to come back to the garrison?" she asked. "Didn't she find it strange that you had just arrived and then were leaving again? Didn't she ask questions?"

"Never mind about my wife," he snapped. "She means nothing to me. Our marriage is a sham. It's been over for a long time. We just stay together for the sake of the kids." His voice softened, and he took a step forward and put out a hand. "It's you I love, Alex. It's always been you."

She looked at him, and wasn't convinced. "Well, I don't love you, John. Not anymore. You lied to me. You lied about your wife, your kids… and you lied to me about Stevie. What you did to him on a daily basis was disgusting. You gas-lighted him at every turn. You physically and verbally abused him. Why did you do that? He didn't deserve it."

"I did nothing to him, Alex."

"I know you did!" she snarled. "Stop lying to me! Tell me the truth."

"Okay, I might have warned him off a couple of times, but I did it for you, Alex," John said, "for us. He was in my way. I wanted you all to myself. He needed to know that, but he just wouldn't give you up. You were his best friend and nobody could stop that."

"Well, you managed it, didn't you? You basically killed him," she said. "Murderer."

"I did no such thing. Stevie took his own life," John said.

"But you pushed him to it," she said. "And now the Military Police know about it and they want to talk to you."

"About what? That I sometimes had to discipline a shoddy squaddy? They'll not believe the likes of you over me, a decorated Major," he sneered.

"They don't need to believe me. It's all written in Stevie's diary: every incident meticulously recorded. You will not get away with this. You're done, John. Your career is over and we are over."

She turned to put her hairbrush back in her bag and was horrified to feel John suddenly behind her, grabbing her hair and pulling her head back. His breath was hot on her cheek as he rasped: "We're not over until I say we are. Now, where is the diary? Give it to me."

"I don't have it," she replied and yowled when he tugged harder. Then she felt the cold hard steel of his British Army issue Glock 17 pistol in her ribs and flinched.

"Where is it then?" he said.

"The Military Police have it," she said.

"Then you're going to go and get it for me," he said, pulling her towards the door.

****

The courtyard was empty save for a few hungry pigeons searching for scraps. John, still holding the firearm at her side, had her by the shoulders and was forcing her across the quad.

"You'll not get away with this," Alex said as they reached the Royal Military Police Office. "You can't just go in there and take it."

"No, but you are," he said, pushing her through the entrance door. They paused in the reception area. "Now where is it?"

Hoping that Rory was somehow still in the building and had not left when she failed to show up, Alex led John to Rory's office. The door was locked when she tried the handle and she was just about to turn to face John when she felt his grip on her being wrenched away and heard an almighty bang as two bodies hit the floor. She quickly turned to see Rory struggling to subdue John on the floor. Someone had kicked aside the handgun, so she picked it up and trained it on the fighting men.

"It's over John," she said, holding the gun on him.

John looked up and immediately stopped struggling. Rory scrambled to his feet and joined Alex.

"Good work," he said, but she wasn't listening. She was staring at her former lover with a look of real contempt.

"You killed Stevie," she said through gritted teeth.

"I didn't. He killed himself," John replied.

"You might not have put the noose around his neck, but your persistent bullying drove him to it." She took the safety off and pointed it back at him. John looked horrified and closed his eyes.

"Alex," Rory said softly. "Put the gun down."

She stared at John again and it seemed like an age passed.

Then she suddenly relented. "You're not worth it," she said, lowering the weapon.

Rory took the gun from her and put the safety cap back on. "I'll keep a hold of this," he said and then he addressed John: "And as for you, Major John Hampton I am arresting you for the kidnap of Lance Corporal Alex Grier, for the bullying of Stevie Puth and for just generally being an arsehole. On your feet."

As a defeated John scrambled to his feet, two RMP soldiers ran up the stairs. They had heard the commotion from outside and come in to find out what was happening. Following a brief explanation from Rory, they cuffed John and took him to a holding cell in the building.

"I thought you might actually have shot him," Rory said as he walked Alex outside a few moments later. "I've heard you're a crack shot. You could easily have done it."

"I seriously thought about it, but killing John doesn't bring Stevie back," she said. She let out a sigh of relief and suddenly felt giddy. She steadied herself against a wall.

"Are you alright?" Rory asked, genuine concern in his eyes.

"Yes, it's all been a bit much, that's all," she said.

"Still up for lunch after this morning's adventure?" he asked.

"Definitely," she replied, smiling.

He grinned back at her. "Would you mind if I did something before we go?"

"Yes, of course. What do you need to do?" she asked, looking up at him.

"This." He drew nearer and put his arm around her waist. Pulling her to him, he bent down and gently kissed her on the lips. Surprised, but happy, Alex returned the kiss and was disappointed when he suddenly pulled back.

"I've been wanting to do that for days," he confessed.

"Well, I'm glad you did," she replied.

He kissed her again, a long, delicious toe-tingling kiss that had her swaying with bliss. They pulled apart and gazed at each other for a few moments, smiling into each other's eyes. Then Rory let her go, stuck out his hand, and she took it. Together, they walked across the courtyard and into a whole new world of possibilities.

****

One year later…

Alex carefully cleaned her rifle before breaking it down and placing it in a black backpack. She had been shooting well, but did not expect to pick gold this time. The inter-military shooting competition was taking place this year at a gorgeous country estate complete with Elizabethan manor house and, for the first time, civilians could spectate. Slinging her backpack across her shoulder, she made her way to a large white marquee that had been set up to serve refreshments.

The marquee was busy with both military and civilian diners and it took her a full ten minutes to collect a cup of tea and a plate of sandwiches from the servers. Taking them to the marquee entranceway, she looked for an unoccupied seat at the tables outside. There were none. She would just have to stand.

Alex was happy to be taking part in a competition, but had already decided that this would be her last one. She was planning to leave the British Army and do something else. What, she didn't know. She placed her cup and saucer on a nearby table and picked up a sandwich. Standing at the entrance gave her a good view of the event and she was delighted to see someone arrive, driving a vintage silver Aston Martin. The car looked like something straight out of a James Bond movie, and she stared at it hungrily.

"You know you could have one of those if you want," a plummy voice said from behind.

Alex turned to see a beautifully dressed older woman with white-blonde hair cut in a stylish bob. She was smiling.

"Oh, I couldn't afford something like that," Alex replied. "Though it is beautiful."

"You could if you came and worked for me," the woman said matter-of-factly. "In fact, you could have a whole fleet of them." Alex frowned. The woman continued: "You know how to handle a gun and you shoot well."

"Thank you," Alex replied uncertainly.

"I could use someone like you and you'd make a lot of money," the woman said. She waved at someone she knew.

Alex frowned. "What do you mean?"

"Well, I'm sure you don't want to live on a British Army salary all your days," the woman said. "No, you could use your rifle skills and earn more for one job than you do in an entire year."

Intrigued, Alex said: "And how would I do that?"

"By joining an elite group of women who carry out a range of international jobs for top money," she replied.

Alex wasn't convinced. "Uh, thanks, but no thanks. I'm not the corporate type."

"Oh, it's not in big business," the woman said. "It's something far… juicier… than that."

She put an expertly manicured hand into the small clutch bag she was carrying and pulled out a pristine white business card. She handed it to Alex. "Call me if you ever get bored with the army and want a change of career. I'll make it worth your while."

With that, she walked away with the panache of a catwalk model. Alex looked down at the card. It exquisitely printed text, it said: Elizabeth Danvers and a mobile number. She turned it over to reveal a gold insignia with the words Sisters of Sin. She looked up, saw the Aston Martin again and smiled.

About the Author

Dawn (D A) Nelson is an award-winning Scottish author of books for both children and adults. She writes action-packed romantic thrillers and dark comedies for adults as well as fantasy adventures for kids. Apart from writing for the SOS series, Dawn is also planning a fantasy/steampunk series for adults too. Her first book was a kids' novel, DarkIsle, which won the Royal Mail Scottish Children's Book Awards (8-12 age group) in 2007.

Dawn lives in a small country village on the banks of the River Clyde, just a stone's throw away from the beautiful Loch Lomond. She lives there with her two kids, three small dogs and three chickens. In her spare time, Dawn loves to read and enjoys both literary, romance and fantasy books. When not writing or reading, Dawn loves to bake, craft, listen to music and watch movies.

Sign up to Dawn's newsletter: https://danelsonauthor.com/

Social Media

Facebook: https://www.facebook.com/authordanelson

Twitter: https://twitter.com/danelsonauthor

LinkedIn: https://www.linkedin.com/in/dawn-nelson-95210221/

Tik Tok: https://www.tiktok.com/@danelson70

Dawn's other books

Pinterest: https://www.pinterest.co.uk/danelsonauthor/

Goodreads: https://www.goodreads.com/author/show/1351494.D_A_Nelson

BOOKS FOR ADULTS

Dusting Down Alcudia

Nina Esposito, archaeologist, is on a mission. She's flying to Mallorca to locate a magnificent Roman treasure that's been lost for centuries.

But, when a former love and a work rival vie for her attention, Nina finds herself locked in romantic rollercoaster. Which one is truly worthy of her? And do they have ulterior motives other than winning her heart?

Added to the mix is a Spanish billionaire who will stop at nothing to get the jewels for himself.

Who will get to the treasure first? Will Nina's heart be broken along the way? And can she really trust either of the men in her life?

Join Nina on a breath-taking journey of discovery that takes her from the dusty fields of Mallorca to the diamond brokers of Amsterdam. As she soon finds out: there's everything to play for when you're Dusting Down Alcudia.

https://geni.us/alcudia

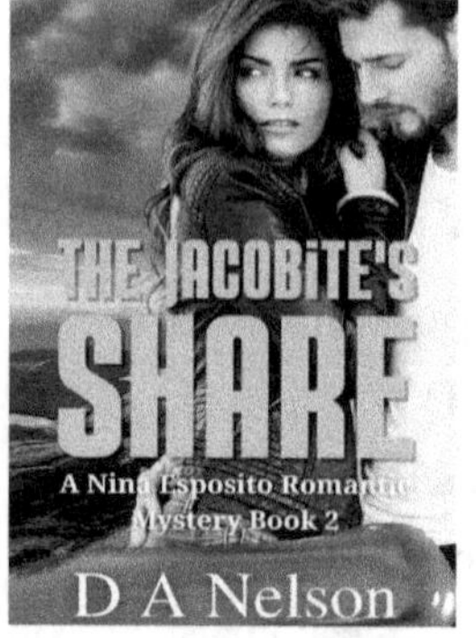

The Jacobite's Share

When an argument leads to estrangement from lover Jay, Nina decides to take a research job at a Scottish castle to get away from her troubles.

Back in her native land, the plucky archaeologist soon finds herself up to her ears in a centuries-old mystery and attempted murder.

Now she's got to find the Jacobite treasure before a would-be assassin picks off the handsome Laird and his equally gorgeous brother… a brother who has taken quite a shine to her.

And when Jay returns to her life, things will only get further complicated as his ex-fiancée shows up tc create mayhem.

The second in the popular Nina Esposito Adventures, The Jacobite's Share is a fast-paced adventure thriller full of darkness and danger.

https://geni.us/jacobitesshare

Everything She Wants

When married Susan decides to run away with a Wham! tribute band as their 'Shirley', little does she know of the consequences it will bring. Fed up with her cold husband, desperate to get away from their spoiled teen daughter, she joins the group to find some happiness in her life. And she gets it - for a while. As the group gets more successful, Susan finds herself falling fo an 80s pop heartthrob. Has she finally f true love and will she get everything she wants?

https://geni.us/everythingshewantsbook

BOOKS FOR KIDS (8-12 years)

THE DARKISLE TRILOGY

DarkIsle

For 10-year-old Morag, there's nothing magical about the cellar of her cruel foster parents' home. But that's where she meets Aldiss, a talking rat and his resourceful companion, Bertie the dodo. She jumps at the chance to run away and join them on their race against time to save their homeland from an evil warlock named Devilish, who is intent on destroying it. But first Bertie and Aldiss will need to stop bickering long enough to free the only guide who knows where to find Devilish: Shona, a dragon who's been turned to stone. Terrifying, touching and funny, DarkIsle is a vivid and fast-paced novel of captivating originality.

https://geni.us/darkislenovel

DarkIsle: Resurrection (The Witch's Revenge)

The 2nd book in the DarkIsle trilogy. Two months after she saved The Eye of Lornish, Morag is adjusting to life in the secret northern kingdom of Marnoch Mor. But dark dreams are troubling her and a spate of unexplained events prove that even with the protection of her friends—Shona the dragon, Bertie the dodo and Aldiss the rat—Morag is still not safe from harm… The 1st book (DarkIsle) WON the 2008 Scottish Children's Book Awards.

https://geni.us/darkisleseriesbook2

DarkIsle: The Final Battle

All seem well in Marnoch Mor. Bertie the dodo, Aldiss the rat and Shona the dragon are looking forward to a relaxing Christmas. However, Morag is having bad dreams – an old enemy is trying to reach her. And when another former foe turns up on her doorstep it is clear something is badly wrong.

Morag and her friends are soon forced to face a powerful new threat, one more terrifying than they have ever encountered before.

The battle for the DarkIsle of Murst must be won…or Marnoch Mor itself will be lost.

https://geni.us/darkisleseriesbook3

A Children's History of Glasgow

Have you ever wondered what it would have been like living in Glasgow when William Wallace was there? What about being a sailor on one of the ships owned by the rich tobacco lords in Georgian times? This book will uncover the important and exciting things that happened in your town. With a helpful timeline, fun imaginary accounts, cool old photos of places you ll recognize in Glasgow and amazing top facts and information, you will discover things in Children s History of (never knew about your

town. Investigate the people and events that have defined your home town: Who was St Mungo? Where was James Watt when he first thought of inventing the steam engine?

https://geni.us/historybookglasgow

www.ingramcontent.com/pod-product-compliance
Lightning Source LLC
Chambersburg PA
CBHW070833250626
47159CB00003B/767

9781916352063